Flashpoint

Agents of Ense

Tess Summers

Seasons Press LLC

Copyright 2021 Tess Summers

Published: 2021

ISBN: 9798726712703

Published by Seasons Press LLC.

Copyright © 2021, Tess Summers.

Edited by Susan Soares, SJS Editorial Services.

Cover by OliviaProDesign.

All rights reserved. No part of this publication may be reproduced, stored in a retrieval system, or transmitted in any form or by any means, electronic, mechanical, recording, or otherwise, without the prior written permission of the author, except in the case of brief quotations within critical reviews and otherwise as permitted by copyright law.

This is a work of fiction. The characters, incidents and dialogues in this book are of the author's imagination and are not to be construed as real. Any resemblance to actual events or persons, living or dead, is completely coincidental.

This book is for mature readers. It contains sexually explicit scenes and graphic language that may be considered offensive by some.

All sexually active characters in this work are eighteen years of age or older.

Blurb

I always get what I want.

He's the ruthless patrón of the Guzman cartel... she's a nerdy, naïve software analyst, nursing a broken heart, poolside in Ensenada.

Their paths should have never crossed, but once they did, Ramon Guzman decided he's keeping his sweet American nerd. One way or another.

Even if that means he has to trick her into marrying him.

Thank you

I can't begin to convey how grateful I am that you took the time to read my work. I still pinch myself when I think about people picking up something I've written and actually reading it—for *enjoyment*! At least, I hope you enjoyed it. ☺

Would you mind leaving me a review on Amazon and/or Goodreads (and Bookbub if it's not too much trouble)? Believe it or not, your review does help get my book seen by other readers, which lets me keep writing.

Don't forget to sign up for my newsletter to get free bonus content and be the first to know about cover reveals, excerpts, and more!

https://www.subscribepage.com/TessSummersNewsletter

xoxo,

Tess

Acknowledgements

Mr. Summers: While I appreciate everything you do for me (making sure I'm fed regularly ranks pretty high up there), thank you especially for being my consultant on all things gun and blood-splatter related. You will always be my real-life hero.

SJS Editorial Services: Thank you for giving this book love and making it that much better.

Alyssa Faye and Truly Trendy PR: Thanks for taking tasks off my plate so I could finish this book. Your help is so appreciated.

Megan Appelt: Thank you for being my Spanish specialist! ¡Eres asombroso! Te quiero, chica!

Cameron and Eric Rau: Thank you for being my go-to gays! I adore you both!

Everyone at Tess Summers' Playhouse: You're the best group a writer could ever ask for. Thank you for showing up and making me laugh every day.

To every single person who has ever bought, recommended, or reviewed my book: I'm able to be on this journey because of you. Thank you.

Lastly, to my readers: You're the reason I get up every day and keep writing. Thank you for giving me purpose. xoxo

Table of Contents

Blurb iii
Thank you iv
Acknowledgements v
Prologue 1
Chapter One 4
Chapter Two 16
Chapter Three 23
Chapter Four 31
Chapter Five 40
Chapter Six 54
Chapter Seven 64
Chapter Eight 80
Chapter Nine 87
Chapter Ten 95
Chapter Eleven 101
Chapter Twelve 110
Chapter Thirteen 116
Chapter Fourteen 121
Chapter Fifteen 128
Chapter Sixteen 133
Chapter Seventeen 138
Chapter Eighteen 150
Chapter Nineteen 160
Chapter Twenty 165
Chapter Twenty-One 170
Chapter Twenty-Two 192

Chapter Twenty-Three	201
Chapter Twenty-Four	209
Chapter Twenty-Five	213
Chapter Twenty-Six	225
Chapter Twenty-Seven	238
Chapter Twenty-Eight	242
Chapter Twenty-Nine	246
Chapter Thirty	251
Chapter Thirty-One	262
Chapter Thirty-Two	268
Chapter Thirty-Three	276
Chapter Thirty-Four	279
Chapter Thirty-Five	289
Chapter Thirty-Six	298
Chapter Thirty-Seven	309
Chapter Thirty-Eight	315
Chapter Thirty-Nine	320
Chapter Forty	332
Chapter Forty-One	337
Chapter Forty-Two	353
Chapter Forty-Three	360
Chapter Forty-Four	367
Chapter Forty-Five	376
Chapter Forty-Six	382
Chapter Forty-Seven	386
Epilogue	388
Bonus scene!	389

Fever	389
Slow Burn	391
Ignition	392
Inferno	393
Combustion	395
Reignited	396
San Diego Social Scene series:	397
About the Author	398
Contact Me!	398

FLASHPOINT

Prologue

Ramon
"Ramon!"

He turned around on instinct at hearing his name and immediately regretted it when he saw a pretty woman wearing a floppy straw hat, bright pink bikini top, and matching sarong. The woman waving wildly as she ran toward him, scuffing her feet while trying to keep her flip-flops on, looked vaguely familiar.

"Oh my God! I'm so glad to see you!" It seemed like she wanted to throw her arms around his neck, but Chachi, one of his bodyguards, stopped her short by stepping in front of her. She was completely undeterred and looked around the wall of a man as she eagerly asked, "How long are you in town for?"

He realized where he knew her from. He'd fucked her in the bathroom at the wedding of one of his captain's daughters the last time he was in Ensenada. But for the life of him, he couldn't remember her name—if he'd even known it in the first place. She'd been a decent enough lay, but nothing worth repeating, that much he did remember.

Ramon nodded at Chachi, who then took a step away from the woman so Ramon could talk to her.

"I'm just in town for the weekend. I have a party tonight, and then I'm leaving tomorrow."

"Are you going to Francisco and Juan Diego's Summer Ball?" she asked excitedly, rocking on her tiptoes like an overstimulated child. The gay couple's themed parties in Ensenada were not to be missed, but it took a lot of clout to garner an invitation.

"I am."

"Um, are you taking anyone?"

"No," he replied curtly. He knew where this was going. The woman thought because she'd sucked Ramon's cock, she'd found a way in.

She batted her eyelashes at him. "Do you think I could go with you? We could go back to your room at the end of the night and…"

Sweetheart, there's a reason I haven't called you. Unapologetically, he replied with one word. "No."

Her mouth opened in surprise. "But…" She tried to touch his sleeve to persuade him.

Chachi intercepted her hand. The man was Ramon's favorite bodyguard for exactly that reason.

Jesús, one of the men in his inner circle, took the lead and stood in front of the woman to block her from following, while Ramon's men ushered him toward the bank of hotel elevators leading to the upper floors.

"I'm sorry, miss," he heard Jesús tell her. "Mr. Guzman is a very busy man."

Flashpoint

Ramon pinched the bridge of his nose as they waited for the car. *Fuck, it's going to be a long night.*

Chapter One

Ramon
His fucking head hurt. He did not want to be at the party—at all. Not even the scantily clad women, who he was sure were hired extras, walking around, chatting up the guests, and pawing at the unaccompanied men made it tolerable. It was all he could do to keep his face neutral and hide his annoyance at being there. But his appearance was necessary: even though he technically lived in San Diego, he needed to maintain a high profile in Ensenada. Tonight's party was the event of the summer, and it was important he made an appearance to remind people he was still a force in Mexico.

He no longer enjoyed public outings—not like he used to. Ever since taking over as *patrón* of the family cartel, he knew there was a permanent target on his back—either from the American government, rival cartels, or maybe even from within his own organization. He no longer trusted anyone, except a few of his captains who were his own flesh and blood, but he was even suspicious of them at times. They'd been part of the coup that had killed his brother, Enrique, and put Ramon into power. Who's to say Ramon wasn't next?

He had no idea what form his would-be assassin may take. Enrique's had been a petite redhead who'd been dating their nephew, but it could just as easily be one of his own bodyguards as a beautiful woman, so Ramon could never completely relax and let his defenses down. Especially not at a venue like this.

His night got a lot more interesting, however, when he noticed the tiny blonde in the long, emerald-green gown with the thigh-high slit the moment she walked into the party. Francisco Flores, the flamboyant host dressed in a yellow sequined jacket and top hat, approached her immediately and demonstratively grabbed both her hands when he greeted her with a broad smile. Her smile in return was demure, but charming, and she moved with an elegant grace as she engaged the man and his partner, Juan Diego Rodriguez, in his coordinated orange jacket and top hat. Despite the theatrics and over-the-top bling on the men talking to her, Ramon couldn't take his eyes off the beautiful woman with the porcelain skin.

He watched, mesmerized, as the hosts each took one of her elbows and started making the rounds, introducing her to the movers and shakers of Ensenada. She smiled graciously as she took their offered hands, then nervously tucked her hair behind her ear as she listened to whatever bullshit that particular guest spewed at her. And it was bullshit, of that Ramon was certain; almost everyone at the party was at least a little dirty in one way or another. Some more than others, but none more than he. On occasion, she'd glance around the room, and that's when she caught him staring at her.

She didn't immediately look away, like most women would coyly do when they noticed they'd caught his attention. Instead, she kept his gaze, almost as if challenging him to be the first to break eye contact. That made his dick move. If there's one thing Ramon loved, it was a good challenge. He hadn't dated anyone in a while whose name he'd bothered to remember the next morning, and he was restless for someone of substance. Her appearance tonight was almost too good to be true.

And that set off alarm bells.

The corner of his mouth turned up, and she finally glanced away.

He'd never seen her before and wondered what her story was. Her fair skin suggested she was probably foreign—given their proximity to California, most likely American. Who was she? And what was she doing in Ensenada? And how did she know Francisco and Juan Diego well enough to get invited to one of their exclusive parties?

He suspected he was about to find out when the hosts, along with their beautiful guest, started his way.

****

Sophia

She'd met Francisco and Juan Diego two days ago at the hotel's swim-up bar. The men were partners in both life and in their high-end international antique and collectibles business. They'd taken an immediate liking to her when she complimented Juan Diego on his sunglasses after popping out of the water next to him and placing her drink order. Once they learned why she was in Mexico—after a few drinks on her part, they became her instant best friends, self-appointed therapists, tour guides, and all-around Ensenada experts.

"Oh, honey, you *have* to come to our party Saturday. It'll be crawling with rich, single, gorgeous men," Francisco declared.

"And you know," Juan Diego added conspiratorially, "the best way to get over a man is to get under a new one."

She'd floated that very idea around in her head as she'd boarded the plane to Mexico. A fling with a dark, mysterious stranger might be just what the doctor ordered. Still, as exciting as that sounded in theory, actually going through with it would be an entirely different thing. She really was a good girl at heart.

"I don't know. I'm only here for another week. I don't think I need to meet anyone new. You two seem to be quite enough."

The two were over-the-top eccentric and absolutely adorable.

"Of course we are, doll," Juan Diego agreed without batting an eyelash. "But we're not going to help you scratch that itch, so to speak, because... ew, boobies! But there will be plenty of male breeders at the party..." He paused when her eyes got big.

Francisco whispered in her ear, "Straight men."

Juan Diego continued without missing a beat, "...who will appreciate *your* perky boobies." He pushed up under her bathing suit top to jiggle her breasts and emphasize his point. "Besides, the whole reason we're here at the hotel is to celebrate with two hundred of our closest fake friends and a handful of real ones, so we insist you come! There will be dancing and free drinks all night long, not to mention a four-course dinner. You'll love it!"

"What are you celebrating?"

"Summer!" they declared in unison.

"You're throwing a catered bash with free drinks, dinner, and dancing to celebrate *summer*?"

"Absolutely. We're gay, fabulous, and rich. We don't need more of a reason."

"Of course you don't," she replied with a laugh. It did sound like fun. "Any idea where I can get a dress on such short notice?"

"As a matter of fact, we do."

They then called a friend of theirs who owned a bridal shop in town and had her come to the hotel with a rack of dresses for Sophia to choose from. She'd wanted to go with an understated soft pink chiffon dress, but the men insisted on the bold emerald-green one with the slit almost to her hip.

She shook her head. "I don't think so."

Flashpoint

"Sweetie, when you have a body like yours, it would be considered a sin not to show it off."

"I'm five foot four. The slit is going to look ridiculous."

"Not when you have these on!" Francisco exclaimed, holding up a pair of sequined, four-inch heels.

"No." Sophia crossed her arms. "I'm not wearing those."

"But they go perfectly with the dress," Juan Diego argued.

"They look like stripper heels. I'll fall flat on my face."

"We'll be around to make sure you don't," Francisco promised.

She pursed her lips but didn't say anything more.

"Yes!" Juan Diego clapped his hands when she didn't refuse. "Girl, we're going to book you an appointment at the salon to get your hair, nails, and makeup done on Saturday afternoon. You're going to be the belle of the ball!"

"It's like you're my fairy godparents."

"Well, you're half-right anyway," Francisco teased.

At the spa two days later, she'd felt like Cinderella. The staff transformed her from the mousy blonde wallflower to a knockout with shimmering blonde highlights that emphasized the tan she'd managed to get in the Mexican sun. She hardly recognized herself in the full-length mirror before she left her hotel room. Feeling like a million bucks, Sophia strutted down the long, carpeted hallway to the elevator like it was a runway—then just before reaching the doors, she stumbled, barely catching herself before she fell flat on her face. She glanced around to see if anyone had witnessed her gaffe, but, thankfully, there was no one in sight, although she was sure whomever was monitoring the security cameras had a good laugh at her expense. Sophia smoothed her gown on the ride down to the lobby, then stepped carefully once she exited the elevator, and there were people around.

Her hosts had been true to their word and approached her the moment she strode into the lavish ballroom with the view of the patio. Beyond the elaborate, crystal-blue pool was the private hotel beach. She'd smelled the salt air from the Pacific Ocean wafting in through the open French doors when she entered the room.

As Francisco spun her around to get a look at her, she caught sight of the most handsome man she'd ever laid eyes on.

Holding onto her new friend's arm to steady herself in her heels after spinning, she tried to be nonchalant as she said, "Don't look right now, but who's that man at the bar in the grey suit?"

"I don't even have to look to know who you're talking about, *chica*," Juan Diego replied. "Ramon Guzman."

"At least she's got good taste," Francisco observed.

"And a thing for bad boys, apparently," his partner added.

"He's a bad boy?" She tried to casually glance at the sophisticated man in the tailored suit at the bar. With a drink in one hand, and the other in his trouser pocket, he looked like a GQ model." "Wow. I never would have guessed that. Your bad boys look quite different than our American ones."

"He's also the most powerful man in Ensenada."

"I think you could make an argument for all of Mexico."

That's interesting.

She stole another glance at him as he raised the glass of amber liquid to his lips, revealing an expensive-looking silver designer watch. His presence oozed he was in command.

"What does he do?" she asked.

"Oh no, no, no, baby girl," Francisco grabbed her arm and escorted her toward the group closest to them. "That's a question you don't want to ask or have answered."

"Yes, better to be in the dark," Juan Diego agreed. "You don't want to complicate things when you're doing the horizontal mambo with him."

"What are you talking about? I'm not going to sleep with him. Talk about out of my league."

"Have you seen yourself tonight? You're the most beautiful woman in the room. Judging by how much he's been looking in this direction, you definitely have his attention. Unless he's converted and is really checking me out, and if that's the case…" Francisco batted his eyelashes at his partner. "I might have to use my hall pass."

Juan Diego rolled his eyes. "I think your hall pass is safe." And like a flip of a switch, he enthusiastically greeted the men and women they'd walked up to. "Angelica! You just get more beautiful every time I see you, you bitch! How's that man of yours treating you?" Followed by, "This is our new American friend, Sophia Castle... Isn't she just the most adorable thing ever? Can you believe someone cheated on her? Poor thing came to Ensenada to mend her broken heart and ended up meeting Francisco and me! So, we're on a mission to find—"

She started coughing to interrupt his word vomit of her sad story and offered an embarrassed smile as she tugged him away.

"Thanks for sharing my dirty laundry with complete strangers, J.D.," she hissed.

"J.D.? Oh, I love it! Wait until I tell Francisco my new nickname!" He looked over her head, trying to capture his lover's attention, completely oblivious to the fact she was annoyed with him.

"Juan Diego. You're missing the point!"

He cocked his head. "What's the point?"

"The point is, you can't just blurt out that I'm in Ensenada to get over being humiliated by my ex. That's nobody's business. Just say I'm here on vacation and leave it at that."

His eyes widened, and he put his hand on his chest. "*Ay, dios mío. Lo siento, mami.* I have a big mouth and like to overshare everything. It won't happen again. Cross my heart." Then, he theatrically made a motion like he was marking an X on his chest. "I'll make it up to you. Come on."

Flashpoint

They started toward the next group, then on to the next. After catching himself a few times, Juan Diego was true to his word about not revealing too much about her stay. Sophia noticed they were getting closer to the gorgeous mystery man at the bar. At one point, she glanced over and found him staring at her. She wasn't sure what came over her, but she didn't look away. Maybe it was how sexy and beautiful she felt in the elegant dress and high heels—like she was someone else, at least for the night. Someone brave enough to return his stare.

His salacious smile quickly brought her back to reality—she was just a nerdy software analyst who couldn't even keep a computer engineer's attention. She'd be completely in over her head with someone like the powerful man at the bar, and she glanced away, not looking in his direction again, until finally ...

"Ramon! You gorgeous hunk of man. So glad you could make it! Have you met our new BFF, Sophia Castle? Sophia, this is Ramon Guzman."

"Nice to meet you," she said with a shy smile and offered her hand.

Ramon stood up straighter and set his drink on the bar. He was more handsome up close, and his bespoke suit fit him like a glove.

He took her extended hand and brought it to his lips, pressing a lingering kiss against her knuckles while holding her gaze with his gorgeous gold-flecked, chocolate-brown eyes. His hand was warm and soft, but his lips were cold—probably from the ice in his drink. She caught a hint of his sandalwood cologne, not overpowering but definitely masculine.

His voice was deep and sexy when he uttered, "Miss Castle, I assure you, the pleasure is all mine," without releasing her hand.

She reluctantly withdrew from his grasp, hypnotized by how charming he was. "Please, call me Sophia."

He nodded and murmured, "Sophia," as if trying it on for size. The sound of her name was like honey dripping from his lips, and she would have loved to hear him say it again.

"Are you visiting Ensenada or living here?"

"Um...." She was having difficulty articulating a thought with his intense gaze on her.

"She's staying here at the hotel for a few weeks," Francisco replied for her. "We met little Miss Soph at the pool a few days ago and adored her immediately."

"I can see why," Ramon said, his eyes still locked on hers.

She'd never been so flustered. Then again, she'd never had a man like Ramon Guzman blatantly interested in her.

Wait.

He *was* interested, right? Or was she jumping to conclusions?

Kevin had told her she tended to do that. Of course, he'd said that in the middle of gaslighting her when he was caught cheating. *Asshole.*

No, she needed to learn how to trust her gut again, and right now her gut was telling her the sexy man she was talking to *was* interested. She wasn't imagining the obvious signals he was giving off.

As if reading her mind and casting away any doubts, he held out his hand. "Care to dance?"

She somehow found her voice as she took his offered hand. "I'd love to."

Chapter Two

Ramon

He'd been right, she was American. At least her accent appeared to be. But then again, so did his. Having gone to boarding school and university in America, he could easily sound 'American' when he wanted. Although when he was in Ensenada for any period of time, his Mexican accent tended to become more pronounced.

It'd been a long time since a woman had caught his attention, but the one dancing in his arms had. There was just something about her that had captivated him the moment he'd laid eyes on her walking in the room. Her shy bumbling at the bar had been enchanting and a breath of fresh air from the women he usually met—those who always had an agenda.

Now, the feel of her bare back against his palm as he held her on the dance floor, the smell of coconut in her hair, and the sound of her laughter made him want to get to know her better. Clothing optional.

"How long are you visiting Ensenada?"

"I'm not sure. I'm booked at the hotel for another week, but I haven't decided if I'll stay longer after that."

That struck him as odd.

"Your job is okay with not knowing when you'll be back?"

"I'm a techie for a software company. I can work from anywhere. I've actually been able to work poolside a little this

Flashpoint

week. I'm guessing you've just arrived. I'm sure I'd have noticed you before if you'd been at the pool or bar."

Now he was really suspicious. It was obvious she'd been sent in ahead of his arrival. Women like her didn't just magically appear in his life. Not unless they'd been strategically placed there by people who wanted to destroy him. The CIA needed to change up their modus operandi. It was almost laughable at how predictable it was.

Still, she was intriguing enough that he'd play along for now. See how far he could push her. The cat and mouse game could be fun, and the sex would probably be incredible. That was one thing the CIA did do right—they always sent agents who liked to fuck, or at least pretend they did.

"Should we continue this in my suite?"

He felt her immediately tense up, then she tilted her head and narrowed her eyes as she created distance between their bodies.

"I, um..." She paused and took a deep breath, then continued, "We just met. I don't really do that."

He couldn't keep the amusement from his voice. "Do what?" He wanted to hear her say it out loud.

"I don't go home, or back to a hotel room, with a man I just met. Call me old-fashioned, but I'm not that kind of girl." As if to soften the blow, she added with a wry smile, "No matter how sexy and gorgeous the man is."

Well, that shocked him. *Is this a new CIA tactic?*

He decided he would walk away and watch her backpedal. There was no way her agency would approve of her letting him off the hook after she'd reeled him in.

"That's a shame. I think we would have had an enjoyable time." The song ended, and he gestured toward the ballroom and guided her in that direction. Once they reached the edge of the dance floor, he dropped his hand from her back. "It was nice meeting you, Sophia Castle."

With that, he headed back to the bar with a smug smile and started counting in his head. He'd reached twenty when he made it to the bar and turned around, surprised she was nowhere to be found.

It took him a second, but he located her with Francisco and Juan Diego again. They were fawning all over her. He made a mental note to have his people look deeper into the two men's dealings. Other than bribing customs officials to get their antiques expedited in and out of the country, Ramon hadn't known them to be affiliated with anyone he would deem troublesome—other than the CIA agents he already knew about circulating throughout the room, but he'd doubted the two men were aware of some of their guests' true identities. If Francisco and Juan Diego had decided to flip, he wasn't the only one in the room who'd put a giant red target on their backs.

No, the gay couple working with the CIA or rival cartels didn't make any sense. They'd been afforded a comfortable lifestyle in Ensenada, why would they jeopardize that? The more likely scenario was that they were an unwitting mark for the beautiful American. She'd found a way in through them.

Still, he would investigate the couple further, just to be safe. And the beautiful blonde who accompanied them.

****

Sophia

Wow. What a jerk.

She'd never been so insulted.

So, because I won't go back to his hotel room ten minutes after meeting him, that's it? He's no longer interested? Whatever. She could only imagine how many diseases he probably had.

She was glad she hadn't wasted more of her time with him. No matter how handsome he was or how sexy he smelled. Good riddance.

"Oh my god, tell us everything!" Juan Diego said, grabbing her arms when she reappeared next to him.

"Nothing to tell," she said dismissively. "It became pretty obvious we aren't compatible and went our separate ways."

"Not even for a vacation fling?" Francisco looked wistfully over at Ramon, who was back at the bar. "Rrrawr. I bet he would tear it up in the sheets."

"I'm sure he would. And I'm sure there are plenty of women here who would love to find out, but I'm not one of them."

Francisco looked at her skeptically. "You need a drink, sweetie. J.D., will you get our little Soph something from the bar?"

"One vodka tonic, extra lime coming right up!" Juan Diego leaned over and said at her shoulder, "We're trying out my new nickname. What do you think?"

"I can't get past that you remembered my drink order."

He winked at her. "My very first boyfriend after I came out used to drink the same thing. That's how I knew you and I were going to be fast friends."

"But he's your *ex*."

"Yeah, but he had great taste," he said with a smile and faraway look, then snapped back to the present and glanced at Francisco, who was now chatting with three men who'd just arrived. "Unfortunately, he was also broke as hell. Not a great combination. Be right back," and he headed to the bar.

Francisco pulled her into the conversation with the group. At first, she thought the men were gay and was surprised when one winked at her as he walked away.

"Okay, so you have to help me. I don't have a good gaydar. Who's straight, and who's gay here?"

"Everyone is straight, except for the lesbians over there." He nodded to a beautiful couple at a table by the French doors. "Well, and there's a couple of guys who are gay but don't know it, but that's a whole other story."

"You don't have gay friends?"

He shot her a look. "Of course we do. But they can get their own straights. We like being the *It* gay couple in Ensenada."

That made her laugh out loud. "You two are definitely *It*. I'm so lucky to have met you."

"We're going to have a blast until you go back to the States. Come on, I want to show you off to some more people."

Sophia danced and flirted with a few different men, trying hard to forget about the jerk at the bar. But it felt like every time she glanced his way, his eyes were on her. She avoided going to the bar until he'd found his seat for dinner at a table with a group of men who were also dressed in impeccable suits, and all equally handsome. But even from his new vantage point, she could feel his eyes on her. Why did he care what she was doing? He'd made it obvious he wasn't interested unless she was willing to sleep with him tonight. She had half a mind to leave with one of the men who'd been paying attention to her. That would serve the asshole right. Except she knew she was full of shit and would never really do it. She'd never actually go through with having a fling on vacation, no matter how much she'd daydreamed about it on the plane, at the pool, or in her hotel while lying alone in her king-sized bed. Or how much her friends—old and new—

encouraged it. She just couldn't envision it happening. Not really. Maybe in her fantasies, but she'd never done something that reckless before.

And maybe that was the problem. Kevin had said she was predictable and boring, not to mention mousy—that was why he'd cheated with his beautiful coworker. *She* was adventurous and glamorous. After he'd told Sophia that, upon her discovering them together naked in his hot tub, she went home, packed a bag, and was wheels up on the next flight out to Mexico. She could be flipping adventurous, too, dammit.

She hadn't yet regretted her spontaneous trip once, and meeting the boys, as she affectionately referred to Francisco and Juan Diego, had been the icing on the cake. Their party was exactly what she'd needed to feel beautiful about herself. She didn't need Kevin—there were plenty of fish in the sea, as this night had quickly shown her.

But there were also a few sharks, and one was headed directly for her.

Chapter Three

Ramon

He'd observed her all through dinner, and she didn't look his way again. Not once. Not to play coy as if she wanted him to change his mind. It was as though she had written him off.

If she was a spy, she was a shitty one. Either that, or a damn genius. Because he was now more intrigued than ever. But ignoring him had been a big gamble on her part.

He was second-guessing his conclusion altogether that Sophia Castle was a spy. Ramon decided, as he watched her dancing with other men, he needed to investigate further to be sure. And until he knew for sure, he sure as fuck wouldn't let someone else have a shot with her.

He noticed her watching him as he walked toward her table. Her lips parted slightly when she realized he was about to sit in the seat next to her.

"Do you need something, *Señor* Guzman?" she asked when he put his arm around the back of her chair.

He didn't even try to hide his smirk as he tilted his head. "*Señor* Guzman? My beautiful Sophia, I'm going to have to insist you call me Ramon. Especially since we're going to be spending so much time together while you're in Ensenada."

She narrowed her eyes at him. "How do you figure that?"

He shrugged with a small smile. "Just a hunch."

"I think you made it pretty clear when we were dancing about the only way you'd want to spend time with me. And I can assure you, *that* isn't going to happen. So, no, we won't be spending *any* time together."

He gave her his most contrite look. "Please forgive me. My behavior was rude and uncalled for. *Mi madre* would have my head if she knew I had behaved like that, God rest her soul. She's probably rolling over in her grave as we speak, waiting to strike me down with a bolt of lightning when I walk outside."

She didn't even try to hide her derision. "Oh, that would be too bad. I suggest you stay away from the windows then."

"I deserved that. But you have to believe me when I say I didn't mean to offend you."

Sophia snorted. "Forgive me if I don't believe you. I find it hard to believe that's the first time you've used that tactic."

He could feel the corners of his mouth turning up. "You are correct. But it's the first time I've been told *no,* and someone walked away insulted."

"How charming." She rolled her eyes and scooted her chair to remove his arm from her seat back. Undeterred, he moved his as well and returned his arm.

"Why don't you try again with someone who will say yes?" She gave an exaggerated glance around the ballroom. "I'm sure there are plenty of women who would be happy to accompany you to your suite after one dance. You're wasting your time with me. I'm not interested."

That just made him even more intrigued. Did she know she'd have that effect on him? Was that why she turned him down?

Ramon stood. "Please. Allow me another chance." He held out his hand. "Dance with me."

****

Sophia

She stared up at his handsome face, shocked at the nerve of the guy. It *was* a really handsome face. But the way he stared into her eyes felt like he could see into her soul was disarming.

He stood next to her with his hand outstretched, refusing to withdraw it when she didn't take it, and people were starting to stare, which made her uncomfortable. Against her better judgment, she took Ramon's offered hand.

He led her onto the dance floor, then wrapped an arm around her, so his hand was on the small of her bare back, while he held her hand in his other, and expertly moved her around the floor.

"Tell me more about yourself, Sophia Castle. Where do you live?"

"I grew up in San Diego, but after college, I moved to San Francisco when I was hired by my company. And you?"

He didn't answer her question but continued with his own. "Who do you work for?"

It was a natural follow-up question to her answer, yet there was an almost urgency when he asked, which made her pause. Why did he care? Was he going to judge her once she told him her company's name? It certainly wasn't big enough for him to be familiar with it.

So, instead of answering his question, and even though Juan Diego and Francisco had warned her not to, she pressed her own questions of him. "What about you, Ramon? Where do you work?"

"I'm the president of Guzman Enterprises. We're a conglomerate with most of our businesses located in Mexico, Central America, and the Western United States, although we've recently branched into the Eastern U.S., South America, Europe, and Canada."

"What does your business do?"

"We're involved in many things. The furniture industry, agriculture, shipping, pot dispensaries, textiles, and manufacturing to name a few."

That didn't sound dangerous. Why did they say Ramon was a 'bad boy?'

"Wow. Do you travel a lot?"

"Only when necessary outside of Ensenada and San Diego. My executive staff usually handles things outside of those territories."

"So, how often would you say you travel to..." She couldn't decide which part of the world sounded most interesting. They all did. Finally, she settled on, "South America?"

He slowed their tempo as they danced and narrowed his eyes.

"A few times a year." There was an unspoken *why?* hanging in the air. Still she continued.

"What about... Europe?"

His words were deliberate, almost cautious. "I've been once this year, and I might go back in the fall."

"Fascinating," she whispered, almost to herself.

Sophia meant it. It sounded like he led an exciting life. A far cry from hers, that was for sure. There was no way they had anything in common, or probably even anything much to talk about.

No wonder he simply wanted to sleep with her. She had a feeling they'd be good at that together. The way he held her reverently in his strong arms while dominantly moving her around the dance floor with their bodies in sync had her imagining him taking charge in other ways. She could feel his muscles under his jacket. They, along with his cocky smile and the scent of his cologne were like an aphrodisiac. The deep timber in his voice, coupled with the way he held her gaze, had her feeling tempted to say yes if he asked again.

Whoa, slut. Where did that come from? You were just muttering about how he probably had a disease.

Juan Diego had encouraged her earlier to make a move on one of the men at their table and *tsked* at her when she told him she didn't do that.

"You're on vacation, getting over catching your man in the act with another woman. If ever there was a time to *do that*, it's now. Go snag one of Ramon's yummy companions if he's not interested. Hell, even his bodyguards are worth getting naked with."

She hadn't told him about Ramon's proposition. She had a feeling if she'd had, he would have marched her over to the sexy man's table and sat her down on his lap.

"It's a beautiful night," Ramon murmured in her ear. "Care to take a stroll on the beach?"

"I'm in four-inch heels."

His smile made it to his beautiful brown eyes. The crinkly lines around them somehow made him look kinder.

"I noticed. You look beautiful in them, but they must be killing your feet. Think about how good the cool, soft sand would feel between your bare toes."

That did sound heavenly. Still, she wasn't sure about being alone with him.

He must have sensed that was her hesitation, because he wrapped one hand at his waist and gave a small bow. "I promise I will be a perfect gentleman."

She couldn't help but laugh. "Okay, just let me tell Juan Diego where we're going."

"He'll vouch for me."

"Yes, he's said you're the most powerful man in Ensenada. But I think that makes you more dangerous, not less."

He cocked his head. "How so?"

"Powerful men often don't have to suffer the consequences of their actions."

That made him stop short, and he took a pregnant pause before he responded, "I suppose you're not wrong about that. But you have my word, no harm will come to you if you're alone with me. Can you say the same?"

Sophia frowned. "I would hardly consider myself a threat. Although, I do have pepper spray in my purse in case we come across anything nefarious."

He grinned at her. "I have a .45 caliber strapped to my ankle. I've got us covered."

She felt her eyes widen. "Really?"

He simply winked in response, not answering either way.

"Do you really have bodyguards here tonight?"

His smirk let her know he did.

Bodyguards? Weapons? She was so out of her comfort zone. And her league.

"Are they going to walk on the beach with us?"

The amusement in his tone was back as he stared at her thoughtfully. "No. I trust you."

"If you have bodyguards, I'm guessing me and my pepper spray are the least of your worries."

"Perhaps. I mean, I don't necessarily want to announce to the room that I'm headed to the beach accompanied only by a beautiful woman."

"Then I probably should tell Francisco where I'm going instead of Juan Diego," she replied with a laugh, trying to make light of the situation.

"That might be best. Francisco will vouch for me, too."

"Be right back."

He winked at her again. "I'll be waiting on the patio."

Chapter Four

Ramon

He was going out on a limb being alone with her, but his men knew where he was, and his watch had a built-in tracking device should she decide to kidnap him instead of kill him. Although the thought of being kidnapped by her had its own appeal.

But his gut was telling him she was as innocent as she portrayed herself. The red flags of her being too good to be true were from years of being suspicious of *everybody*.

"Don't sabotage this based on *you're not sure*. You need to find out for certain who she is before you do anything rash," his nephew, Dante had said at dinner after Ramon had told him about meeting her and his doubts about her identity.

"Isn't that how you knew Bella was CIA? Because she was too good to be true?"

"There were a lot of tells with Bella—one was her eagerness to get to know me and please me. This girl just blew you off because you insulted her. Too good to be true would've been if she'd taken you up on your offer and blown your mind in bed."

Ramon smirked. He knew that was how Bella got to his nephew but chose not to mention that.

"So, you think she's on the up-and-up? Just some beautiful woman on vacation, who innocently ran into the party hosts at the hotel bar, and got invited tonight purely by happenstance?"

"I'm not saying you should let your guard down, and we definitely need to do some digging with our guy on the inside. I'm just suggesting you proceed with caution and leave the door open. I've been telling you for a while now that it'd be good for you to be in a real relationship. Maybe it'd mellow your ass out a little."

Either his nephew was in on another coup attempt—with Ramon's life this time, or he really had his uncle's best interests at heart.

Ramon guessed time would tell and stood to apologize to the stunning blonde who'd captured his attention.

And now here he was, waiting on the patio to take a romantic, moonlit stroll on the beach with her. He either had a death wish, or he'd lost his mind—but he had to get to know the little American better.

He waited patiently while she went to tell one of their hosts that she was going for a walk on the beach with him. Ramon recognized it for what it was... letting someone know where she was and who she was with in case something happened to her. Something every woman should do, frankly.

What was the word she'd used? *Nefarious.*

When she'd said it, it was all he could do to keep from cupping her adorable face in his hands and kissing the hell out of her. God, he hoped she was the real deal because he couldn't get enough of her.

She appeared at his side with her heels in one hand, dangling by their straps from her fingertips, with her dress bunched up to the side in her other hand, and a shy smile. "Ready?"

He offered his elbow. "Absolutely."

She stood, unmoving, looking at him. "When was the last time you walked on a beach? Don't you think you should take your shoes and socks off? Maybe roll up your pantlegs?"

He didn't make a move to do any of those things. He really did have a gun strapped to his ankle. Whenever he left the house, he was sure to always have one on him. Usually two. But he left the one he normally wore in his waistband in the safe tonight.

Sophia sighed and rolled her eyes, transferring her shoes to the fingertips of the hand holding her dress, and looped her free arm through his.

"Oh my god. You've just committed an epic beach fail. I'm almost embarrassed for you, it's so bad."

She's busting my balls.

Women didn't bust his balls. They fawned over him. Bent over backwards to stroke his male ego. Hung on his every word, laughed at anything he said that could remotely be construed as funny. Worshipped him on their knees when he snapped his fingers.

Not this girl.

He fucking loved it.

They made it to the ocean's shoreline and walked on the hard sand as the waves ebbed and flowed, just out of their path.

"Tell you what. I'll walk on the beach properly with you tomorrow, after we've had breakfast."

"If you weren't prepared to walk on the beach tonight, why'd you suggest it?"

Ramon noticed she didn't balk at his innuendo they'd be together in the morning.

"I was tired of sharing you with the rest of the room. I wanted you all to myself. Besides, I was sincere when I suggested you get out of those shoes."

And that dress.

"Well, I have to admit, you were right. The sand feels wonderful on my feet. These shoes were taking their toll. I'm not used to wearing heels, or fancy dresses for that matter. My wardrobe consists mostly of yoga pants and flip flops."

An image of her in yoga pants flashed in his mind, and his cock jumped. He'd been semi-hard since holding her on the dance floor the first time. Having her hands wrapped possessively around his arm with the smell of her hair wafting up to his nose as they walked along the beach alone together hadn't done much to change that.

"I think I'd like to see you in yoga pants."

She rewarded him with her beautiful laughter.

"I think you may have a false impression of me. Tonight's version of Sophia Castle is sexy and sophisticated, and not at all the real me. In real life, I'm a nerdy wallflower. In fact, I tripped in the hallway on my way to the elevator tonight. I guarantee if we'd met under different circumstances, when I wasn't made up by professionals, you wouldn't have looked twice at me."

"I find that hard to believe."

She shrugged. "It's true. I'm normally a giant geek, complete with glasses and everything."

He ceased walking and pulled her against him, encircling her body in his arms while he looked down at her.

"I'm perfectly capable of seeing past some makeup and hairspray, my little American nerd. And you're stunning, Sophia Castle."

Without an ounce of hesitation, he lowered his mouth to nip at her lips gently. When she nipped back, that was all the invitation Ramon needed, and he held her firmly against him as his tongue sought to tangle with hers.

He heard the thud of her shoes hit the sand and felt her arms come around his neck. Her body was soft and pliant as she molded her frame against his.

Ramon wove his fingers into her hair with one hand while the other remained against her bare back. Sophia flexed her hips against his hard cock, and he deepened the kiss. He was completely lost in the feeling of her soft mouth as she returned his urgent kiss and the heat generating between them. It was dangerous how enthralled he was, but her sweet lips tasted too good. Her body felt like she was made for him.

And they were still completely clothed. However, the longer he kissed her, the more he wanted to remedy that.

The sound of a group of partygoers approaching slowed things down between them, although they remained entwined in each other's embrace with their foreheads touching, as the group passed with a nod and smile.

"I think I better get you back to the hotel before I propose fucking you in the sand."

Her sigh indicated she was conflicted about not doing exactly that. Finally, she murmured, "You're probably right."

Ramon wanted to ask her to come back to his room with him. It was on the tip of his tongue to suggest it, but he decided to wait. He had a feeling if she spent the night with him tonight, she'd disappear before morning, and he wanted to see her again.

They walked hand in hand back to where the party was still going strong. As they approached the lights, Sophia tried smoothing down her messy hair while musing, "I must look like I've been making out on the beach."

He smiled when he looked down at her well-kissed face. She had no lipstick left, and her sensitive skin was red from his five-o'clock shadow rubbing against it.

"Yes, you do."

"I think I'm just going to go to my room."

"I'll walk you. I want to make sure you get there safe and sound." If anyone saw her leave with him, he might have just inadvertently put a target on her back too. *Fuck.*

Flashpoint

At first, he thought she would argue, but she must have realized it would be useless.

"I'm this way."

Good girl.

****

Sophia

She could say with certainty that she'd never been kissed like Ramon Guzman had kissed her on the beach. She felt like she was still in a daze as they walked toward her room. She found herself wondering if she could be brave enough to invite him in. He'd awoken something in her. Sophia decided that if he asked to come in, she would say yes.

Except he didn't ask. Just dropped a kiss on her forehead and said, "Breakfast on the patio tomorrow? Say, nine o'clock? I'll be properly dressed this time for a walk on the beach, then maybe we can hang out by the pool in the afternoon."

"Um, yeah." She had to admit she was a little disappointed that he didn't even try to come inside. "That sounds like a plan."

"Good night, my sweet *nerdicita*," he said with a grin. "Sleep well."

He stood in the hall as she opened the door with her key.

"Make sure you throw the security lock when you close the door, along with the deadbolt."

"I will."

Ramon leaned down and kissed her lips softly. "Dream of me," he whispered when he finally pulled away.

"I could say the same," she sassily retorted.

His smile was crooked. "Oh, there's no doubt about that." He gave her a wink and stepped back. "See you in the morning."

Closing the door behind her, she did as he instructed, then leaned against the wooden barrier, touching her swollen lips absentmindedly.

Her phone dinged as soon as she'd slipped her dress off and washed her face.

Juan Diego: Tell me everything! The normally immaculate Ramon looks a little disheveled; I can only imagine what you look like!

He went back to the party?

Sophia: We kissed on the beach—that's all. I went back to my room alone and am now in my pajamas. My good-girl reputation is still rightfully intact.

Juan Diego: Oh, honey. You need a new rep. And I bet Ramon Guzman is just the man to help you with that! Do you want me to send him back to your room to try again?

Sophia glanced down at her white, cotton nightgown with the tiny yellow flower pattern and high, lace neckline. A far cry from the sexy dress she'd donned earlier.

Sophia: No!

Juan Diego: Okay, fine. He already left anyway.

Juan Diego: Breakfast tomorrow?

Sophia: I'm having breakfast with Ramon.

Juan Diego: I love it! I will gladly concede my time with you to the sexy *capo*. But I want details!

She smiled when she read his text. She loved his theatrics.

Sophia: I'll talk to you tomorrow, my friend.

Juan Diego: Sweet dreams, *mami*.

She had no doubt that her sleep would be filled with images of the gorgeous, rich Mexican. Hopefully doing dirty things to her body. Naughty things none of her boyfriends had ever done before. Because there was no doubt in her mind, he'd know what he was doing.

Chapter Five

Ramon

She looked vastly different from last night when she appeared for breakfast dressed in an orange, pink, and blue plaid sundress, and nothing but mascara and lip gloss for makeup, yet was still adorable. Her hair was pulled back in a loose ponytail with a pair of big, white sunglasses on top of her head.

"Good morning," he said with a welcoming smile when he stood and pulled out her chair. He'd gotten a table under an umbrella near the pool. He could make out the freckles on her nose, something he hadn't noticed last night under her makeup. They suited her. "You look beautiful. How'd you sleep?"

She placed the big, multi-colored straw beach bag she had slung over her shoulder onto the back of the chair and sat. "Surprisingly well."

"Did you dream about me?"

The blush on her cheeks as she quickly looked down while putting the napkin in her lap suggested she may have done more than just dream about him. That made two of them. He'd jerked off before going to bed last night, and again in the shower that morning, thinking about how soft her body had felt against his as they kissed on the beach, and as he imagined how amazing she'd feel as he was sinking himself balls deep inside her. He had fallen under her spell.

Flashpoint

Ramon had been on the phone with Pedro Ruiz, one of his top lieutenants, the minute he'd returned to his room last night—directing him to start a background search on the self-proclaimed nerdy American. He also had Dante check with his men about what they could find about her. Ramon wanted different sources confirming her identity, in case one of his men was scheming against him. If both men were working together... well, then sweet Sophia was probably the least of Ramon's worries.

He didn't think his men were conspiring against him; he'd given them no reason to. He listened to their recommendations about ways they could legitimize the cartel and authorized the money to make it happen. Being on the up and up was especially important to Dante. Ramon's nephew had promised his former-CIA wife that the organization would be 'more legal than not' within five years. That's the best he could offer her, and she loved him enough to take it.

There'd been no reply from either man before Ramon headed to breakfast, not that he had expected something that soon, but he kept his phone in his pocket in case the call or text came later.

Their server arrived immediately once Sophia sat. One of the perks of being head of the Guzman family, he supposed. Either that or the occupant of the Presidential Suite in the hotel, it was hard to tell. Either way, he appreciated the prompt, attentive service.

Once they'd placed their order, he asked her about what she'd seen so far while in Ensenada.

"I've only been here a few days and have just wanted to unwind and relax and try to forget why I came until I absolutely have to face it again."

That made his ears perk up. "Why did you come?"

Her smile was phony when she vaguely reiterated what she'd just said. "To get away and not think about things."

"Get away from what?"

"San Francisco."

He cocked his head and opened his mouth to ask more questions, but she put her hand on top of his.

"I'd really rather not think about it right now; it just upsets me. I hope you understand. I'd much rather talk about you, and maybe what we're going to do today."

Her cryptic response left him very unsatisfied and suspicious, especially once they started talking about other things, and he found himself more smitten with her by the minute.

She is too good to be true.

There hadn't been a lull in their conversation once. No awkward silences as they searched for something to keep the conversation going. And her apparent lack of filter was like a breath of fresh air. She was unapologetically herself, in the most endearing way possible. When she offered to pay for her fifteen-dollar breakfast, he couldn't help but smile. No one ever offered to pay their own way around him. They all stood around waiting for him to open his wallet. Not that paying was ever a hardship for Ramon, but the gesture would have been nice once in a while.

"I appreciate the offer, really. But please let me spoil you while you're in Ensenada. You're a guest in my city; it's the least I can do."

"Well, next time you're in San Francisco, you'll have to let me return the favor."

He didn't agree, just simply smiled at her. It dawned on him that if she really was who she said she was, then she probably had no idea how much he was worth.

"Are you ready for the beach?" she asked as she stood and slipped the large bag over her shoulder.

Ramon stood as well. "Absolutely."

"You look ready."

He'd dressed casually in tan pleated linen shorts, a plain white linen button-up shirt with cutaway collar, and most important for a day at the beach—flip flops. While not being strapped left him uneasy, her company made up for it.

They put their sunglasses on at the same time, and he gestured toward the walkway leading to the ocean—the same one they'd used last night. "Shall we?"

She nodded her head, and they started toward the turquoise blue water. After taking only a few steps, he reached for her petite hand, not looking at her as he did. From his peripheral vision, he could tell she didn't look his way but entwined her fingers with his like it was the most natural thing in the world to do.

It felt like it was.

If she was a spy or an assassin or a decoy, he was going to be so disappointed.

****

Sophia

After walking along the beach hand in hand, laughing and talking the entire time, they arrived back at the hotel.

"We probably should have put our stuff on a few lounge chairs before we left. I hope we can still find two together," she mused as she surveyed the busy pool area.

"That shouldn't be a problem. We have our own cabana for the day."

She looked at him with raised eyebrows, and he shrugged. "One of the perks of my room."

A hotel staff member greeted him by name the second they approached the area where the towels were distributed.

"*Señor* Guzman. May I show you and Ms. Castle to your cabana?"

"Wow. They know who I am, too?"

She noticed a tick in his jaw at the observation and wondered what that was about.

From an analytical perspective, Sophia knew the two of them didn't make sense. He was a rich and powerful tycoon,

Flashpoint

and she was a plain Jane computer software analyst who lived alone in a studio apartment because that was all she could afford in San Francisco. She'd put this whole vacation on her credit card, and it would take her months to pay it off. Ramon wasn't just out of her league; they weren't even in the same universe. And still somehow, he'd made her feel like she was enough just as she was.

Granted, he'd been an ass when they first met, but she suspected he wasn't lying when he said that approach usually worked. But he'd apologized and had since made her feel like he was interested in more than a quick fuck with her.

The time she'd spent with him after he apologized last night had been like something from a movie. He was brilliant, witty, obviously gorgeous, and easy to talk to. All while making her feel comfortable in her own skin—something Kevin never once did in their three years together.

Now they were lounging poolside in a private cabana with their own personal server who dropped everything when either she or Ramon buzzed the bar. Sophia noticed the other cabanas didn't have their own designated server—just two waiters running ragged to accommodate everyone's requests. Luckily, neither she nor Ramon were high maintenance, freeing up their server's time to help the others.

"I feel like someone should be feeding us grapes right now. I think this is the most decadent thing I've ever done," Sophia said as she took a sip of her piña colada and adjusted her big floppy hat to shield her face from the sun peeking in their tent.

Although he joined her in the pool whenever she got in, Ramon had been working on and off on his tablet throughout the day and would occasionally excuse himself to take a phone call, but he was currently taking a break in the lounger next to her with a drink in his hand.

He tilted his head on the seat cushion to lazily look over at her with his sunglasses hiding his gorgeous eyes. "Stick with me, *cariña*. This is nothing."

"I don't think I could afford to keep up with you. You and I live in two very different worlds."

"First of all, *you* wouldn't have to be able to afford anything. I'm obscenely wealthy and am happy to pay for things. I would actually get great enjoyment at being able to spend my money on you."

She wrinkled her nose. "I would feel like a freeloader."

Ramon frowned. "You're anything but. Not to mention, you make me happy with your company, so just let me spend my money on you, please."

"Now I just sound like a sugar baby. I don't know which is worse."

That made him laugh out loud, and he reached for her hand. "If it will make you feel any better, you can buy breakfast tomorrow."

"Okay, good."

They'd sat with their eyes closed for a few minutes when Ramon wondered out loud, "Don't sugar babies usually provide sex for their daddies? If that's the case, we should probably look closer at that dynamic."

She pulled her glasses down the tip of her nose and looked at him, unenthused.

He matched her gesture and said with a devilish grin. "I'm just saying... I wouldn't be opposed."

Staring at his washboard abs all day as he walked around shirtless, she had to admit, she wasn't exactly opposed either. Not the sex-for-gifts-and-money part, just the sex part.

"You couldn't handle me," she quipped as she pushed her sunglasses back up and pulled her hat further down her eyes to hide her true feelings. Which were really, *I would be in so over my head with you.*

"Maybe not. But I wouldn't mind trying my best to keep up." He lowered his voice and leaned closer. "I can't think of anything I'd enjoy more than spending all night pleasuring you."

Sophia felt her nipples stiffen at the idea, and she heard a little whimper escape her lips. His smug smile when he put his head back against the lounger told her he'd heard it too.

****

Ramon

Pedro's call that afternoon had been great news. Everything his lieutenant could find on Sophia Castle seemed to match the Sophia he'd spent the day with.

Sophia Leigh Castle. Middle child—two brothers, Liam—married, two kids, and Greyson—single. Born and raised in San Diego where her still-married, middle-class parents resided. That bode well for Ramon since his primary residence was also in San Diego. Thirty-four years old, never married, no children, Stanford-educated, making barely one hundred grand a year as a software analyst. He shook his head. *And she's living in one of the most expensive cities in the United States.* Ramon could only imagine the shoebox she had to be living in. Why would she live in San Francisco? It sounded like her job would allow her to work from anywhere.

Her only debts seemed to be her student loans, small amounts on a loan for a Volkswagen Jetta, and a few credit cards. Nothing that seemed suspicious or would cause her to do anything out of character. She did have a tidy amount, for someone in her early thirties, tucked away in a 401K. That made him smile, but also confirmed she had to be living in a studio or commuting three hours daily to have been able to save that much of her salary.

She had a strong social media presence, and all her photos seemed to be authentic. Her *Throwback Thursday* photos of when she was a child were fucking adorable.

He'd finally been able to relax with her. Well, as much as he could with her in that goddamn black bikini.

When she walked out of the changing room, he was sure his jaw hit the floor just as his dick sprang to attention, wanting a better look.

She had to know she was torturing him when she asked him to put lotion on her back. At least he knew she was as affected by him when her skin broke out in goose pimples at his touch.

They'd been trading long looks all afternoon and subtle touches, not to mention his outright sharing verbally of his attraction to her.

He needed to get her to his place in town. It was on a cliff overlooking the ocean, much like his home in San Diego—only smaller and much more secure than the hotel. His guards would appreciate it.

Even though everyone who knew him knew he traveled with a large security detail, he'd still asked his men to try to blend in as much as they could this weekend. It'd been easy last night at the party—everyone was wearing suits, making for easy weapons concealment. Poolside today in shorts, made it a little more difficult, although he'd rented the cabanas immediately surrounding theirs to help with containment.

Ramon hadn't planned on staying overnight at the hotel—the suite had been more of a staging area, and he'd been planning on heading back to San Diego Monday morning. Then he met a little nerdy blonde from California, so he extended his stay not only in Ensenada, but at the hotel. Still. He'd rather be at his home.

"Would you like to have dinner with me tonight? At my house? I have a wonderful cook who rivals any top chef."

She eyed him with a small smile. "If I say yes, you're not expecting me to spend the night, are you? You'll bring me back to my room tonight, right?"

He'd rather not. He'd much rather she slept in his bed. Not that they'd do much sleeping.

Still, Ramon replied with, "If that's what you want. You'd be welcome to stay, too, of course."

Sophia nervously pulled at a thread on her towel. "I don't know. Maybe we should just have dinner at the hotel's restaurant. I don't want to give you the wrong impression."

"And what impression would that be?"

"That I sleep with men after knowing them for only one day."

"Sophia, I think we've established that you don't make a habit out of taking men home." A small grin escaped his lips as he decided to push the envelope, just a little. "However, since you're on vacation, I do think you should seriously consider making an exception for me. I promise to dote on you until you leave Ensenada. I want to have as much of your time as you'll allow me while you're here."

Her pursed lips told him she wasn't convinced.

"Okay, how about this? Pack an overnight bag, and I promise you can sleep in the guest room if you decide to stay at my place."

"*Alone.*"

Ramon shrugged. "If you decide that's what you want."

She bit her bottom lip as she looked at him, like she was struggling with her decision.

"Or you can come back to the hotel if you'd rather. Whatever you're comfortable with."

"Okay."

He didn't know which scenario exactly she was agreeing to but decided to quit while he was ahead and closed his eyes.

He heard a little gasp from her. "Oh! I promised Francisco and Juan Diego I'd have drinks with them at five though. I'd invite you along, but I suspect they just want to hear all about our day together."

Thinking about those two theatrically grilling her made him chuckle.

"That's okay, I have some more work I can do in my suite. Can you be ready to leave the hotel at seven? It's just a short drive to my house."

She glanced at her watch. "Yes. I probably should go get ready." She sat up, slipped a black cover-up over her head, and gathered her things.

When she had everything in her straw bag, she put her hands on his lounger and leaned down.

"Thank you for a perfect day," she whispered, inches from his face, then softly kissed his lips. Her mouth was warm, and he could smell her suntan lotion. She controlled the tempo of the kiss, leaving him wanting more. Much more. It was all he could do not to close the tent's flaps and pull her onto the couch in the rear of the cabana.

"I'll pick you up at the hotel bar at seven," he promised when she finally pulled back.

She seemed reluctant to leave and murmured, "Okay," before leaning down and kissing him again.

When she pulled away a second time and looked into his eyes, Ramon growled, "You better leave now, little one, or you may not make drinks. As a matter of fact, we might not even make dinner."

He thought that would scare her, but she didn't make a move to leave, and the corners of her mouth turned up in amusement.

"That's not much of a threat, you know."

She was challenging him. It made his cock want to punch a hole in his board shorts.

He sat up taller, so he was in her space and said in a low voice, "How about this, then? If you don't leave now, I'm closing the tent and laying you down on the couch. Then I'm going to spread your legs, move that tiny swimsuit to the side, and lick your pussy until you're shaking with ecstasy and calling out my name for everyone to hear."

Her pupils dilated, and she swallowed hard. Still, she didn't move. It was as if she were either imagining it, or contemplating it, or both.

She took a deep breath through her nose until her chest rose high, tempting him to bury his face between her tits. He was just about to bite her nipples over the cover up, when her chest lowered, and she stepped back.

"I'll see you at seven," she said as she continued walking backward. "Thank you again for a wonderful day." She then turned and scurried away, his hard dick calling after her to come back.

"We'll see her again, soon, buddy," he mumbled to his appendage as he stood to gather his belongings and head back to his suite to get some more work done before dinner.

Chapter Six

Sophia

She wore a baby pink sleeveless romper that showed off her tan with a pair of nude, strappy sandals. Sophia thought it worked for both drinks at the bar and dinner at his house.

Her hair was piled on her head in a messy bun, and she slipped on a simple gold chain that shimmered against her tan skin and matching small hoop earrings. She went with understated makeup—just a swipe of mascara, a touch of eyeliner, and pale pink lipstick that matched her outfit almost perfectly.

As she looked herself over in the mirror before heading down to the bar, Sophia decided that beach life suited her.

She'd been having the time of her life so far. Ignoring Kevin's apology texts had been easier than she'd thought it would be. Between Juan Diego and Francisco, and that sexy man who'd kissed the hell out of her, she'd had no trouble occupying her mind with other things.

Her phone buzzed as she waited for the elevator.

Kevin: Baby, I'm sorry. She means nothing to me. You're the one I want to be with. Tell me where you are and let me come apologize in person.

Ha! Fat chance, dick.

Rolling her eyes, she threw her phone in her purse and got on the elevator—feeling strangely liberated at not even wanting his lame apology as she hit the button for the main floor. She didn't give a damn anymore what he had to say, and it felt great.

"Wow, look at you," Francisco declared, grabbing both hands and looking her up and down before kissing one cheek, then the other. "Someone got some sun today. You look fabulous."

"Thanks, and you two are looking very GQ, as always," she said with a broad smile as she took her seat at the high-top table where Juan Diego was seated. "Hi, J.D."

He ignored her greeting and with narrowed eyes, accused, "You got laid, didn't you?"

"What?" she said with a coy smile while twisting her body to hang her bag from the back of her chair. "Don't be silly."

She knew her vague answer would torment him.

"Listen." He pointed a finger ominously at her. "Since we introduced you to him, it is mandatory that you tell us everything. Don't leave out a single, sordid detail."

Sophia erupted in giggles at Juan Diego's distress over the thought of not being in the know and leaned over to give him a peck on his cheek. The sour look on his face lessened but didn't completely subside.

"There's nothing to tell, I promise. We kissed in the cabana by the pool before I left, that's it."

"What about last night? You were gone an awfully long time before he reappeared, and you, noticeably, did not. One can only presume—based on his appearance—it's because you were no longer presentable. Maybe had a little sand in your hair?"

"We just kissed last night, too."

Juan Diego looked over at his partner in disgust. "That man is being wasted being straight." He looked back at her, his eyes wide with drama. "Do you have any idea what I would have let him do to me?"

"No, actually, I don't," she said with a laugh as she shook her head. "But I think I could probably figure it out."

He frowned and shook his head slowly. "Girl. You better ride that stallion. You owe it to hetero women and gay men everywhere."

Francisco, who had been looking on with amusement, squeezed the top of her hand and said, "You take your time. Don't do anything until you're ready."

Juan Diego waved his hand dismissively and sat back in his chair. "Don't listen to him. He pressured me on our first date."

Francisco looked at his lover with a small grin and a twinkle in his eye. "Funny. That's not how I remember our first date at all."

"Well..." a small grin escaped Juan Diego's lips, as if involuntarily. "That's how it would have gone if I wasn't so easy."

"You? Easy?" Sophia teased. "I never would have guessed."

Flashpoint

"And…" He looked at Francisco demonstratively then back at her. "It worked, didn't it? He was putty in my hands afterward. You might want to reconsider your tactics."

She laughed at how blatant he was being in front of Francisco. That's how she knew he was full of it.

"My situation is different. You seem to forget I'm leaving soon. There's no long-term potential there."

"Besides, sex shouldn't be a tactic," Francisco admonished.

Juan Diego rolled his eyes. "Please. Like there would have been a second date otherwise."

Francisco shot him a look and countered, "On either part."

"Touché." Juan Diego turned back to her, resting his palms together on the table in front of him and wiggling in his chair like he was about to dish some gossip. "So, when are you seeing him again?"

"We're having dinner tonight."

"Oh reeeeeallly? Where is he taking you?"

She hesitated, knowing her friend would screech and draw attention to the table if she told him she was going to Ramon's house for dinner.

"Um, I'm not sure. He just said it'd be casual."

The two men speculated about where Ramon would take her that would be considered casual.

"I'll let you know tomorrow," she said while trying to keep her face neutral so as not to give away she already knew their destination. Changing the subject, she asked, "So, what's the tea from last night? Spill." before taking a sip of the vodka tonic with extra lime they'd had waiting for her when she sat down.

That did the trick because they quickly changed their focus to giving her the gossip about all the partygoers from last night.

She had no idea who any of the people they talked about were, but she oohed, ahhhed, and tsked at all the appropriate times. Her ear perked up, however, when Juan Diego said, "Did you see Raquel Torres?" He turned to Sophia to give her some back story. "Rumor has it she and Ramon dated for like, a hot minute. Anyway, you should have seen her face when she noticed you and Ramon leave the party. I thought I was about to witness some real Joan Collins shit when she marched right up to him once he came back. I expected her to slap his face or throw her drink at him, and I don't mind telling you, I was a little disappointed when they just seemed to have a civil conversation. Although I was glad to see him shut her down when she pawed at him and tried to fix his hair."

"The hair I'm betting *you* messed up," Francisco added.

Despite the irrational pang of jealousy she felt over another woman touching him, Sophia smiled at the memory of how his hair had gotten messed up. His thick, black hair had felt so soft when she ran her fingers through it as she kissed him on the beach. Not to mention, *that kiss.*

Flashpoint

"Oh, speak of the devil," Juan Diego gushed and lifted his chin toward the bar entrance where Ramon stood, looking sexy as sin wearing an open-collared, white button-down shirt he'd left untucked and a pair of old, faded jeans.

He noticed all three of them staring at him and smiled as he started toward them; his perfect white teeth and white shirt were a sexy contrast to his tan skin.

"Oh my god, girl. If you don't fuck him tonight, there is seriously something wrong with you."

"There's nothing wrong with taking it slow," Francisco told her, then hissed, "Juan Diego, stop it."

Although, if she were honest with herself, Juan Diego wasn't exactly wrong.

Her toes curled when he greeted her by putting his hand at her waist and kissing right below the ear, then whispered, "You look beautiful."

"Thank you." She could feel herself beaming up at him. "You look very handsome."

He didn't take his hand from her waist when he nodded. "Gentlemen. Thank you again for the invitation last night. I enjoyed your party."

"We're so glad you could make it and that you enjoyed yourself," Francisco graciously replied.

"Well, of course you enjoyed yourself. You met our little Soph there. Where are you taking her to dinner?"

Ramon glanced at her like he was confused, looking at her face when he answered, "We're eating at my house, remember? My personal cook is preparing an authentic Mexican dinner for us."

Juan Diego looked at her with pursed lips. "Oh, really? You forgot that?"

She hopped off her chair, carefully avoiding looking at either of the men who she could feel staring—no, glaring at her, and responded with more enthusiasm than was necessary. "Well, that sounds yummy! Shall we go?"

After slinging her bag on her shoulder, she snuck a glance at Francisco. He stood and had a warm smile with his arms stretched out, like he was waiting to hug her. She put her arm around his shoulder and kissed his cheek.

"Thank you for the drinks."

"Of course. If you're around tomorrow, we'd love to have brunch before we check out."

"It's a date."

Juan Diego was next, and he grumbled in her ear when he hugged her tight—maybe a little too tight. "Dinner at his house, huh? Remember what I told you, *mami*. Make Uncle J.D. proud. I want the dirt tomorrow."

She kissed his cheek, then patted it with a smile. "I'll see you tomorrow. Take Francisco somewhere nice for dinner."

Ramon reached for her hand and nodded his head. "Francisco. Juan Diego. Have a great night," he said, before ushering her out the door where his driver stood outside a black Cadillac Escalade with tinted windows.

Ramon

He didn't understand why he felt so happy to be taking Sophia to his home, but he was. He rarely brought women back to his house. In fact, now that he thought about it, he'd never brought a woman to his new estate in Ensenada. He was having a hard time remembering if he'd ever brought someone to any of his other properties. He seemed to recall Dante telling him at their last business meeting that Ramon owned ten, spread throughout the world.

Of course, he wasn't sure if he'd visited all the homes he knew he owned, but right now, he wanted to show Sophia each and every one.

When he became *capo* of his family's organization, he moved his primary residences in both Ensenada and San Diego, so they were more easily secured by just their location alone. Moving hadn't been a hardship. Both his new luxurious homes were high on a cliff above the Pacific Ocean.

The catch of her breath was exactly the reaction he'd hoped for when they walked to the end of his expansive patio that overlooked the water and meticulous grounds.

"Oh, Ramon," she turned to him with wide eyes. "This is so beautiful. I don't think I'd ever want to leave if I lived here."

That was strangely comforting to him.

"You should see my place in San Diego," he said with a smile. Ramon was a lot of things, but humble wasn't one of them.

"Can we have dinner out here?"

"Of course." He reached for her hand. "Come on, let me show you the inside."

They stepped through the French doors into the large foyer; their footsteps echoed off the black, blue, and white Encaustic tile and twenty-foot domed ceiling. While the outdoor area had a modern flair, the inside was very much Old Mexican charm.

She ran her hands along the ornate, black, wrought-iron railing for the wide, curved staircase that ran along the cream wall.

"Wow. I love it."

She echoed that sentiment in every room they walked through. When they entered his kitchen, his long-time cook, Maribel, and two of his fulltime housekeepers, Antonia and Consuela, that he'd brought over from his parents' home, greeted them with a smile.

"*Señor* Guzman! Welcome home!" Antonia cried, standing up from the large, eat-in island where she and Consuela were seated, to meet him and Sofia at the kitchen entry. The other women followed, obviously curious about who he brought home for dinner.

"*Hola, señoras. Cómo están?* This is my friend, Sophia Castle. Sophia, this is Antonia, Maribel, and Consuela."

Flashpoint

The ladies looked her over with an approving smile as they welcomed her.

Sophia smiled brightly and replied in broken Spanish, "Nice to meet you."

"Dinner will be ready shortly," Maribel said in Spanish as she returned to her place in front of the stove.

"I think we'd like to eat on the patio."

Ramon chuckled as the *abuelas* clucked their approval of that idea and scurried to set the patio table.

He grabbed her hand once again. "Let's have a drink before dinner."

"Okay but make mine weak. I had two at the bar with Juan Diego and Francisco, and I haven't eaten anything since lunch."

"And you were in the sun all day," he observed. "Maybe you should just have water or soda until you get something in your stomach."

"No, I'll be okay. Besides, I'm a fun drunk."

That made him grin. "I'll bet you are."

Chapter Seven

Sophia

She kept pinching herself all through dinner. She was having dinner at the estate—there was no other way to describe it—of a gorgeous, rich man who couldn't stop smiling as he looked across the table at her. This after having spent the day being spoiled in his private cabana at a swanky resort where she also happened to be a guest herself.

How was this her life?

A week ago, she was in her pajamas by seven p.m., eating a microwave dinner over the sink in her postage stamp-size apartment after her boyfriend had canceled their dinner plans, citing he had to work late. Of course, she found out the next night that 'working late' was a big, fat lie.

She'd left San Francisco on a whim after Kevin humiliated her when she walked outside to his back patio and found his bare ass thrusting into someone whose feet she could see on his shoulders.

When he heard her gasp, he turned around, his hard cock jutting out, still slick from the woman he was cheating on her with. Sophia recognized her as Jessica Hill, from the accounting department at the company both Kevin and Sophia worked at.

His response at seeing her there, stunned with her mouth open and tears in her eyes? "What are you doing here?"

"Are you fucking kidding me?" she'd screamed before throwing a lit candle at his head and storming back inside to gather anything she'd been keeping there.

He came inside about ten minutes later with a towel wrapped around his waist—she hadn't been sure if he'd gone ahead and finished first—just as she was walking toward the front door with two plastic grocery bags filled with what belongings of hers she could find.

"Soph, look. Let me explain."

She spun around and spat out, "Fuck you, Kevin. There's no explanation for what you did other than you're a lying, cheating asshole. I hope you get herpes."

Then a horrified thought occurred to her. He hadn't had a condom on when he turned around, and he'd talked Sophia into going on the pill, so they didn't have to use one.

"Oh my god. How many times have you cheated on me? I swear, if you've given me a disease, I'm going to cut your dick off with a rusty kitchen knife."

Who knew she had such a propensity for violence? Certainly not Sophia. But then again, she'd never caught her boyfriend in the middle of fucking another woman before.

"It's just been Jess, I swear."

"How long have you been seeing her?"

He stared at her, not answering.

Sophia glared at him, surprised at the dead calm in her voice when she asked again. "How. Long."

"A few months."

A few months? Things were starting to make a lot more sense. The nights he canceled on her because he was 'working late.' Why he didn't want to have lunch with her in the cafeteria anymore or wasn't interested in sleeping with her—telling her he was 'too tired.' Why he seemed to criticize everything she did lately.

"I see."

He stepped toward her, adjusting the towel and retucking it in at the waist. "Come on, Soph. We drifted apart a long time ago. You had to know this was coming."

"No, I didn't. Certainly not *this*. I just figured we'd hit a rough patch but would work through it. I had no idea you'd go out and fuck the first slut that came along."

"Jess isn't a slut."

That's when it hit her. He hadn't come inside to apologize and try to get her back; he'd come inside to officially end things between them. Not that they weren't already over the minute she saw him fucking the skank in the hot tub, but he was attempting to do it on his terms.

Well, fuck him.

"I don't know, her freaking legs were spread wide open for another woman's boyfriend. In my book, that makes her the worst kind of tramp."

"Well, maybe if you weren't such an uptight, mousy bitch who just laid there, I wouldn't have gone looking for her."

"Of course, you went looking for her before breaking up with me. Because that's the kind of lowlife you are. And, oh, yes, the way she was lying there with her legs spread looked like it took real talent."

"At least she's willing to be adventurous."

She opened the front door and had one foot on the doormat when she snarled, "Fuck you. It's not like you were any good anyway."

He got the parting shot in. "Well, consider what I was working with. Miss boring Priss."

"Go to hell," she choked out and slammed the door behind her.

Screw him. She wasn't boring. And that bastard better not have given her a venereal disease.

She had all kinds of revenge fantasies that night about what—and who—she would do while on her Mexican getaway. She even stopped to get tested at the walk-in health clinic the next day on her way to the airport—in part so she wouldn't stress the entire time that he'd given her gonorrhea, but also just in case she did meet her dream man who wanted to sleep with her on the beach, like the scene in her favorite classic movie, *From Here to Eternity*. Even though it was doubtful she'd meet her Mexican Burt Lancaster who'd sweep her off her feet, but even if she did, could she go through with having sex on the beach with someone she'd just met? Maybe Kevin was right—she was uptight. Still, it'd been fun to at least dream about when she was alone.

She'd decided by the second day in Ensenada that she would just focus on healing and not worry about meeting anyone. She didn't need a wild fling with a Latin lover to make herself feel better. Meeting two gay men that she instantly adored almost seemed like a sign that was the right decision about how to proceed.

Then along came Ramon Guzman, who kissed her on the beach like she'd never been kissed, and her world flipped upside down.

*

It was probably the vodka talking, and the *From Here to Eternity* scene she'd been playing in her head since before she even boarded the plane almost a week ago, but Sophia looked across the table at Ramon once their dinner plates had been cleared and with a coquettish smile, asked, "Wanna kiss me in the sand again?"

The right corner of his mouth turned up. "I would love to kiss you again. But it's going to have to be on the patio. It's high tide, so the beach is inaccessible from here."

"Oh." She tried to hide her disappointment but knew she wasn't doing a very good job.

He tugged her chair, so it was next to him, and caressed her cheek while looking into her eyes.

"I haven't stopped thinking about last night's kiss."

She stared back at him, her voice barely above a whisper when she replied, "Me neither." Then confessed, "I've never been kissed like that."

Raising one sexy eyebrow, he asked, "Never?"

"No."

Ramon leaned over the arm of her chair, bringing his face within inches of hers.

"What kind of idiots have you been kissing then? I promise, I will kiss you like that every chance I get."

She closed her eyes as he lowered his mouth on hers. His lips were soft and tender, while still managing to be assertive. Last night's kiss had been no fluke.

His tongue sought hers out and left her no choice but to tangle with his. Not like she wanted another choice. She loved how dominant he was, yet how she still felt safe and in control, knowing he'd respect her boundaries. Although those seemed to be crumbling by the second.

"Let's go inside," he whispered against her lips.

Is that a good idea? Her lady parts screamed, "Do it!" Her tipsy brain screamed, "Do it!" Yet, there was a tiny part that wondered if that was a good idea.

"Um..."

He shook his head and smiled. "Not to my bedroom, my sweet *nerdicita*. But we might be more comfortable on the couch." He gestured to the guards making their rounds along the perimeter of the property. "And not have such an audience."

Still, she hesitated. Not because she didn't want to, but rather because she *did*. Badly. She knew once she kicked off her shoes and got comfortable, she'd be begging him to take her to bed.

She heard Juan Diego's voice in her head, asking, "And why would that be a bad thing? Live a little."

"How about this?" he suggested. "I promise, I'll only kiss you. Nothing more. You have my word."

"It's not you I'm worried about. I get horny when I've been drinking."

He pulled his head back with a frown, like she'd surprised him with her admission, then a smile slowly spread across his face.

"I see. Then it wouldn't be very gentlemanly of me to take advantage of that, would it?"

She traced her finger along his chest. "But that's just it—I think I'd *want* you to take advantage of me and would be offended if you turned me down."

Sophia waited for him to take her back inside, maybe offer her one last chance to say no, before pouncing. She didn't want to say no. She wanted to be adventurous with a man, just once. Ramon Guzman was definitely the right man to be adventurous with.

He looked at her in silence for a few beats. Long enough to make her fidget uncomfortably, until he finally said softly, "Maybe I should take you back to the hotel."

She knew he was trying to be a good guy, but his rejection felt like a slap. She wanted him to find her so desirable, he couldn't help himself. That obviously wasn't the case. Kevin's words echoed in her mind. *Consider what I was working with. Miss boring Priss.*

Then her pride kicked in, and she stood abruptly, needing to get away from him.

"Oh. Yeah. That's a good idea." She gestured to the house with her thumb. "I'm just, um, going to use the restroom before we go," then turned and blindly made her way back inside as the tears of humiliation filled her eyes.

She put the lid down on the toilet and sat with her head in her hands. Why was she upset? She'd basically told him she wasn't the type of girl who had a fling with a stranger. Except now she wanted to be that girl. He thought she'd had too much to drink. He was just honoring her wishes. She'd be happy a month from now that he rejected her. That way she wouldn't be filled with regret at having slept with him.

But she knew it would be the other way around. Ramon had turned her on like no one ever had simply by kissing her. She would regret letting the opportunity pass her by to do something that, deep down, she wanted to do.

And why was she letting the opportunity pass her by? Why had she said she wasn't that kind of girl when she clearly wanted to be? Because she worried about what other people might think? And the sadder thing was, she didn't even know *who* would judge her—it's not like anyone knew her in Mexico, but it had been so ingrained in her that *someone* would, and that she shouldn't let that happen.

What a cruel twist of fate that when she decided to let loose, the object of her affection was more interested in being the good guy.

At least she'd have a fun story about having dinner with a multi-millionaire when she got back home. Too bad she didn't have some hilarious supplement, like she threw up on his thousand-dollar shoes.

Sophia went to the bathroom, since she was already there, washed her hands, and looked at herself in the mirror. After doing a quick swipe under eyes with a Kleenex and smoothing her hair, she took a deep breath, put on a fake *I don't give a damn* smile, and walked out into the beautiful foyer, where Ramon waited with a frown.

"Ready?" she said sweetly and started toward the door.

"Sophia, wait."

She wanted to do just that. Give him an opportunity to explain. Offer her anything to salvage her pride.

But, ironically, her pride wouldn't allow that, and she walked out as if she hadn't heard him.

She heard his approaching footsteps on the cobblestone, then felt the tug on her elbow as he spun her around.

"I said *wait*."

It was obvious by his impatient tone and furrowed brows that he wasn't used to his commands being ignored.

"What?" she challenged, yanking out of his grasp.

Ramon glowered at her with his mouth slightly agape, as if he were at a loss for words, then he reached for her again,

Flashpoint

one hand at her waist to pull her tight against him while the other grabbed a fistful of hair to hold her still as he lowered his mouth on hers and kissed her. It wasn't soft and tender like his other kisses. It was rough and hard, as if he intended to punish her with his lips. Remind her who was in charge.

And it was hot as hell.

He tightened his grip on her hair while she clung to his shoulders and whimpered softly when his tongue ravaged her mouth.

Sophia wove her fingers into his jet-black hair as he loosened his hold of her long tresses and growled into her ear, "Just so we understand each other, little one. There hasn't been a second I haven't wanted you. But you're not going to be intoxicated the first time I finally do have you." His lips were inches from hers again. "Do you understand?"

"I'm not drunk," she argued. "I'm perfectly capable of giving consent."

"It's not your consent I'm worried about," he said with an arrogant smile.

"Then what are you worried about?"

Ramon squeezed her breast over her top and sucked her bottom lip between his. "You remembering." He then nipped her top lip. "Every." Back to her bottom. "Single." And her top again. "Thing I do to you," before consuming her mouth again with his.

Sophia felt herself surrender completely to his kiss; her eyes still closed when he broke away and whispered in her ear, "So that you crave me."

She finally opened her eyes and stared up at him. "I already do."

The corner of his mouth lifted. "Good."

God, he was a sexy, arrogant jerk. And she really thought he would scoop her up and take her back inside. So, it felt like she'd been doused with ice water when he added, "Let's get you back to the hotel."

****

Ramon

The hurt look on her face had him reconsidering what to do. He knew she wasn't too drunk to know what she was doing, and God knew he wanted her, badly.

Truth was, had she been someone he was simply interested in fucking, she'd already be bent over naked on his bed. Well, not *his* bed, more than likely a hotel bed. But, after reading everything Pedro and Dante had sent over about her, coupled with just how freaking adorable she was as he got to know her, Ramon found himself wanting to own more than just her pussy. He wanted all of her: mind, body, and soul.

So this must be what Dante was talking about when he said someday a woman would come along and knock him on his ass. But how was that even possible? He'd only known her for twenty-four hours. Yet it didn't matter—he wanted her. And Ramon always got what he wanted.

"Little one," he said softly as he smoothed her hair from her face. "I know you don't do one-night stands. When I take you upstairs to my bed, I'm not letting you leave."

That's why he needed her to crave him.

Her smile was obviously fake as she stepped out of his embrace. "Then it's a good thing we're going back to the hotel, since I had more of a vacation fling in mind. I leave in a week; never leaving isn't really an option."

That wasn't going to work for him. He had his work cut out if he only had a short time to convince her to stay.

****

Sophia

Her head spun. She had no idea how Ramon really felt about her. One minute, he curled her toes with his passionate kisses, and the next he was rejecting her. Was he being sincere when he said if she went back to his room, he wasn't letting her leave? Or was it a safe thing to say because he knew she was only here for another week?

She had been planning to ride back to the resort in silence, then thanking him for dinner when the hotel was in in sight and exiting the car as soon as they pulled up.

And that would be that, as far as spending any more time with Ramon Guzman.

He foiled her plan somewhat when he decided to forego his driver and the Cadillac and take her back to the hotel in his brand-spanking-new royal blue McLaren Senna. She tried not to look impressed when he pulled it out of his ten-stall garage. The sound of the engine as he revved it gave her goosebumps; she knew it could go from zero to over one hundred twenty in less than seven seconds. Her dad was a mechanic and all-around automobile enthusiast who passed on his love for cars to all three of his children.

Her father would lose his mind if he knew she was on a date with a man who owned the million-dollar car.

Ramon opened his dihedral door to help her with hers, making her feel like she was getting into a spaceship. Appropriate—since meeting Ramon had been an out-of-this-world experience.

"She's quite a bit different than the Escalade," Sophia quipped when she tucked herself in the passenger seat. The low-ground clearance made her glad she wasn't wearing a skirt.

"This was my birthday present to myself," he replied as he lowered the driver door.

"When was your birthday?"

"Last month."

"A May baby. Taurus or Gemini?"

Although, based on his luxurious tastes, she already suspected he was a Taurus.

"I don't know. Whatever May Eleventh is."

"A Taurus. I thought so."

The car roared out of the house gates and onto the streets as he muttered, "I don't believe in that hocus pocus stuff."

She stared out the unique window in the car door as they drove along the city streets and said curtly, "Of course you don't."

Sophia could feel him looking at her but didn't look back. "Do you?"

She shrugged. "I've found it to be pretty accurate."

"What does it mean to be a Taurus then?"

Looking over at him with pursed lips, she deadpanned, "Stubborn, opinionated, flirty, shopaholic." Then felt bad and added, "Homebody. Loyal. Sensual lover. Passionate about food and money."

He nodded his head as he listened. "Huh. That does sound like me. How do you know so much about that?"

"My last boyfriend was a Taurus." She tried not to sound bitter, but it was no use. Just the thought of Kevin annoyed her.

"That doesn't sound like it ended well."

"No." There was nothing more to add.

His tone was light when he asked, "Can I take you to breakfast tomorrow? Then we can go sightseeing afterwards. I'll take you to my family's vineyard, then we can stop at the oldest vineyard in Baja—*Bodegas de Santo Tomas*. Then, if you're not too tired, maybe we can do some shopping downtown?"

Through the windshield, she could make out the hotel's lights in the distance. She stared straight ahead when she replied, "No. I have plans for the day with Juan Diego and Francisco."

Okay, so technically, it was only for brunch, but he didn't need to know that.

"I see. How about dinner then?"

"You know, the rest of my time here is pretty booked. But thank you for dinner, and today. And letting me ride in your beautiful McLaren. My father will definitely be jealous." She put her hand on the door handle in preparation and offered a polite smile. "It was nice meeting you, Ramon."

Instead of pulling into the resort's entrance with the lighted palm trees, he drove right past, speeding up as he did.

"Um…? I think you missed our turn."

He glanced in his rearview mirror, headlights from the car behind them reflected in his eyes.

"No, I didn't," he said before taking the next corner at the last second like they were on rails.

The vehicle following attempted to also take the turn, but its suspension wasn't that of a million-dollar sports car and didn't quite make it. Ramon proceeded to drive through the dark streets of the city like he was in a rally car race.

"Call Jesús," he said out loud.

A woman's computer voice responded with, "Calling Jesús," before the sound of a ringing phone filled the cabin of the car.

"What's up, Boss?"

Ramon had both hands on the wheel as he maneuvered the car at a high rate of speed. "I had some company on my way back to the resort. Pretty sure I lost them, but I need you to bring a team to the winery along with a driver and an unaffiliated car to take my date back to the hotel."

"Wouldn't she be safer at your house?"

He glanced at her, as if trying to gauge her reaction to the idea. She knew her eyes were wide, but otherwise she didn't respond. Ramon turned his attention back to the road.

"No. She'll be fine once she gets back to her hotel room."

The man was bound and determined not to spend the night with her. A far cry from how he was earlier today.

Kevin's words echoed in her head. "You're a mousy, uptight bitch."

Of course Ramon wouldn't want to be with her. Why would he?

Chapter Eight

Ramon
He'd gotten them to the winery in record time. It was one of the cartel's legitimate businesses with barely a trace to the organization, so it was a perfect place to hole up until reinforcements arrived.

He killed the lights and backed into the garage located next to the barrel warehouse.

"I'm sorry about this. I should have known better than to go out without my men." He lifted his door. "Let's wait inside; it's safer," then went around to help her out of the passenger side, not letting go of her hand once she stood.

After letting his eyes adjust to the moonless night, he led her to the tasting room door and pressed his thumb against the key reader on the state-of-the-art alarm system until a green light beeped, and the sound of the doors unlocking resonated loudly in the quiet, country night. Ramon hit the soft lights behind the tasting bar and lifted her onto a bar stool, then stood between her legs and pulled her against his chest. He could feel her heart beating fast and realized she hadn't uttered a word since he noticed the tail and drove past the resort.

"Are you okay?"

Her voice was shaky when she replied, "I'm not sure. That was quite an adventure."

Flashpoint

Stroking the back of her long, blonde hair, he whispered, "I know, baby. I'm sorry."

"What's this all about?"

Ramon let out a deep sigh at the realization she truly had no idea who he was. She was so beautifully innocent. That only made him want to corrupt her beyond redemption and tie her to him forever. He could be a selfish prick, and he was okay with that. He didn't get to his position of *capo* by being a boy scout.

Still, he needed to tread lightly, for now. He wasn't willing to scare her off.

"To be honest, I'm not sure. It could be nothing more than my rivals keeping tabs on me, but I can never be too careful."

It could be a rival cartel, but a rival cartel in his city would be a pretty ballsy move on their part—especially with everyone on high alert after what had happened with Dante's daughter. The more likely scenario was that it was the CIA. Ramon knew there had been agents at the party last night. What he didn't know was if they were simply spying on him or had more sinister ideas, and he hadn't been willing to find out—especially not with Sophia in the car.

Sophia looked up at him through her lashes. "I've never seen anyone drive like you did."

"I'm so sorry. I didn't mean to scare you. The car is built for performance. I promise I didn't push it harder than I could handle."

She shook her head. "I know. I wasn't scared."

"You weren't?"

"No, it was sexy. The way you were in control of everything—the situation. The car. I was, um..." Her voice trailed off, leaving her thought unfinished, and she glanced away.

Ramon tipped her chin, so she looked at him again. "You were what?"

Sophia hesitated, then whispered, "Turned on. Again."

He could feel the smile spread across his face. She just kept getting more perfect. Ramon leaned down to kiss her and was surprised when she moved her face and spun the bar stool away from his body.

"No! You're not doing this to me again. I'm not some toy you can take out to play with, then put away when you're bored. You can't mess with my emotions—turn me on, only to reject me."

He spun the stool so that he was back between her thighs, his hands on her waist while his eyes searched hers. "Is that what you think? That I was bored, so I rejected you?"

The tears welling up in her eyes answered for her.

Ramon rubbed her bare arms up and down, then pulled her tight against his chest and stroked her hair, kissing her temple. "Oh, my sweet *nerdicita*. You couldn't be more wrong."

****

Sophia

She was mad at herself for not only confessing his driving had turned her on, but then letting her tears fall in front of him. She attempted to pull away from his embrace.

Ramon was relentless and wouldn't let go of his hold on her. She tried at first to push him away, but then his lips crashed down on hers in another punishing kiss, and he held her even tighter against him.

Sophia whimpered against his mouth and gripped the material of his shirt in her fists. Alarm bells went off, telling her he would stop like he did before and leave her filled with desire for him. But the warnings in her head were no match for what he was doing to her.

He opened the top buttons of her outfit, so her bra was on full display. Ramon pulled the cups of the silky garment below her tits and dipped his mouth to her pebbled peaks. She threw her head back and ran her fingers through his hair, moaning out loud. While his mouth concentrated on her nipples, she felt his hand slide up her inner thigh, past the opening in her romper, to caress her slit over her underwear. She knew she had to be soaked. He moved her panties to the slide to run one finger up and down her slick folds and then pushed inside her while circling her clit with his thumb.

Sophia gasped at the intrusion, then arched her boob into his mouth while holding onto the back of his head.

"Oh my god. Yes. That feels so good."

If she'd thought Ramon kissed better than any other man, that was nothing compared to his technique on her pussy. She usually struggled to come with a partner and often when she was with Kevin, Sophia preferred to just go home and finish the job herself—alone.

That was not the case with the Mexican sex god who currently manipulated her clit in ways no one ever had, herself included.

"Oh fuck! Yes, just like that. Oh my god," Sophia chanted while her body tensed as the orgasm crept up from her toes.

He finger fucked her faster, and she tightened her grip on his hair when she approached the orgasmic cliff, until she flew over it—her whole body shuddering as she floated through her release.

Ramon burrowed his face in her neck and held her close, waiting for her to catch her breath.

"Wow," she panted with her eyes closed. "You're amazing. No one has ever touched me like that."

He lifted his head like she'd shocked him.

"You're not—?"

She tilted her head while she tried to figure out what he was referring to. Suddenly, it dawned on her, and she let out a little gasp, followed by a chuckle.

"No, I'm not a virgin. I just meant, no one has ever touched me quite like that and made me... you know."

The corner of his mouth lifted in his sexy, signature grin.

Flashpoint

"I liked touching you and making you, you know. It was sexy as fuck."

Sophia put her hand on his hard cock over his trousers and rubbed his entire length against her palm. And it was an impressive length.

At the same time, headlights flashed in the tasting room window, and he buttoned the blouse of her romper.

"We'll continue this later," he murmured in her ear when the last button was fastened, and he took a step back, just as a group of handsome, dark-haired men walked through the door. Their guns were in shoulder holsters, with a few having a second tucked conspicuously in their waistbands, like Ramon's. She'd noticed it when he'd pressed against her earlier.

A few of the men she recognized from the party last night.

"We scoured the road here, Boss. There's nobody."

"I figured I lost them; otherwise, I wouldn't have come here."

A phone rang, and Gabriel, the man he'd introduced earlier as his head of security, looked at his screen with furrowed brows, then answered it.

"Yeah?"

Gabriel glanced at Ramon, then spoke into the receiver. "Yes. He's right here."

He looked at Ramon nervously, then put his hand over the mouthpiece and held out the phone.

"They want to talk to you."

Chapter Nine

Ramon

He and his men, along with his beautiful companion, convoyed back to the hotel, and he walked Sophia to her room. The CIA already knew about her, so it was a waste of time to try to pretend she hadn't been with him. At this point, they probably assumed she was just someone he was getting his dick wet with and was inconsequential.

He'd let them keep thinking that.

As they stood at her hotel room door, she bit her bottom lip while looking up at him through her lashes and purred, "Do you want to stop by for a nightcap after your meeting?"

He shook his head. "I don't know how late it's going to be." Or how messy. But he kept that point to himself. "But, maybe we could have breakfast before you go out with Francisco and Juan Diego. What time are you getting together with them?"

"Um..." Her hesitation confirmed what he'd guessed earlier. She didn't really have plans with the two men. She surprised him when she continued, "I'm supposed to have brunch with them before they check out. But I can see if they can meet Tuesday instead."

"But not plans for the day?"

She shook her head no, and he bit back a smile.

"We'll talk more at breakfast."

Her nervous fidgeting made him want to hug her, but he had CIA assholes to contend with at the moment.

One of the said assholes had called his head of security's phone while they were at the winery, wanting to talk to Ramon.

He'd taken the phone and walked outside, away from Sophia, snarling into the phone, "What the fuck do you want?"

With a chuckle, the arrogant agent said, "We just want to talk to you. We were going to suggest maybe grabbing a drink at the resort's bar, then you disappeared on us. You should think about entering next year's Rally Mexico with those driving skills. Although, I'm sure being in the McLaren helped."

"Yeah, you should consider getting one yourself—maybe you'd be able to keep up. And unfortunately, tonight's not really good for me. Why don't you have your people call my people and schedule an appointment like fucking civilized professionals do."

Again with the chuckle on the other end. "Ramon. You're not actually suggesting your business is civilized, are you? Rumor has it you have a meeting in New Orleans coming up. If you can't meet tonight, maybe we can talk there."

Not many people knew about his meeting with the Colombians at the end of the month. Either he had a mole, or the Colombians did.

He decided to take the bait.

"I'll be at the hotel bar in an hour. You get fifteen minutes—the clock starts when I sit down. I suggest you not be late."

"See you then."

With that, he hung up the phone and went back inside. Sophia still sat on the stool where he'd made her come not more than fifteen minutes earlier.

He'd approached her, wrapped his arm her waist and whispered in her ear, "Little one, I want you to wait in the car for a few minutes while I talk to my men. Alejandro will stand guard to make sure you're safe until I take you back to the resort."

She immediately slid off the bar stool so Alejandro could escort her to the car. There were questions behind her eyes, but she said nothing.

Good girl.

He hadn't made her wait long as he apprised his men of the impending meeting later tonight, and they established a plan to keep him protected. They then made the trek back to the hotel—where he walked Sophia to her door and kissed her goodnight, after reluctantly declining her invitation to return later.

He'd thought about taking her to his suite, so she'd be there when he finished. But he wasn't one hundred percent certain he wouldn't have blood on his hands—literally, when he got back to his room.

As much as he wanted to hold Sophia in his arms tonight, he needed to take care of business first.

*

The second he sat down, 'Raquel Torres' appeared.

Ramon shook his head in disgust. "I should have known they'd send you."

She ran a long, manicured finger down his shoulder and leaned down to flash her ample cleavage at him.

"*Papi,* I'm starting to feel like you don't love me anymore."

Playing along, he reached up and twisted a long strand of her hair around his finger, staring into her eyes.

"Sweetheart, you were a decent fuck—much better than you are a spy, but I have no interest in dipping my dick into that well twice, so I suggest you cut to the chase because you have..." Ramon looked at his watch. "Thirteen minutes and thirty-six seconds left before I get up and walk out."

He wasn't lying—she was a good lay, but unfortunately for her, he knew who she was before she had even gotten on her knees, so the only thing she gained by putting out that night was an orgasm, his cum plastered in her hair, and bogus information before being shown the door.

Her icy smile suggested his words hit the intended mark. Still, she slid onto his lap like they were lovers and traced her fingers down his cheek as she proceeded to whisper in his ear,

Flashpoint

"We know the Colombians are asking for a meeting in New Orleans later this month, and we'd like to make you a little proposition."

He pulled his head back and looked at her skeptically, but didn't remove her from his lap. "I'm listening."

"We both have a mutual interest in crippling the Colombians' operation before it gets back to full speed. I've been authorized to make a deal with you to work together and do just that."

Ramon noticed her earpiece and knew she had to be wired, so he put one arm around her middle and nuzzled her ear while holding her neck still with his other hand.

"Listen carefully because I'm only going to say this once. I'm not a rat, and I'm certainly not your pawn. You assholes are going to have to do your own dirty work."

With a patronizing kiss to her temple, he lifted her off his lap with a pat to her rear. "Run along now."

With a wicked smile that seemed out of place, she leaned forward to display her boobs again and theatrically handed him her room key as she purred in his ear. "When you change your mind," then walked away with a smug smile on her face.

His hackles immediately went up. She'd been way too confident, and he knew something was amiss.

****

Sophia

Between the sun and alcohol earlier today, along with the roller coaster of emotions tonight, she had a headache. Juan Diego's shriek when she explained why she was postponing lunch hadn't helped. Although the orgasm Ramon had given her should have quelled it, as she got ready for bed, she found herself filled with worry that something bad was going to happen to him. Looking through her bag, she realized that in her hurry to pack to leave San Francisco, she hadn't included any pain reliever. If she didn't deal with this tonight, it was liable to turn into a full-blown migraine by morning.

Piling her hair on her head, she slipped on a pair of running shorts and a tank top along with some flip flops and headed down to the front desk. She wasn't sure if the gift shop was still open but assumed someone on staff would be able to help her.

Walking through the lobby, she glanced at the French doors leading into the bar and noticed Alejandro, the man who'd stood guard over her at the winery, mulling around by the hostess stand.

Curiosity got the better of her, and she decided to go inside, under the pretense of seeing if the bar hostess could help her with pain reliever.

She padded inside the dimly lit bar and glanced around, hoping to catch a glimpse of Ramon's business rival so she knew who to watch out for this week. Tears welled up in her eyes when she saw a buxom blonde sitting on Ramon's lap, with his hands all over her as he whispered in her ear.

Business meeting, my ass.

Sophia stood there stunned for a moment, hardly believing what she was seeing. How could this have happened to her twice in one week's time?

The woman slid off Ramon's lap, and he patted her butt as she handed him her room key.

Bile burned in Sophia's throat as she watched him touch the beautiful woman—not less than ninety minutes after having touched Sophia even more intimately. She felt like such a fool. She'd practically begged him to come to her room after his 'meeting,' but he'd declined. Now she understood why. He'd gotten a better offer.

She needed to get out of there before Alejandro or any of Ramon's other men noticed her. The last thing she needed was that added humiliation.

Spinning on the ball of her flip flop, she scurried toward the elevators, completely forgetting her original reason for coming downstairs.

"I'm so stupid," she muttered as she looked at her reflection in the elevator doors. There was no way she came close to measuring up to the woman on Ramon's lap. Just like she hadn't with Jessica Hill—the woman she'd watched Kevin drilling in his hot tub. She stared at the woman in the mirrored doors with no makeup and her hair in a messy bun. Kevin was right—she was just a mousy priss. Of course, when given the choice, Ramon would pick the buxom blonde to spend the night with.

Changing her scenery hadn't changed anything at all. It was time to go home and back to reality.

Chapter Ten

Ramon

He arrived for breakfast before Sophia, and the hostess immediately seated him on the patio under an umbrella. His men were seated at three different tables close by, but out of earshot.

He'd thought about her all night and had even considered stopping by her room after leaving his meeting with Raquel, but then decided against it. He didn't want to wake her although he'd desperately wanted to hold her and continue where they'd left off.

That was on today's agenda.

After twenty minutes of waiting, he asked the hostess to call her room. The young woman returned to his table minutes later with a grimace on her face, and timidly told him, "I'm sorry, Señor Guzman. Miss Castle checked out early this morning. The front desk said she got on the shuttle to the airport about an hour ago."

It felt like the floor had just dropped out from under him.

What the hell was going on? Had the CIA gotten to her? Why would she just leave? Did Francisco and Juan Diego know anything about this?

He got Pedro on the phone to find out what the gay couple knew about her sudden departure. His lieutenant called him back within minutes.

"They seemed as surprised as you to learn she had left. She'd rescheduled their brunch for tomorrow."

Ramon couldn't let her just leave like this. He needed to keep her in Ensenada where he controlled, well, everything.

"Get Chief Villasenor on the phone. She is not to get on that plane."

"Um, what should I tell him is the reason to stop her?"

"Have him call me on his way to the airport."

****

Sophia

Men sucked.

She had managed to change her departure when she got back to her room last night. The earliest flight out was at noon the next day, but she left for the airport as soon as she was up and packed. She wasn't sure if Ramon would even show up for breakfast the next morning, but in case he did, it would just be easier if she was already gone before he arrived. Sophia didn't trust herself not to make a scene while giving him a piece of her mind.

Arriving at the airport hours before her plane was supposed to take off, she checked her bags, grabbed a coffee and a bagel, and flipped open her Kindle while she waited for her flight at the deserted terminal. The latest cowboy shifter romance by Renee Rose and Vanessa Vale was exactly what she needed to try to forget the shitshow that was her reality.

She was engrossed in the story and imaging what her life would be like if she had her own sexy alpha wolf shifter, so she wasn't paying much attention to her surroundings. She felt someone's presence invading her personal space and glanced down to find two pairs of shiny, black shoes. Looking up, there were two stern-looking men in *Federales* uniforms standing directly in front of her.

Her Spanish was limited to her three years of classes in high school, but she managed to understand they were asking her if her name was Sophia Castle.

She tilted her head and simply responded, "*Sí?*"

The taller of the two men said in clipped English, "Will you come with us, please?" He waited for her to stand and gather her purse and carry-on bags before grabbing her by the elbow and escorting her away.

"Is there a problem, officer?"

"Yes, ma'am."

She did a mental calculation of how much money she had in her wallet. She remembered reading about tourists being stopped and detained for fabricated offenses but were then let go if they paid their 'fine' to the officer looking for a bribe.

The airport seemed an odd location for this to take place, yet she couldn't think of what other reason they had to pull her aside other than to shake her down. She was as squeaky clean as they came.

They entered a small, windowless room where an older man with thick, salt-and-pepper hair and a matching mustache in grey trousers, a starched white shirt, navy blue blazer, and red tie casually leaned against a metal desk. The way the uniformed officers straightened their shoulders and looked straight ahead the second they entered the room let her know this man outranked them, by a lot.

"Thank you, gentlemen. I will take it from here." He stood straight and focused on her with a scowl.

"Senorita, I am Roberto Villasenor—Ensenada chief of police. Please, be seated." He gestured to one of two pea-green vinyl chairs in the small room. His English was good, but very formal, like he'd learned it in a classroom and didn't use it much otherwise.

She sat on the edge of the cushion with her hands in her lap and ankles crossed as she looked up at him, wondering what this was all about.

"Senorita Castle, you have a problem."

She cocked her head. What kind of problem could she possibly have that would require the chief of police's involvement? Her mind raced. Had he somehow found out she was a passenger in the car that flew through his city last night like a bat out of hell? It didn't seem likely, but that was the only illegal thing she'd even been remotely involved with.

"What problem?"

"You left the hotel without paying your bill."

That wasn't at all what she expected, and her mind immediately began to regroup.

"What? That's not true. I have my receipt..." She opened her bag to fish for the full sheet of paper that the front desk lady gave her after she checked out. Finding it folded in quarters, she opened it up and handed it to him.

He barely glanced at it before giving it back to her.

"The credit card company declined the sale. It seems you used a stolen credit card."

"That's not possible. The transaction wouldn't have gone through. I have a receipt. My card wasn't stolen. I have identification proving who I am. This is obviously all a big misunderstanding." She pulled her cell from her bag. "I can call my credit card company and get this straightened out right now."

Chief Villasenor reached for her phone, which she handed to him without thinking. He pocketed it and sat on the corner of the desk, staring down at her.

She was pissed off, frustrated, and a little scared.

"I don't take kindly when Americans come into my city and try to steal from my citizens, then try to skate out of town. The hotel said you checked out over a week early after spending a lot of time with Ramon Guzman. Did you steal from *Señor* Guzman? Is that why you're leaving town so quickly?"

"Of course I didn't steal from him. Are you insane?"

He stood with such a start that Sophia recoiled. She was in a foreign country, she probably ought to tone her sass down a little.

"Let's just see about that, shall we?" he snarled as he crossed the room toward the door.

"Go right ahead," she replied, crossing her arms defiantly and slumping back in her seat when he walked out the door.

That's not toning it down, her inner voice scolded.

Sophia was left waiting in the little room for what felt like forever. The longer she waited, the more she stewed.

How dare they detain her! The American Consulate would hear about this!

The chief had pocketed her phone, and there was no clock on the wall, so she couldn't be sure just how long she'd been in the windowless room, but she was sure she'd missed her flight. As more time passed, however, her anger subsided into fear. They could throw her in a Mexican prison, and no one would even know until at least the end of the week, when her best friend expected her back stateside. And even then, who knew how long until anyone located her?

Sophia decided when—or if, she was starting to wonder at that point—Chief Villasenor came back, she would lay on the charm. She couldn't go to Mexican prison. When the door finally opened, she was waiting with a humble smile. Only instead of the chief walking through the door, Ramon Guzman sauntered in with his stupid, crooked grin that still made her stomach do flips.

"Sophia Castle, what on earth have you gotten yourself into?"

Chapter Eleven

Sophia

Ramon wore a grey, silk, custom-made suit and looked as gorgeous as he did the night of the party, when she first met him.

She should have listened to her instincts that night that he was nothing but a player.

"What are you doing here, Ramon?"

He didn't answer her question, just said quietly, "We have about thirty seconds before the chief comes back. I've told him you're my fiancée, so you probably want to act the part."

"You did *what*? Why?"

"Trust me, it's in your best interest to go along with this, Sophia."

"Fiancée? You're insane. I'll just tell the chief there's been a huge mistake and explain everything."

He shrugged and turned to leave. "Suit yourself."

All the movies she'd watched with Mexican prison scenes in them flashed in her mind. What could one little white lie hurt? It wasn't like she actually had to marry him.

She reached for his arm that was just out of reach. "Wait!"

Ramon paused, and the chief walked in with a manila file folder, tossing it on the desk when he sat in the black leather office chair, opposite her uncomfortable green vinyl one.

"Ms. Castle," he started. "Why didn't you tell me you were Ramon's fiancée? We could have cleared this up in a matter of minutes."

Her pissed-off mood was back, and she felt braver with Ramon standing next to her, so she snorted, "Yeah, I'm sure you would have believed me."

"I apologize for the inconvenience."

"Can I get on a plane now?" she asked impatiently, standing and putting her purse over her shoulder.

"It's not that easy. There's still the matter of your hotel bill. And, unfortunately, you've already been put on a no-fly list. It's going to take some time until things get cleared up."

"I've been put on a no-fly list? Are you serious? Over a misunderstanding about a hotel bill?" That was the most absurd thing she'd ever heard.

"Once you and Ramon get married, it should get cleared up rather quickly. Being the wife of a Mexican citizen—particularly someone like Ramon Guzman—will move the process along a lot faster."

"Well, that's good." Whatever he needed to hear so she was free to go. She just wanted to leave here and find another way home, whether it be by bus, boat, or renting a car.

"Being his wife will definitely help smooth things over with the hotel. Being Sophia Guzman will go a long way to help convince them to drop the charges of skating out on your room bill."

Flashpoint

"I did no such thing," she said through gritted teeth. "There was obviously a mix-up with my credit card company. They gave. Me. A. Receipt."

Her inner voice chided, "Good grief, woman, just play along!" She glanced at Ramon, then ran her hand up and down his arm before briefly resting her head against his shoulder. "But I'm thankful my fiancé will be able to help me clear things up with the hotel."

Ramon cleared his throat. "Yes, of course." It was the first thing he'd said since the chief came into the room.

The chief narrowed his eyes. "Why weren't you staying at Ramon's in the first place?"

"I, um..." She always folded like a cheap suit when put on the spot.

"She needed to get some work done, and I tend to distract her when she stays at the house."

"From what the hotel has told me, you were spending a lot of time at the hotel, too."

He grinned and slid his arm around her waist, kissing her hair. "Yeah, well. I can't keep away from her."

"So, why did she have her own room?"

"What can I say? She's an independent woman."

He smelled nice. Damn him.

Ramon might be helping her out right now, but he was still an asshole that she wanted nothing to do with.

"Just tell me what I need to do to help this process along," she said politely. "I have to get back to my job in California."

"You aren't going to be free to leave Ramon's house until this is cleared up with the government."

"Like I'm on house arrest?" Sophia tried not to shriek, but even to her own ears, it sounded shrill. "How long am I stuck there?"

Chief Villasenor narrowed his eyes at them both. "*Stuck there?* Are you two really engaged?"

"Roberto," Ramon said with a patient smile. "Can't you tell a couple in love when you see one?" For emphasis, he smiled down at her and traced the backs of his fingers along her jaw while staring into her eyes, then leaned down to kiss her gently on the mouth. She couldn't help but sigh once he pulled away. The man knew how to kiss. "Of course we are."

"Absolutely," she echoed, looking up at Ramon with a tender look to help sell it.

"And you're sure about this?" he seemed to ask Ramon.

"Never surer."

"Okay, if you're sure," the older man said, pulling out a form. "Sign here. Both of you."

They both signed the form, followed by Roberto's signature, then the chief smiled. "Congratulations. I never thought I'd see the day." He added with a scowl. "Go pay her hotel bill and make sure she stays out of trouble. She can move about the city if you're willing to vouch for her, but that's it—no farther."

"Consider the hotel bill already taken care of, Roberto. I'll make sure she doesn't leave Ensenada until she's cleared. You have my word," Ramon said, shaking the man's hand. Then he put his hand at the small of her back and escorted her out the door.

****

Ramon

Best hundred grand he'd ever spent.

Hell, he would have been willing to pay ten times that if he'd known it would end like it did.

Once they'd walked out of the security office, she shrugged away from his touch and refused to look at him as she collected her luggage from the airline staff. He reached for one of her suitcases, and she brusquely said, "I've got it," while ripping it away from his grasp.

Her anger seemed to be directed at him, not her situation. Did she have any idea he'd bribed the chief? Or the hotel? Or what she'd just signed?

Ramon looked at her pursed lips as she struggled with her bags. Some of her hair had fallen in her face, and she let out a breath to try to move it, but he knew better than to offer his assistance again as they exited the airport doors to his waiting car.

His driver got out and helped her with the luggage, which she readily accepted, so it was obvious she was pissed at Ramon.

"Mind telling me why you left this morning without even saying goodbye?" he asked once they were situated in the back of his car.

"I just assumed you'd be too busy with your company from last night to even notice I was gone."

He tried not to have a physical reaction to her words. He needed to know what she was talking about before he offered any explanation. So, he played dumb.

"My company from last night? You were my company last night."

"I'm not a fucking idiot." Her voice rose with her ire. He watched her carefully, trying to size up what she knew, without replying. If he were quiet long enough, she'd continue yelling at him and reveal what exactly she was upset about.

Sophia shook her head in disgust. "Pfft. Whatever. You know what? It doesn't even matter." She then turned her attention to the passing scenery out the window, effectively dismissing him.

Okay, *that* had obviously been the wrong tactic.

He reached for her hand. "My sweet nerdicita. I'm not sure what you're upset about, but I went back to my hotel room alone."

She wrenched away from his grasp. "Don't gaslight me. I know what I saw."

Okay, now they were getting somewhere.

"Are you talking about Raquel—the woman at the bar?"

"Raquel? *That's* who you were with? Oh my god, I'm such an idiot."

"Sweetheart. How do you know Raquel?"

"Juan Diego and Francisco said they saw you two together after you came back to the party once you dropped me off at my room. They said you're lovers."

He nodded his head slowly. "That's only partially true—we *were* lovers once. But she's a liar and was only using me to try to get secrets about my business in an attempt to destroy what I've built."

That part wasn't exactly a lie. He just omitted that she was a U.S. government agent, and he was the leader of a drug cartel.

"So why was she sitting on your lap, Ramon? I *saw* you. Kissing her neck and grabbing her butt. God, you must think I'm such a naïve fool."

Fuuuck.

Naïve? Yes. A fool? Absolutely not.

"Sophia." He said her name with a quiet sternness. "She was sent by the people who followed us last night. It was all a power game. I have absolutely no interest in that woman. I didn't leave the bar with her or see her again once she left.

Besides, why would I agree to marry you today if that were the case? Without a pre-nup even."

She stared at him with her mouth open, like there were so many things she wanted to say but couldn't find the words for any of them. Finally, she squeaked out, "Look, I appreciate you coming to my rescue. I'd be a jerk if I suggested otherwise. You didn't owe me your help, but you showed up anyway."

Well, I kind of owed you my help, since I was the cause of your problems... He didn't say that, of course; he just let her continue.

"And I'm sorry you've gotten roped into me having to stay with you. I will absolutely pay you back for the hotel. I have no idea how this has even happened. I'm going to call the credit card company and get it straightened out—shoot, can we go back? The chief still has my phone. But in the meantime, I promise I will try to be as invisible as possible until I can go home."

Ramon shook his head. "I'll send one of my men to retrieve your phone. And you need to be as visible as possible—around the estate and around town. I need to get you a ring. Oh, we should have a party, too. We could have it at the winery. It won't be as big as the one where we met, but it will still be nice. Maybe we could even invite your friends and family."

She looked at him like he'd gone mad—and maybe he had, a little.

Flashpoint

"You're acting like this is real."

He shrugged. "We might as well make the best of it. I think I'll enjoy being married to you. It will be good for my image. Come to think of it, let's put something in the paper."

"Ramon. No, that's insane. We need to keep this quiet."

"Why?"

"I'm only thinking of you. So you don't have to explain why we aren't married once I'm back in San Francisco."

He cocked his head as if confused. "But, Mrs. Guzman, that doesn't make any sense. We already *are* married."

Chapter Twelve

Sophia
What did he just say?

"What are you talking about? No, we're not."

He cocked his head. "Of course we are. We just signed our marriage license not more than ten minutes ago—witnessed by the chief of police even."

"I signed a *marriage license*? That can't be possible."

"You have some basic Spanish skills, Sophia. Surely you would understand what *licencia de matrimonio* means."

She did know what that meant. Had she just not been paying attention to what she was signing?

"I don't recall signing any such thing."

He pulled out a piece of paper from his jacket pocket. It was the yellow carbonless copy with a heading in bold letters that said 'Marriage License' in Spanish right at the top, and although her signature was faint, it was right there above *novia*.

How could she have missed that?

Glossing over the fact that they were only married because she hadn't known what she'd agreed to, he grabbed her hand, kissed her fingertips, and continued with, "Let's celebrate tonight with dinner at Franco's Steak House. It's one of my favorite restaurants, and I can't wait to introduce you as my wife. But right now, we need to stop and buy your ring before we even go home."

Sophia shook her head as if to help wake up from what was happening.

"You—you can't be serious?"

"Of course I'm serious. Why wouldn't I be serious? I want everyone to know you're my wife."

"Please stop saying that," she whispered.

"Saying what?"

"That I'm your wife."

"But you are. I don't understand. Do you want to keep your maiden name? I'm okay with that, but I think having my last name will only help you. It buys a lot of clout in this town and in San Diego. Speaking of which, my main residence is in San Diego, so I'd prefer we live there. I'm guessing since that's where you grew up and where your family is, you won't mind that."

"I love San Diego," she said automatically, then put her fingertips to her temples. "But, no! I'm not living there—with you. I live in San Francisco—where my job is."

"I thought you said your work was flexible. It's how you were able to come down here."

"It is, but I still have to report to the office on occasion." She closed her eyes for a long second. "But that's not the point! We aren't really married, Ramon. I had no idea that's what I was signing. I thought I was just signing papers so I could leave with you, like a promise I'd stay put—not a marriage license. We need to go back and have Chief Villasenor tear that up."

"Sweetheart, he wouldn't have let you go otherwise."

"This is crazy," she whispered. "How can we get it annulled?"

"Well, we can't. Mexico isn't like the United States. We fall under Roman Catholic influence, I'm afraid, and divorces aren't so easy to get here."

"So we'll have to do it in the U.S."

He smiled patiently. "Maybe we should try being married? Who knows, you might like me. I obviously like you—I married you without a pre-nup."

"I don't want your money, Ramon."

"I know you don't, mi nerdicita." He tapped her nose with the tip of his finger. "If I thought that, I never would have married you. But I don't think you understand just how much money—and power—I have."

"If you have so much power, why can't you get this annulled?"

His forehead wrinkled like the answer to her question was obvious. "Because I don't want to." He threw his arm around her shoulder and drew her to him. "Let's go pick out your ring."

Sophia was in the twilight zone, that's all there was to it.

****

Ramon

She bristled against his touch and moved to the other side of the car. "Might I remind you, that you were just with another woman last night—after, um, spending time with me at the winery. How can you possibly think I'd not want to get this mistake annulled?"

He could only imagine what his exchange with Raquel must have looked like to her, so he needed to do everything he could to convince her nothing happened. And do it with patience—something he wasn't used to having to do.

Ramon moved closer to her, tentatively reaching for her delicate hand and placing it between both of his while looking her directly in the eye. With a low voice, he said, "I promise you, Sophia. What you saw in the bar was not what it seemed. I'm not interested in any woman but you. I wouldn't have married you if I wanted to be with other women. There's a reason I've been single until now. I take my vows seriously and don't make commitments I don't intend to honor."

She narrowed her eyes and pulled her hand back. "You're not making any sense. We've known each other *two* days. There were no vows between us—I didn't even know it was happening! How can you say you made a commitment to me? You helped me out of apparently getting arrested by marrying me; that's hardly worthy of a life-long promise. And, last night, I mean, it's none of my business who you were with after you left me. Just because you made me... you know, at the winery, doesn't mean you owed me anything."

"Damn it, Sophia, I'm not interested in anyone but you! I only want you. What do I need to do to convince you I couldn't give a damn about Raquel or any other woman?"

"I don't know, not have her sit on your lap or grab her ass might be a good place to start."

"Agreed, and done. Last night was not what it looked like. I know that sounds cliché, but it's the truth. And there will be no other woman in my life, I promise you that."

Ramon knew he needed to give her more than assurances in the back of his Cadillac. She'd had a point that they hadn't technically made vows to each other… probably because she didn't know what she was getting herself into when she signed their marriage license, thanks to some well-placed Post-It notes. Still, the vows needed to be remedied.

"Do you want to have another ceremony in the church, or would you prefer to do it in our backyard?"

"Neither! This is crazy, Ramon. This marriage isn't real. We're getting it annulled. And it's *your* backyard."

He shrugged, undeterred. "We'll see," then grabbed her hand and kissed her knuckles with a smirk. "And sorry, love, but legally, it's your backyard now, too. No pre-nup, remember?"

She sighed but didn't withdraw her hand this time. "I don't want your money, or your houses…"

"You might want to hold off on that statement until you've seen all of them. I have some amazing properties throughout the world. I can't wait to show them all to you."

Sophia murmured softly. "We can't stay married, Ramon. I don't belong here with you."

"It's okay. We'll spend most of our time in San Diego."

He knew he had his work cut out for him, but he was determined to make Sophia see by his side was *exactly* where she belonged—whatever city they were in. Because she'd captivated him in just the two days he'd known her.

Chapter Thirteen

Sophia
She recognized Juan Diego and Francisco's storefront as they drove through the high-end shops of Ensenada. They were nowhere near the hotel.

"Aren't we going back to the resort so I can take care of my bill?"

Ramon waved his hand dismissively. "I already took care of it."

"You did? When?"

"Right after the chief called me."

"I promise I will pay you back."

He chuckled. "I appreciate the sentiment, really. But again, my money is your money. There's nothing to *pay back*."

There was no use arguing with him, so she let it drop—for now. "So, where are we going?"

He cocked his head. "I told you. You need to pick out a ring. I cannot have my wife walking around Ensenada without my ring on her finger."

"Ramon! This. Isn't. A. Real. Marriage."

He brought his shoulders up and opened his hands wide like he was acquiescing. "Okay. But we still need to make people believe it is, don't we? The bureaucrats will tie your paperwork up forever if they think we're conning them. For as big a city as Ensenada is, it's still a small town in many

Flashpoint

ways. People talk. It's in your best interest to act like you enjoy my company and want to be married to me. At least until you're back on U.S. soil."

She stared at his handsome face and conceded; it wouldn't be too hard to pretend. She had enjoyed his company yesterday—a lot, right up until she saw Raquel sitting on his lap in the bar.

Why would he even want to be married to her? There obviously had to be something in it for him. If he wanted to be married to help his image, she was sure he could have his pick of any of the most beautiful women in the world. Why Sophia? What was so special about her that would help his image?

Ring shopping with Ramon was like something out of a movie. Salespeople were lined up the minute they walked in—ready to show them the finest rings in the store, and he said, "Choose whatever you want."

He then, of course, vetoed her first choice with a tender smile. "Sweetheart, my wife needs a bigger diamond than that."

He picked out a seven-carat, colorless diamond, which Sophia quickly declined.

"That is way too big, Ramon. I'll be banging it on everything and won't want to wear it."

Hearing the words come out of her mouth was surreal. How did she agree to this again?

"Well," he said with a wink. "We can't have that, can we?"

They compromised on a flawless three-and-a-half-carat, emerald-cut diamond with two larger, tapered baguette-cut diamonds framing the center stone. The wedding band was a simple platinum band.

"Are you getting one?" she asked with a smirk, expecting him to offer an excuse why he wasn't.

"Of course. I was just waiting to see what you picked so I could match yours."

She hadn't anticipated that response. Seeing the platinum band on his strong hand did something to her insides that surprised her.

This isn't real, Sophia. Don't get any ideas.

But Ramon made it hard not to get caught up in the daydream of what being his wife would feel like. The staff at the jewelry store had treated her like royalty. Several times, she had to remind herself she was a middle-class nerd from California, and he was a rich playboy. This was all just a game of pretend until she was cleared to leave Mexico—whenever that was. And she was confident he'd be sick of her by then and eager to sign the annulment papers. She just needed to keep everything in perspective until then.

****

Ramon

His driver brought her luggage inside, and Ramon instructed him to take it upstairs to the master bedroom.

"Um, don't you mean the guest bedroom?" Sophia asked with a nervous lilt in her voice.

"No. We need to sleep in the same bedroom—keep up appearances."

"Appearances for your staff?" she asked incredulously. Her skepticism was founded—he knew he could trust his staff implicitly, but he wasn't about to tell her that.

"They take good care of me, but they're still gossips. Something as juicy as Ramon Guzman and his new wife sleeping in separate beds would spread like wildfire."

Sophia narrowed her eyes and opened her mouth like she was about to argue, but he cut her off.

"I'll be a perfect gentleman." Then added, "Until you ask me not to be." He changed the subject, letting her know the discussion on the topic was closed. "You must be hungry. Go get ready for our celebratory dinner at Franco's. I hope you don't mind, but I've invited a few people to join us."

"You've invited people? Who?"

"Just some of the men in my inner circle that I want to introduce you to. We can ask Juan Diego and Francisco if you'd like. And, by the way, do you want to call your parents?"

"Ramon, no. I don't want anyone to know. My parents would be crushed, not to mention suspicious, if I called and announced that I'd married a man I met on vacation two days ago."

"Okay, we'll keep your picture out of the paper and tabloids—for now. I'd like them to come for the ceremony where we exchange vows, though."

"Stop it. Stop saying that. We are *not* exchanging vows. We aren't doing anything other than co-existing until I can leave the country. When I get back to the U.S., I'll file for an annulment."

"Annulments are only possible if we haven't consummated the marriage, Sophia."

"We haven't. I don't count the winery as consummation."

The corner of his mouth turned up. "Neither do I."

"Well, then there won't be a problem, since we won't be sleeping together as husband and wife—in the biblical sense."

Challenge accepted, sweetheart.

Chapter Fourteen

Sophia

Walking into the restaurant, the staff practically fell over themselves trying to assist Ramon. Just like they had at the jewelry store. And the hotel. And anywhere else they went.

She had to admit, his power was sexy as hell.

And so was the way he looked at her as he doted on her throughout dinner.

He made sure to pull her into the conversation with their dinner companions, who left as soon as dinner was over, while the two of them stayed, talking until they were the only patrons left in the restaurant. Still, the owner assured them they could stay as long as they'd like and even brought out dessert for them.

Their conversation was easy, just like it'd been yesterday, and she found herself laughing out loud at Ramon's stories. With every sip of the expensive red wine he'd ordered, Sophia could feel herself relaxing and falling under his charms again. Then the picture of him patting Raquel's butt entered her mind, just in time to remind her that he was nothing but a player. Just like Kevin.

And she would be a fool to think otherwise.

She was a little tipsy when they arrived back at the estate. The wine had gone down easily, and she lost count of how many bottles had been opened. She was in store for a hangover tomorrow. Red wine tended to do that to her.

"Thank you for dinner. And for keeping me out of jail," she said quietly as they walked slowly up the ornate staircase toward what she assumed was his room. As they approached double wooden doors at the end of the hall, she became nervous. What if he made a move on her? She didn't think she'd be able to resist him in her current state.

"I had wonderful evening. Thank you for your company." With a wink, he added, "It was absolutely worth marrying you for."

She dished it back. "Without a pre-nup, even."

Sophia had overheard him earlier telling someone on the phone that he'd gotten married, and the person on the other end had been concerned about that detail.

"She's not like that," she'd heard him say. That had made her glad that he really believed she was a good person and wouldn't manipulate the situation. He'd done her a favor, for goodness sake. What kind of horrible woman would she be if she turned around and tried to take his money?

They walked into his beautiful bedroom suite. It was very masculine with the dark wood and rich fabrics in navy and forest hues. His four-poster, king-size bed was on a raised platform; the ornate carved wood was a work of art and made it the focal point of the room.

"Is that where the magic happens?" she asked with a nervous laugh as she gestured to the bed.

His face was solemn as he stared back at her. "I told you yesterday, I've never brought a woman here before. But yes, that's where the magic between us will happen, when you're sober."

Not this again.

"I'm not drunk."

The corner of his mouth turned up. "So, are you offering?"

Shit. *Was* she offering?

"I, uh..."

He threw his head back and laughed at her, which made her feel embarrassed, especially when he tapped her nose.

"Don't worry, little one. I told you I'd be a gentleman."

Without another word, he turned toward the bathroom, leaving her to look for her suitcases that their driver had brought up earlier. She found them empty in the walk-in closet that was bigger than her entire apartment back in San Francisco. Upon further inspection, all her belongings had been unpacked and put away in drawers or hung up neatly.

Having people to do things like that for her would take some getting used to. As soon as the thought entered her head, she chided herself under her breath. "You're not going to be here that long... don't get used to it."

She sighed out loud when she pulled the frumpy white cotton nightgown with the tiny yellow flower pattern from the top drawer of the dresser. Why did she care that it screamed *grandma* instead of *sex kitten*? It wasn't *really* her wedding night, after all.

Ramon had said he'd be a gentleman, and she believed him. So, why did she wish she had something sexier to wear to bed?

It had to be her pride—nothing more. He was a playboy; he was interested in every female—she wasn't special.

Yet, at the restaurant tonight, the beautiful hostess practically shoved her boobs in his face, and he didn't look twice at the woman. And Sophia had been watching to see if he would. He hadn't—even when the other men at the table had discreetly watched the woman strut away. Ramon only had eyes for Sophia.

His attention should have unnerved her. Had it been any other handsome, powerful man, it probably would have. She would have been tongue tied and fidgety, but with Ramon, his attention felt empowering. Like maybe she was interesting and beautiful after all, just as he'd told her on more than occasion.

He's a playboy—that's his superpower; make women feel like they're the exception.

But she had been the exception—he married her. And she still had no idea why he would have done that just to help her. She kept coming back to something he'd said about her being good for his image.

That had to be it. She was innocent enough, she supposed. If he needed to look like he'd settled down, she'd be the perfect candidate.

Flashpoint

Things still didn't make sense though. If he was the most powerful man in Ensenada, or all of Mexico as the boys had suggested, who would he need to clean his image up for?

He walked out of the bathroom, and her stomach felt like it was doing somersaults. He was dressed in blue plaid pajama bottoms and was shirtless. He was as stunning to look at as he'd been at the pool yesterday.

And here she was, the queen of frump.

At least he wouldn't be interested in doing anything with her that she'd regret tomorrow.

That thought didn't provide much comfort, and she scurried into the bathroom, where she found her toiletries organized.

She stared at her freshly washed face in the mirror and murmured out loud, "Girl, you are in way over your head."

****

Ramon

It was hard to believe the woman in the modest nightgown that had scampered into the bathroom was the siren from Francisco and Juan Diego's party. Or the woman in the black bikini yesterday. Or the one he'd made come on a bar stool in his winery last night.

Or his *wife*.

But she was, and he fucking loved it.

Sophia Castle Guzman was an enigma. Fortunately, he'd tethered her to him—at least legally, so he could take his time learning all there was to know about her.

Yet every layer he'd discovered only proved to intrigue him more.

He was sitting up in bed when she appeared, one arm behind his neck as he read his tablet. She didn't have a stitch of makeup on and yet, as she approached his bed—their bed—in her high-collared, cotton nightgown, all he could think was, *that's my wife*, and his dick moved at the idea of her lying next to him all night.

He hadn't thoroughly thought through what it would be like to have her so close, yet so far, when he'd insisted they sleep in the same bed. His ego had been certain they'd be naked by the time they got into bed together, he hadn't considered the alternative. It would now be torture having her next to him, fully clothed, without being able to hold her. In his original vision, they were naked, fucking, then she'd fall asleep in his arms—still naked. Maybe waking up and fucking some more.

Reality sucked.

She pulled the covers back and slid between the sheets with a shy smile, and he wanted nothing more than to kiss her, pull her under him, and slide that nightgown right up her sexy little body and over her head.

Even though his dick screamed, "Do it!" he knew it wasn't the right play. If anything, he should have just taken her up here last night, then he wouldn't have had the run in with Raquel.

Then again, they wouldn't be married. Maybe things had worked out for the best, after all. He just needed to gain her trust again.

Trying to seduce her when he'd told her he would be a gentleman didn't feel like the way to go about that.

Regardless, his cock was not pleased and made sure to let him know—all goddamn night long. Every time she moved or made a noise, his dick was on high alert, wondering what the hell he was still doing on his side of the bed.

Dawn couldn't get there soon enough.

Chapter Fifteen

Sophia

She woke up in the middle of the night and found herself snuggled next to Ramon's side with his arm draped over her hip. Rolling over, she nestled her ass against his groin without a second thought. Her eyes flew open at the realization of what was hard against her backside, and what she was doing to, um, *encourage* said hardness.

"Go back to sleep, Sophia," came his gruff voice. When he pulled her tighter, she realized he'd moved his hand to her abdomen. "And you can breathe, you know. It's not going to bite." He kissed her hair and whispered, "But it does do other things if you want it to."

She took a shallow gulp of air, embarrassed that she had, indeed, been holding her breath, then rolled away from him, immediately missing his warmth and the protected feeling she'd felt in his embrace.

"I'm sorry," she mumbled awkwardly. "I must have… when I was sleeping… I didn't mean to…"

He cut her off, "I'm not sorry." Then he reached for her and pulled her back into the warm spot she'd previously occupied and tucked her into the spoon position with him. "Now go back to sleep."

"Are you always this bossy?" she grumbled, but inside, she sighed with contentment. It felt good to be lying next to him again.

"Yes, I am. Get used to it."

Normally, arrogance was a turnoff for her, but Ramon Guzman was all-alpha, and it worked for him.

And her, she recognized with a smile as she drifted back to sleep.

Sophia was alone in bed when she woke up again. She lay in the luxurious sheets, staring up at the ceiling fan spinning round and round with so many thoughts running through her head.

She needed to try to get some work done today.

She should do some yoga and maybe some laps in the pool.

A repeat of last night could *not* happen again.

You didn't even do anything, she reminded herself.

Oh, but she'd wanted to. And that would only complicate things because she knew Ramon was right. Sleeping together would take an annulment off the table. She couldn't afford to not have the option of annulment when she returned to the States. No, she'd be best served avoiding Ramon altogether for the rest of her time in Ensenada.

As it turned out, that was easier said than done.

****

Ramon

Falling asleep next to Sophia last night hadn't been easy, then he woke up to her snuggled against him with her nightgown bunched around her waist and her toned legs wrapped around his. He had to pinch himself to make sure he wasn't dreaming.

It had been natural to put his hand on her hip and hold her. Then she woke up and froze. It was then that he realized she'd snuggled next to him in her sleep. He didn't give a shit, he'd take it. When she tried to pull away, he wasn't having it. Fortunately, she didn't argue, and he got to sleep with her in his arms all night after all. Tonight, he was shooting for her to be naked, too.

He woke up before dawn like he always did; only that morning, he didn't immediately hop out of bed but rather breathed in the coconut scent of her hair as he listened to her breathing and admitted to himself, he liked sharing his bed with her.

Never in a million years did he think he'd want to wake up with a woman every day—let alone the same woman. But the little nerd had done something to his heart. Dante had a hearty laugh at Ramon's expense when he'd told him on the phone last night. That was, until he found out there'd been no pre-nup.

"*Tío*, I appreciate that you've finally found someone you want to spend time with, but you *married* her? Things just aren't adding up. I'm not convinced you meeting her at that party wasn't a setup after all... just not with the CIA. How did she convince you to do something so crazy—and without a pre-nup?"

"You're right, there wasn't a pre-nup. But she's not like that." Then he noticed her in the hall and told his nephew in Spanish that he'd explain how it happened later. But clarified in the interim that it had been Ramon's doing—not Sophia's.

Begrudgingly, he slipped out of bed and quietly got ready without disturbing her.

Kissing Maribel on the cheek when he entered the kitchen for his morning coffee, he explained he wasn't sure how late his bride would sleep, but when she came down, he wanted to have breakfast with her on the patio.

"*Claro que sí, Señor* Guzman," she said, grinning ear to ear.

With a spring in his step, he walked to the office wing of the estate. Jesús, the man who ran his day-to-day dealings and was part of Ramon's inner circle, would be in later—although his men were always at his beck and call. The men didn't punch a timeclock, just got shit done and were paid handsomely for it. Although Ramon wouldn't be surprised if Jesús didn't show up until late morning. The man had drunk a lot of wine at dinner last night where Ramon had officially introduced Sophia to those she'd see on a daily basis.

In the quiet office, he got a lot accomplished before Consuela knocked on his office door to tell him Sophia was on the patio, and breakfast would be ready in ten minutes.

He thanked his housekeeper and locked his computer screen before heading to the patio with a smile on his face. He was happy to be having breakfast with Sophia and wanted to make starting their day together over a meal a habit. He also wanted to make ending their day naked in bed a habit too, but first things first.

Chapter Sixteen

Sophia
He's probably not even going to bother coming to breakfast, she scolded herself as she pulled her bathing suit and cover-up on, then swiped her eyes with mascara and her lips with pink lip gloss.

I'm not trying too hard. I'd do this even if he weren't here.

Maribel gave Sophia a knowing smile when she walked in the kitchen and asked in her rudimentary Spanish if she could have breakfast.

"*Claro que sí, Señora* Guzman. It would be my pleasure. *Señor* Guzman asked that he be informed when you came down for breakfast."

Sophia tried to be nonchalant when she asked, "Will Ramon be joining me?"

"*Sí, Señora.* He wants to eat on the patio this morning."

She shouldn't be smiling so brightly at the news, but she couldn't help herself.

****

Ramon
He stopped short at the tall French doors leading to the patio. Sophia was already seated at the table, and she looked like a vision in the morning sunlight with her face turned up

toward the sun, wearing a smile of contentment. He liked the idea of her feeling content here.

He rolled up his sleeves, cracked his neck, and took a deep breath before stepping out into the Ensenada morning.

The soles of his expensive leather shoes made a tapping sound on the brickwork as he strolled toward the table like he didn't have a care in the world.

He kissed her cheek and murmured, "Good morning, *mi mujer*," before sitting opposite her. "Do you want to do some shopping today? I can go with you or give you my credit card and send you with a driver. Whatever you'd like."

She shook her head. "No, I think I'm going to lie by the pool one last day before I report back to work."

"That sounds like a nice way to spend your first full day at the estate. But, you know, you don't need to work anymore. You could do that every day…"

She cut him off. "Even if this marriage were real—which it's not, I would want to work. And since we're just faking things until I am cleared to leave, I definitely cannot jeopardize my job."

He ignored her comment about faking it. "Be sure to wear sunscreen and drink plenty of water. The Mexican sun can creep up on you."

"I've discovered that."

She reached into her bag and produced a bottle of SPF 50, then pulled the cover-up over her head. His cock jumped when he got another glimpse of how hot his wife's body was.

He knew he would be finding several reasons to leave his office today and walk by the pool.

"Would you mind putting some on my back, since you're here? That way I won't have to ask anyone else."

The idea of anyone on his staff, other than the *abuelas*, touching her made his blood boil, and judging by the smirk on her face, she knew it.

Still, he played it cool, pretending to be unaffected when he murmured, "Yeah, I can help you," like his cock hadn't jumped to attention at the thought of touching her.

He wasn't, however, going to pass up an opportunity to give her a taste of her own medicine. He stood and took the offered lotion, squirting some in his hands, while she turned around and lifted her hair off her neck. The neck he wanted nothing more than to bury his face in and inhale her scent before kissing his way to her ear.

Soon, he promised his inquisitive dick who wanted to come out and take a better look around.

He took his time applying the slippery substance with a lover's touch. He bit back a grin when he noticed the goosebumps on her skin while he sensually rubbed his hands over her body. Encouraged by her reaction, he lingered at her outer boobs, stroking her tanned flesh reverently. He wasn't sure, but he thought she moaned softly when he'd made his way to her lower back and slipped his fingers under her waistband—all in the name of making sure she was adequately covered in sunscreen, of course.

His hand lingered, giving her the opportunity to greenlight going further. He would have taken anything at that point—a whisper, a head nod, a simple please... Hell, even a subtle shift in her body toward him, and he would have her laid out on the nearest chaise lounge.

Instead, she went stiff and moved away from him, murmuring, "Thank you."

"Of course," he replied like she'd just thanked him for passing the salt and sat back down to pour coffee from the carafe on the table into his fancy china cup.

He did glance at her body out of the corner of his eye when she put the cover-up over her head, but he quickly looked away when her head poked through the neck of the fabric.

"Will you be working all day? Do you want to swim with me later?"

This was a good sign. She may have said she was faking it, but still wanting to spend time with him spoke volumes. There was no way she'd be able to resist his charms for much longer. Still, he didn't want to appear too eager.

"I'm not sure. I might be able to get away in the afternoon for a long lunch."

"Aren't you like, the boss?"

He chuckled at her observation.

"Being the boss is a double-edge sword. It means you have to know everything that's going on."

His captains, lieutenants, and planted spies did a damn good job of keeping him in the know, so yeah, he could get away—all day if he wanted. Not like he could tell her that.

Sophia shrugged. "It seems like you had free time when we first met."

There was a challenge embedded in her comment.

"That was the weekend. It's a new work week."

"That makes sense." Her mouth turned down in obvious disappointment, and his ego was stoked.

He wanted nothing more than to spend the day poolside with her in that fucking bikini—in the privacy of his home. Although he was having serious doubts about his ability to keep his hands off her. Especially when he got the distinct feeling that wasn't what she wanted.

Maybe today was the perfect opportunity to help her realize that she belonged with him.

"After breakfast, I'll let Jesús know that if he needs me, I'll be at the pool today."

Chapter Seventeen

Sophia
What's the saying? Be careful what you wish for?

She had turned to mush when he showed up at breakfast with his shirt sleeves rolled up, revealing his sexy arms and expensive watch. When he'd put suntan lotion on her, there was no doubt he'd purposefully applied it in such a way that it turned her on. Then she goaded him into spending the day with her, and she was now left wondering what the hell she'd just done.

Lying back in the lounger with her eyes closed, she felt his presence the second he walked into the pool area and slowly opened her eyes to find him shirtless and in board shorts. A lazy grin spread across his face when he noticed her gawking at him.

And she was gawking—there was no other way to describe it. The 'V' right above his hip bones made her mouth water. It seemed like it formed an arrow directing her attention to his cock, and she couldn't help but look at the area hidden underneath the fabric of his swimsuit.

And he's your husband, the devil on her shoulder whispered. *Anything you do with him would be perfectly acceptable.*

Not anything, the angel on the other shoulder warned. Certainly not the things she fantasized about him doing to her, anyway. Besides, doing those things negated getting an annulment.

But damn, looking at him walking toward her, she had to admit... losing the annulment option might be worth it if it meant the rest of her time in Ensenada was spent being intimate with Ramon.

And why did he have to be so damn *likable*?

"Hey. You made it! I thought for sure you'd have a work emergency and wouldn't be able to get away."

He sat in the lounger next to hers. Consuela had served their breakfast as they'd discussed spending time at the pool, and not ten minutes later, the older woman walked by with a stack of fluffy beach towels before they'd even finished with breakfast. When Sophia arrived in the pool area, she found two towels laid out on loungers and the remaining stack in the pool house, along with a basket containing bottles of water—sparkling, purified, and spring, and varying SPFs, aloe vera, and other lotions. She was still getting used to people taking care of her.

"Like you said, I'm the boss. And it's not like I'm far away if I'm needed."

"So, I have you all to myself today?"

The corner of his mouth turned up. "You sound happy about that."

She thought about what he said for a second before responding. "I guess I am. I enjoy spending time with you."

Her admission seemed to surprise him; he nodded his head with raised eyebrows. "Good to know." Then he grinned. "Enough to want to stay married to me?"

"Well..." she smirked. "Let's not get crazy. You're still a bazillionaire man slut, and I'm still a mousy nerd scraping by."

"You're fucking sexy, Sophia. Don't ever doubt that for a second. And my playboy ways are over—I told you that. What happened with Raquel was not what you think."

She wanted to believe him. But she also didn't want to be a fool like she had been with Kevin.

"How about we just pretend we're two friends who are hanging out at the pool today?"

As if to seal the deal, Sophia offered her hand for a handshake. Ramon took it with a smirk, but instead of shaking it, he brought it to his lips and tenderly kissed her knuckles as he looked into her eyes. She swallowed hard, trying to keep her composure. He softly swiped his thumb over the backs of her fingers, then released her hand with a wink.

Siding with the devil on her shoulder just kept getting more and more appealing.

Picking up his phone, he punched some buttons while asking, "So, *friend*, what are you drinking?"

"It's, um..." She looked at the Fitbit on her wrist. "Eleven o'clock."

"Mimosas it is."

Flashpoint

Minutes later, Consuela appeared with a tray carrying a carafe of orange juice, a bottle of champagne in an ice bucket, and two champagne glasses, along with a plate of cheeses and fruits.

"Aw, thank you so much," Sophia told the older woman once she set the tray down on the table under an umbrella by the pool.

Consuela patted her hand with a smile, approval in her eyes as she said something in Spanish that Sophia didn't understand. Out of all the older women, Consuela understood the least amount of English.

"She said she loves having you here," Ramon translated.

Sophia beamed at the woman while answering Ramon. "Tell her everyone has made me feel very welcome."

Ramon translated for her, and Consuela patted her hand again, then walked away, grinning ear to ear.

"I should take another Spanish class," Sophia said wistfully, wishing she could communicate better with the women who had been so kind to her.

"We can get you a tutor," Ramon suggested. "Or I can teach you."

She wrinkled her nose. "I think you trying to teach me would be as bad an idea as my father trying to teach me to drive. Some things you should just leave to neutral third-party professionals. But maybe I could practice what I learn on you."

"Fair enough." He eyed her carefully for a beat before saying softly, "Consuela's not the only one who loves having you here, you know."

"Really? Give it a week, you'll be sick of me by then."

He shook his head. "I don't see that ever happening."

Ramon filled the flutes halfway with champagne then added the orange juice. "What should we toast to?" he asked as he handed her a glass.

Sophia swirled the contents to mix them as she tried to think of something clever but came up blank. Finally, she raised her glass. "To Mexico. You meet the most interesting people here."

"Indeed." The look he gave her when he clinked his glass against hers sent a shiver down her spine.

She took a big gulp of her drink; she had a feeling she would need some liquid courage to get through the day with her clothes still on.

****

Ramon

She had to know the effect she had on him. He subtly adjusted himself as he approached her lounging next to the pool, with her hair piled high on her head and her bikini-clad body displayed like a buffet just for him. He'd never been so twisted up over a woman before. Ever.

Flashpoint

Sure, the opposite sex was nice to look at, they almost always smelled nice, and he certainly enjoyed fucking them, but it was as if Sophia Castle had cast a spell on him. Enough to make her Sophia Castle *Guzman*. He never thought he'd get married, yet he'd married her the second an opportunity presented itself—without even a second thought.

Granted, he'd done so through deceptive practices, but that didn't weigh on his conscience in the slightest. It was a small cost to get what he wanted—and what he wanted was her.

Ramon always got his way—it was the means on how he achieved it that varied, but he didn't become one of the most powerful men in Mexico by being a nice guy. How he'd achieved his power he knew might be a sticking point with his new bride, so he needed to keep her in the dark about most of Guzman Enterprises' dealings. At least until she was so in love with him that she'd forgive him once she found out. Hopefully by then, more of the family business would be legitimate business. Dante had continued working on that, but there was no escaping there would always be an element of criminal activity to what they did—if for no other reason than it would keep them alive.

Illegal activities equaled money, and there were those who wanted the Guzmans' share of the pie and would have no problem killing for it. Fortunately for him, money also equaled power, and that kept him and those around him safe. Ramon wasn't willing to give up that money or power.

Allowing another cartel control of the drug trade in Ensenada would be like signing his—and his men's—death warrants. It wasn't happening.

Still, Dante had been right. There was nothing wrong with diversifying their dealings to include legal ones, too.

But now, Ramon had taken a wife, and she made him vulnerable. It was for the best that she'd made him slow down and not announce their marriage—even though he'd wanted to right away as another form of 'sealing the deal.'

Now, as they sat poolside, laughing and talking—even flirting a little, he realized spending time with her was all he needed to seal the deal. She was meant for him; Ramon knew she felt it, too. She'd just gotten spooked because of Raquel.

The fucking CIA. He'd take them intercepting one hundred of his shipments if they hadn't messed this up with Sophia.

Still, as he reapplied her lotion, he knew this was nothing he couldn't overcome.

Kissing her shoulder, he slid his hands under her black bikini top and paused, giving her the opportunity to object. She didn't, and he brushed his thumb over her rock-hard nipples as he moved his lips from her shoulder to the back of her neck. Sophia dropped her chin to give him better access while rounding her back into him as he kneaded her breasts.

Her skin felt like silk in his hands, and her scent drove him crazy. Then she turned to look at him, her eyes hooded with lust, and he quickly captured her mouth with his, wasting no time seeking out her tongue.

She twisted in the lounger to situate herself in his lap as she fervently returned the kiss—her arms wrapped around his neck while her fingertips sought purchase in his short hair as she ground her hips into his. Their bathing suits created a barrier to what he wanted most—to be inside her.

Suddenly, she broke the kiss and slid off his lap onto the cement, panting, "We can't."

With a rock-hard cock, he struggled to find his bearings as to what just happened.

"Did I hurt you?" He had no idea how he could have, but anything was possible.

"No," came her strangled response. "We just can't do *that*. You said it yourself; it would take an annulment off the table."

Yeah, which is exactly why they should do *that*.

He helped her back onto the lounger.

"Would being married to me—for real, be so bad, Sophia? You'd never want for anything."

"I've told you, Ramon, I don't care about your money."

He believed her—to an extent. But money opened a lot of doors to a lot of different possibilities. Not that he wanted his wife to only want him for his bank account, but if she would allow herself to see what their life could be like, maybe she'd agree.

"What do you care about?"

"Love. Companionship. Having someone who supports me. Someone I can see myself having a family with."

"And you can't see that with me?"

"No."

It was just one word, but it felt like a swift kick to the nuts—and to his pride. And if it was one thing Ramon had a lot of, it was pride.

"I see," he said curtly as he stood. He didn't need to be here any longer. "Enjoy the rest of your day."

****

Sophia

She wanted to run after him and tell him she didn't mean it. She could see all that with him—and it scared the daylights out of her.

But there was no way this could work in the long run. Ramon was bound to grow bored of her once the shine of a new relationship wore off. How could he not? She was the definition of middle class. She didn't belong in his world. He'd realize it, too, soon enough.

Sophia didn't see him for the rest of the day, but only realized she hadn't gotten her phone back until after he left, and there was no way she was chasing after him now.

The sun began to set so she moved inside the pool house and flipped through a magazine when Maribel came in to ask if she'd like to eat dinner in the dining room or on the patio.

Flashpoint

"Wherever Ramon would prefer is fine."

She felt a pang of disappointment when Maribel explained in broken English that he wouldn't be joining Sophia for dinner but was eating in his office instead.

"Oh, I can just eat in the kitchen then. I don't want you to go to any trouble."

"It's no trouble, *Señora*."

"Then I guess I'll just eat in here, if that's okay."

Maybe she could hide out in the pool house until she could go back to the U.S.

"*Sí*. Ready in..." Sophia knew she was struggling for the right English word until she gave up and reverted back to Spanish as she held up one hand with three fingers raised and the other in the shape of a zero. "*Treinta minutos*."

"*Gracias*, Maribel."

After dinner, she decided she wouldn't risk a repeat of snuggling up to Ramon in her sleep, and instead would 'accidentally' fall asleep on the pool house couch and just sleep there for the night.

She should have known the *abuelas* wouldn't let her get away with that. Around nine-thirty, Sophia lay on the couch reading a book she'd found on the coffee table when she heard the soft click of the door. She looked up to see Antonia collecting her dinner dishes.

"*Hola*. Are you coming inside, *Señora? Señor* Guzman wouldn't want you to fall asleep out here."

"I'll be in a bit."

The older woman hesitated.

"What is it, Antonia?"

"I can't go to bed until I'm sure you've come inside."

Oh, FFS. He's seriously using the sweet old ladies working for him to babysit me?

Sophia wanted to tell Antonia to tell Ramon that if he had a problem with her sleeping in the pool house, he could come out and tell her himself, but then thought better of it. She didn't need to bring the staff, who doted on their employer, into this.

Swinging her legs to the edge of the couch, she stood with as genuine a smile as she could muster.

"I'm right behind you."

"*Gracias, Señora.* I'm sorry to bother you."

"It's no bother at all. I should probably get ready for bed anyway. I have a long day tomorrow."

"Oh, are you going into town?"

"No, I need to work on my project from my job."

The fact that Sophia had a job seemed to surprise the housekeeper. With raised eyebrows, she asked, "*Usted tiene un trabajo?*"

She knew enough basic Spanish to know Antonia was confirming she had a job.

"I'm a software analyst for a tech company." She had no idea if that translated, so she added, "*Para computadora.*"

Antonia lips parted, as she took a breath of recognition. "Ahhh*, sí. Computadora. Muy bien.*"

Flashpoint

They walked back into the main house, and Sophia bid the older woman goodnight, then headed up the stairs. She was annoyed at Ramon for sending Antonia to bring her inside and foiling her plan to sleep in the pool house. Why did he even care?

Then she realized, he didn't want to look bad. Not having his wife in his room anxiously awaiting his arrival when he finished work wouldn't reflect well on him. After all, if a mousy, American nerd wasn't falling over herself to be with him, what would that say about the Mexican playboy?

She almost ducked into one of the guest rooms off the hallway leading to the master suite, but asked herself what that would accomplish. The point of her being here was to sell the idea that they were truly husband and wife so she'd be allowed to go home—where she could get an annulment.

No, it was better to keep up pretenses.

Although, when she rolled over and looked at the clock at one a.m., she was annoyed to find his side of the bed empty. What was the point of keeping up pretenses if he wasn't going to keep up his side of the bargain while she looked a fool?

Chapter Eighteen

Ramon
It had been late when he finally climbed the stairs to bed. He regretted offering one hundred of his shipments to be intercepted to the universe, because just dealing with one big one tonight was a huge pain in the ass.

Having a shipment seized wasn't unusual in his line of work, but they were normally smaller, less expensive loads that his lieutenants dealt with. But this had been a major import from one of his suppliers, and the impact of it being confiscated would be felt for a while and trickle down to a lot of supply.

His captains and local lieutenants had all assembled in his office just before dinner, and even though they hadn't finished formulating a plan, Ramon decided to call it a night a little after two a.m. The idea of Sophia waiting in his bed, even though they'd had a falling out earlier, was his main motivation.

"We'll look at this with fresh eyes in the morning. We've rerouted the next shipment, we have extra security in place at our current locations, and we have people working on how the feds obtained the intel. There's not much more we can do tonight, gentlemen."

"I'll bet if his new bride wasn't upstairs waiting for him, he'd have found things we could do," Jesús quipped.

"Oh, yes. Congratulations. I assume my invitation got lost in the mail?" snarled Luis Ramirez. Although Luis' mother was Ramon's sister, he wasn't in Ramon's inner circle, something his nephew clearly resented.

Still, tonight wasn't the time to have one of his captains acting like a little bitch over a perceived slight, so Ramon attempted to smooth the man's feathers.

"No one was invited; it was just her and I—sort of a spur of the moment thing. But we're planning a ceremony and party soon. Once we have a date, you'll be the first to get an invitation."

"Well, since I also have a wife waiting for me," Dante said as he stood, "I'm happy to call it a night and start fresh tomorrow morning."

"Those of you who want to stay are welcome to one of the guest rooms," Ramon said as he followed Dante out the door. He knew he could trust Jesús to lock up and not leave his office until everyone was out.

He took the stairs two at a time but gingerly opened his bedroom door so not to disturb Sophia. It took his eyes a minute to adjust to the dark room, but once they had, he looked at his bed, expecting to see his pretty wife fast asleep.

Instead, he found an unmade bed, but no Sophia. He walked into the dark bathroom and flipped on the light; she wasn't there either.

A sense of panic swelled up in him, especially after dealing with someone betraying them tonight. Had someone come into his home and taken his wife right under his nose?

No. He was being irrational. He had security—men he trusted. Maybe she was just getting a snack. But the men in his office had brought their own security, too. Maybe one of them...

Ramon turned on his heel and rushed out the door, down the hall, only to run smack dab into Luis, coming out of one of the guest rooms.

"Did you lose something?" he asked with smug grin and gestured to the door he'd just come out of. "Because, if not, you've definitely stepped up your hospitality game."

He strode past his smirking nephew, into the guest room, and found Sophia fast asleep under the covers in her lace-collar nightgown, her hands in a prayer pose under her head. She looked like a fucking angel, which worked in her favor because he was as mad as the devil.

Gently scooping her up in his arms, he marched out the door.

"I take it the honeymoon is over?"

It was a good thing Ramon loved Luis' mother, because he might consider having him killed otherwise.

"I'm sure she was just upset that I worked so late." He paused before walking back to his room. "And if you ever refer to my wife as 'hospitality' again, I'll knock your goddamn teeth down your throat."

Sophia

She could feel his anger vibrating off his body as he carried her down the hall, so Sophia pretended to be sound asleep, not daring to open her eyes to even sneak a glance at him.

When the guest room door had opened, she'd assumed it was Ramon coming to find her. Then she heard a voice she didn't recognize chuckle sinisterly as he said, "Well, well, well. What do we have here?"

Fortunately, his remark was immediately followed by a slamming door and fast footsteps coming down the hall. Footsteps that she realized were Ramon's when she heard the exchange between the men before he came in and scooped her up.

Now he marched down the hall with her in his arms, and he was *mad*.

"I know you're awake," he snarled as he pushed the door open with his knee. "But it's probably very smart of you to pretend not to be."

"I'm sorry," she whispered just before he set her on the bed.

"What were you thinking? You embarrassed me, Sophia." His voice was low and calm—scary calm. "In front of a man who answers to *me*. How do you think it makes me look, my new bride sleeping in a guest room?"

"I don't know… like a man who had a fight with his wife? Like a normal married couple?"

"Not a couple who *just* got married. And *not me*. No one disrespects me."

She jumped to her feet. "Well, I didn't even know you had people here. How was I supposed to know someone would be sleeping in the guest room?" Her voice went up an octave. "Shouldn't you have told *your wife* we were having overnight guests?"

"These are my business associates, Sophia. I have no obligation to tell you they're staying; you're not expected to feed them or clean up after them—we have staff for that. Nor are you expected to even interact with them."

"It's common courtesy, Ramon. Along the lines of 'I'm working late, don't wait up.' Something a husband should tell his wife. Ruse or no ruse."

He stared at her for a beat, then his features softened, and his shoulders relaxed.

"You're right. But regardless of overnight guests, it was still disrespectful."

"You were disrespectful first." She felt like a petulant child with her response.

"I should have told you I was working late, but I'm in the middle of a mess right now—hence the reason my entire team

Flashpoint

of men is here. It was an oversight on my part. What you did was blatant."

"You had Antonia come get me from the pool house like I was a child. You couldn't have had her tell me you had people here?"

She could tell by the look on his face, he was confused.

"I never asked Antonia to come get you—but it's probably for the best she did. And she wouldn't have told you my men are here, because my staff knows better than to discuss my business dealings *with anyone*."

"Isn't it *our* staff, Ramon?" she threw his words back at him.

"Fine. *Our* staff. But it's *my* business, Sophia. And they do not discuss it. Ever. Period."

"What if they did?"

"They'd be fired. Any family member they have working for me would be fired. Any standing they had in Ensenada by being associated with the Guzmans would be ruined."

Jesus, no wonder Antonia didn't say anything.

"Well, you're going to have to make an exception for them when it comes to me, Ramon. I deserve to know who's in my house."

"No exceptions, Sophia. Not when it comes to business. It's better for everyone this way."

"Better for everyone? How is it better for me to have people in my home without me even knowing?"

His ire was back, and he glared at her before lifting his head toward the ceiling and taking a deep breath through his nose.

"We can make an exception that you know when there are outside visitors here. But that's it. Not who they are, or where they're from."

She snorted. "Well, won't that be convenient when your girlfriend comes for a visit?"

He grabbed her elbow and got within inches of her face. She caught his masculine sent, and her stomach dipped. Or maybe it was the intensity with which he delivered his next words.

"I would never disrespect you like that. Ever."

She shrugged out of his grip, unnerved at being so close to him. "I wouldn't blame you. Our marriage isn't real, why wouldn't you have a girlfriend?"

He got back in her space, the furrowed line between his brows conveyed his mood, but he kept his hands off her. "Consummated or not, this marriage is real. You're my wife, Sophia. Until you're not, I will be faithful to you."

She stared at his mouth as he uttered the words that she believed without a doubt. His beautiful, kissable lips were mere inches from hers. She could just lean in and...

He stepped back abruptly.

"I have to get some sleep; I've got a lot of work ahead of me tomorrow."

Ramon retreated to the bathroom, reappearing moments later in nothing but pajama pants. Good grief, he was gorgeous.

He got in bed, switched the lamp on his bedside table off, and rolled over on his side—facing away from her.

She lay on her side of the bed, staring at his muscular back in the moonlight. It was tempting to slide over, hug his middle, and lay kisses along his spine. She wanted him to tell her everything was okay. Maybe ask her again if she wanted to be married for real.

"I really am sorry," she whispered as she scooted closer to him.

"Thank you," came his reply—his back still to her. "I accept your apology."

He made no move to roll over, so she tried again.

"Goodnight."

"Goodnight, Sophia."

It was clear she'd been dismissed. She didn't like it very much.

*

Sleep was hard to come by as she lay next to him. Listening to his even breathing, it was painfully obvious he wasn't nearly as affected by her presence in bed next to him as she was his.

Although he was quiet, she heard him get up only a few hours later, well before dawn. After hearing the bedroom door close, she finally fell into a fitful sleep, filled with dreams of her being old and alone, while Ramon was remarried with children and grandchildren surrounding him in his old age.

She woke up feeling more tired than ever.

When he sat opposite her at the patio table and murmured a polite, "Good morning, Sophia," she tried to hide her surprise.

"Good morning. I didn't expect to see you. I thought you'd be busy working."

"I am, but I thought it important that we be seen having breakfast together." He placed his napkin in his lap and asked, "What are your plans today? I can have Jesús arrange for a driver to take you into town if you'd like."

"No, I really do need to do some work. They're going to fire me if I don't report in soon."

Instead of his usual reply, reminding her that she no longer needed to work, he murmured a disinterested, "Well, we wouldn't want that, would we," as he opened his phone.

"No, that would be bad."

"Mmm hmm…" She thought he wasn't listening, but he added without looking up, "Jesús will provide you with the Wi-Fi information and anything else you need."

"Great. Thanks. But, I do need my phone, too. I never got it back from when Chief Villasenor took it."

He furrowed his brows but kept his eyes on the screen in front of him. "You didn't get that back? I'll be sure to have Jesús look into it."

Maribel served their breakfast, looking back and forth between them as they sat in awkward silence.

They continued that way through breakfast until Ramon set his fork down, took another sip of coffee from the dainty china cup, then wiped his mouth with his napkin, and stood.

"I will be late again tonight," he said as he pushed in his chair. "Have a nice day."

He didn't wait for her reply, although she offered it even though he had already left the patio. "You, too."

Chapter Nineteen

Sophia

Jesús found her before she even left the patio after breakfast to give her back her phone and provide her with the Wi-Fi information. She was surprised to see she had no missed calls or texts. Not even from Kevin or her boss. And she needed to contact Juan Diego and Francisco with an apology. Perhaps seeing them in person would be better.

She did her best to concentrate on her work project and was able to make some progress, but her mind kept going back to breakfast and Ramon's cool demeanor toward her.

She'd thought that she'd wanted him to accept that they were married on paper only. Now, that he seemed to have agreed, she wasn't so sure that was what she wanted. Him giving up so easily had left her feeling unbalanced.

Which was stupid, if she stopped to analyze it. She'd known him for what—five days? Hardly enough time to develop feelings for the man.

Yet, here she was married to him and wasn't that mad about it. Actually, she wasn't upset at all. Maybe because she knew it wasn't real and could get fixed, or maybe...

She shook her head. To even think this could work was preposterous. If she thought Kevin had crushed her, it would be child's play compared to what Ramon could do if she let him in her heart.

Kevin... funny how little she'd thought of him. She certainly didn't miss him. Sophia huffed a small laugh under her breath at the realization that she hadn't really loved Kevin. Not even in the beginning. The hurt she'd felt at seeing Ramon pat Raquel's butt far outweighed the hurt at seeing Kevin naked and pounding Jessica in his hot tub.

She wondered why... She'd only spent one day with Ramon before she saw him with the beautiful, buxom woman. But during that time, she may have allowed herself at least the daydream that there could be something with the Mexican. Especially after the orgasm he gave her in the winery tasting room. Learning he was just another playboy had closed the door on any possibility of a future with him—whereas in her heart, she'd already known there was no future with Kevin.

Ramon's insistence that it wasn't what she thought had left her as confused as ever, partly because she wanted to believe it wasn't what it seemed. Then he *married* her—the eternal bachelor—without even batting an eye.

But now, just as quickly, he seemed to have written her off. Not even putting up a fight for her.

It's for the best, she thought with a sigh. But deep down in her gut, it didn't feel that way. Not even a little.

She didn't see him again that day and had dinner alone in the kitchen as she practiced her Spanish with Maribel. Bedtime came without having seen him all day, and she wondered if she would sleep alone, but heard him come in sometime after two a.m. He was quiet as he prepared for bed, then was careful to stay on his side of the mattress—even placing a pillow between them. Sophia suspected it was supposed to be a barrier in case she tried to cuddle him in her sleep again.

He was gone when she woke up.

He did, however, arrive at the patio before Maribel served breakfast.

"Good morning, Sophia," he said brusquely as he sat down. Placing his napkin in his lap without looking at her, he asked with a polite tone, "Would you like for me to arrange a driver for you to go into town today?"

When he finally glanced her way, his expression was neutral—almost bored—while he waited for her reply.

"No, thank you. I still have to work on my project."

"Very well. Should you change your mind, stop and speak with Jesús. He'll arrange a driver for you."

He hadn't offered money or his credit cards since her first day at the estate.

Whatever. She didn't want them anyway. She had a job; she didn't need his money. She would, however, like someone to talk to that understood more than basic English, so she attempted to engage him in conversation.

"How's work for you going? I'm guessing things are still busy; I didn't hear you come to bed until late."

"I'm always busy," was his clipped response as he scrolled through his phone without looking at her.

"How did you find time to go to Francisco and Juan Diego's party then?"

She hoped to remind him of the night they'd met—when he'd pursued her.

"Their party is an important social event in Ensenada every year. It was important that I and my associates attended—for appearances."

"Ah, yes, appearances. Those seem important to you."

She tried to keep her tone even, so her observation didn't sound like a criticism—although maybe in a way, it was.

He leveled her with his stare. Obviously, he'd taken it as an insult.

He chose his next words carefully. "In my line of work, it's important that I maintain a certain level of… visibility. To be seen when the occasion calls for it, and invisible when necessary."

Cryptic much? Still, she nodded her head like he'd made perfect sense.

She wanted to keep him talking, so she followed up with, "Is it like that for you in San Diego, too?"

He was back to scrolling through his phone, not looking at her. "Nothing like here."

"Do you go back and forth a lot?"

"Having a helicopter helps."

"You have a helicopter?"

He was engrossed in something on his phone now, and absentmindedly murmured, "Mmm hmm," effectively dismissing her.

She didn't like that at all.

"Will you be around for dinner tonight?"

He glanced up at her then back down at the screen. "I think it's best that I'm not, don't you?"

"No, I don't."

That got his attention.

"Oh? Why's that?"

"Um…"

That pride… she could be such a bitch.

"Tell me why you don't think that's for the best, Sophia."

She knew he wanted to hear her say she wanted to spend time with him—and all it would take to make that happen would be to say it.

Still, she hemmed and hawed. Her ego just wouldn't let her utter it out loud.

He took a sip of coffee from the china cup, set it on the saucer, then stood with a wry smile. "Have a nice day, Sophia Castle. Let Jesús know if you need anything."

He was gone before she could even respond.

Sophia *Castle*. He wasn't adding the *Guzman* anymore. It was probably for the best.

Chapter Twenty

Ramon

It took everything in him not to leave his office at six thirty when Consuela came in and asked if he wanted dinner in the dining room or patio.

"I'll have a plate delivered here later, thank you."

"Would you like *Señora* Guzman..."

He cut off whatever his longtime housekeeper was about to suggest. "I'm quite busy. She should have dinner without me."

"Of course, *Señor*." She lowered her eyes, and he realized he may have sounded harsher than he'd intended.

"*Gracias*, Consuela," he replied with a soft smile, making sure to give her his full attention. "I'll call down later."

"My pleasure. It will be Antonia. I'll be leaving soon."

"Have a nice evening."

She patted his hand. "You, too, *Señor*."

He was leaving Sophia to eat alone for the third night in a row. He should just fly her back to San Francisco and end this farce. But, something told him to be patient and not throw in the towel—not yet.

When he slipped into his bedroom a little after one a.m., the first thing he noticed was that she'd left his bedside lamp on for him. Then he glanced at her asleep on the bed and bit back a groan. *What the hell was she wearing?*

Oh, that little minx. He should have known she wouldn't fight fair.

With the comforter at her waist, her hair was fanned out on her pillow and with one toned leg sticking out from under the covers, he caught sight of her pastel pink panties. She was dressed in the white button-down shirt he'd worn yesterday—while generously leaving several buttons undone so that the swell of her breasts and the curve of her waist peeked out. She had to be the sexiest thing he'd ever laid eyes on.

Ramon stood frozen in place, staring at her. That was *his wife*. And he couldn't fucking touch her. Not yet, anyway.

He wanted nothing more than to kneel at the side of the bed and wake her with kisses—starting from her ankle and taking his time as he worked up her leg, licking behind her knees and leaving love bites on her inner thighs. He'd breathe in the scent of her pussy before licking the crease at the top of her thigh, taking his time to lightly mouth her slit over the fabric of her panties. When she'd tortuously try to make contact with his mouth, he'd move up her stomach and get lost in her perfect tits. Eventually, he'd make his way to her neck and her mouth, but he'd take his time and explore every inch of her skin before getting there. And when he was sure she was soaked for him, only then would he feast on her cunt.

Fuuuck. His dick was so damn hard. There was no way he was going to be able to keep his hands off her if he lay down in the same bed in his current state of arousal.

No fucking way. And he suspected she knew it.

Flashpoint

Goddamn her.

And yet, knowing she was a worthy adversary only made his cock harder, if that were possible.

No, he absolutely was not flying her back to San Francisco anytime soon. Her fighting dirty only proved that she did want something to happen between them.

She didn't know it—but her little trick had made Ramon more determined than ever to keep her by his side.

Starting a hot shower, he imagined all the dirty things he was going to do to her once she admitted she wanted him. They wouldn't be coming out of their bedroom suite for days—not until she couldn't walk straight.

With the water shooting at him from the many jets on the grey slate walls, he wrapped his hand around his shaft and stroked his cock as he pictured himself on the shower bench with Sophia on her knees between his thighs, looking up at him with her lips around his cock. She'd take his length deep in her throat with his fingers tugging her golden silk hair while she bobbed her head up and down. Her pretty eyes would water while she hungrily sucked him, moaning around his shaft.

It was imagining her moaning that did him in, and he spurted rope after rope of cum down the shower drain. There was a lot. He hadn't jacked off since the morning after the first night he met her, and he'd been perpetually horny ever since.

Getting out and toweling off, he opted for only his boxer briefs tonight, no pajama pants. Two could play at her game. Although, he conceded, being half naked next to her could backfire; whacking off had only been a temporary easing of his desire. Once he got in bed with her, he wasn't so confident what would happen if his bare skin touched hers.

He was willing to take the chance though.

****

Sophia

She'd heard him come in after she'd gone to bed and felt him looking at her, like she'd hoped when she positioned herself in bed like she had while making sure to leave the lamp on. But she didn't dare open her eyes to be sure. She had no idea what had compelled her to put on his shirt, other than she knew she'd look sexy in it as opposed to her frumpy nightgown, and maybe she'd get a reaction from him. Once she had the button-down on, his lingering scent on the fabric did things to her. She knew then that she was playing with fire, and maybe secretly hoping to get burned.

He came to bed but made no move to touch her, and Sophia suddenly felt stupid and immature for trying to get his attention like that. She was so out of her league with him. What had she been thinking?

She fought the tears, but knew she'd lost the battle when she felt them trickle over her nose and down the side of her face to uncomfortably collect in her ear.

Do not sniffle. Do not sniffle. For the love of God, Sophia, do NOT sniffle.

She feigned a cough to disguise her sniffling and eventually fell asleep with a heavy heart. She was yet again with a man who didn't want her. Only she was married to this one, which complicated things exponentially.

Chapter Twenty-One

Sophia
You aren't making any sense! she scolded herself in the shower before going down to breakfast.

You wanted him to leave you alone, remember? It's a good thing he doesn't want you!

You're going to use your time here to work, do some yoga, and maybe get a little sun and exercise. You'll relax and read by the pool, and not worry about Ramon Guzman, got it?

He barely acknowledged her when he sat down at breakfast. And although she tried telling herself it was for the best, being ignored by him was the worst. Her little pity party last night proved that.

His eyes were glued to his phone, not looking at her while she spread jelly on her toast.

She murmured, "I think I will take you up on going into town to do a little shopping."

His brusque answer of, "I'll have Jesús arrange a driver for when you want to go," before taking a sip from his expensive china teacup without even glancing up, wasn't the reaction she hoped for. There was a tiny part of her that even hoped he'd offer to take her himself.

Having him act like he didn't care about her hurt more than she'd like to admit. She tried again to engage him in conversation. "So, do you have any suggestions where I should go?"

He swiped on the screen. "No, but I'm sure Alejandro has some good ideas."

"Alejandro is going with me?"

For the first time, he looked up from his phone to make eye contact. "Yes. Is that a problem?"

Alejandro was close to Sophia's age and very good looking. Somehow, this seemed like the perfect opportunity to poke the bear.

She smiled like she was trying to hide excitement but made sure enthusiasm oozed from her lips when she replied, "Oh, no. Not at all. I'm sure we'll have a good time."

Ramon narrowed his eyes and glared at her for a moment, then softened his features with a fake smile. It sounded forced when he said politely, "Yes, I'm sure you will. He knows the city like the back of his hand," before directing his attention once again to his phone, like he couldn't care less what she did.

His set jaw indicated otherwise though.

It was funny, but she'd prefer him pissed off rather than indifferent. Indifferent meant he didn't care. The idea of him not caring bothered her more than it should.

"Great. I'll need some money." Maybe a reminder that, since he'd married her without a pre-nup, his money was now hers.

He seemed engrossed in whatever he was reading and murmured, "Stop by my office before you go and see Jesús. I think your credit cards arrived yesterday. If not, he'll give you mine, along with some money."

She felt like being a brat, if for no other reason than she wanted his attention.

"I hope I don't have to go to you whenever I need money. I'm happy to pay you back when my accounts are unfrozen, but right now, it feels like I'm going to you for my allowance."

She wanted him to assure her again that she wouldn't have to pay him back, what's his was hers now. At least, until they got the marriage annulled.

He did no such thing, but at least he looked at her when he replied, "Your new cards have high credit limits. It should get you through until you leave. I'll have Jesús transfer the billing address once you're settled back in California."

"Okay, yeah, that sounds good."

So, shopping would be more like *window* shopping. That was fine. She didn't want his stupid money anyway. At least she'd get out of the house and talk to people who would at least act like they liked her—if for no other reason than she was a potential customer.

They ate the rest of their breakfast in silence, until she stood and cleared her plate then reached for his.

"I have help to do that," he said brusquely. "Put the plates down."

I—not *we* have help.

Flashpoint

"I know you do," Sophia replied with a defiant tone as she clanged the silverware against the china while repositioning it in her hand. "But they're busy, and it's no trouble for me to carry our dishes inside."

She walked away with her head held high, feeling satisfied that she'd deliberately defied his command. Sophia knew Ramon was used to having his orders followed exactly, without question, and she liked the idea of not letting him boss her around, like he did everyone else.

I don't give a damn what he wants. I'll be out of here soon.

That thought seemed to instill more sorrow than comfort. Even with how coldly Ramon was now treating her.

Sophia took her time getting ready. She wanted Ramon to eat his heart out when she stopped by his office before going into town.

Dressed in a royal blue and white polka dot skater dress and strappy white heels with her hair perfectly styled and more makeup than she wore around the estate, she stood in the entry of his office suite and knocked on the open door. Jesús looked up from his desk outside Ramon's office, then immediately moved to close the door leading to the room where Ramon's large mahogany desk sat. But not before her husband looked up from his computer to see her standing in the outer office.

His parted lips and intense gaze when he noticed her made the effort to get ready worth it—even if she only saw him for a second.

"Alejandro is ready whenever you are." Jesús reached in his top drawer and pulled something out of an envelope. "Your cards, *Señora* Guzman," he said as he handed her a Mastercard and Visa with the name *Sophia Castle Guzman*. Opening another desk drawer, he pulled out a wad of American money as well as pesos. "Ramon asked me to order a debit card for you that should be here tomorrow, but here's some cash to tide you over until then."

She started to protest she didn't need the money, but he must have interpreted her objection as a complaint because he cut her off. "Don't worry. If that's not enough, you should be able to buy whatever you want with those." He gestured to the plastic now in her hands. "I think you could even buy a new yacht with the credit line you have."

She smiled at the man who obviously had no idea she had no intention of using her new cards for anything more than what her salary could afford—which was basically lunch and maybe a new blouse and a pair of shorts.

"Thank you. I don't really need a driver though; I can call a cab, it's no problem."

"Absolutely not. Ramon has made it clear that you're not to go out without a body—" He stopped and corrected himself. "A driver and translator."

Flashpoint

"I'm sure I would get along fine in the shops with my basic Spanish skills."

Jesús picked up the phone and punched some numbers before directing his attention back to her with a patient smile.

"I don't want to lose my job, so, humor me..." Then he spoke Spanish into the phone when the person on the other end answered.

He disconnected the call and said, "Alejandro will be waiting with a car out front. Enjoy your shopping."

She tried getting in the front seat of the blacked-out Escalade, but Alejandro wagged his finger at her and opened the back door.

"The boss would have my hide if he saw you in the front seat, *Señora*."

She didn't want to make waves for him, so she acquiesced and got in back.

"Where would you like to go today?" he asked as he looked at her through his rearview mirror.

"I don't really know, to be honest. I know I'd like to stop by and see my friends at their antiques boutique, but other than that, I don't know Ensenada very well. Where would you recommend I do a little clothes shopping?"

He nodded thoughtfully while contemplating her question, then finally replied. "I think I know a few places you'd like."

They chatted during the drive, but the younger man did his best to maintain a professional demeanor and seemed extra cautious to keep their conversation superficial. Sophia recalled Ramon's comment about firing someone—and any family who worked for him—if they talked about his business. Alejandro answered her questions about Ensenada, but any other information she tried to draw out of him was quickly shut down as politely as possible. And he ended or started almost every sentence with *Señora* or Mrs. Guzman—no doubt, Ramon's doing. The young man had been much friendlier the night he stood guard over her at the winery, when he thought she was just a one-night stand of Ramon's.

He eased the Cadillac into a metered parking space along the street, shut the car off, and got out. She was already standing on the sidewalk when he came around to her door at the curb, so he fed the silver machine quarters and gestured for her to walk toward a two-story boutique in the swanky part of town. It was the same area where the boys had their antiques storefront, and where Ramon had purchased her ring just days earlier.

Thinking about their visit to the jewelry store made her run her thumb over the smooth part of her wedding band as she remembered with a smile how pampered she'd felt that day—even if she had been in shock picking out a wedding band set.

Her treatment at the jewelry store was a far cry from how the overdressed clerks at the boutique treated her. The moment she walked in, they looked at her like something they'd find on the bottom of their shoe. Alejandro stood outside to make a phone call before entering a few moments later.

He stood at the front as she walked around the store, running her hand along garments that caught her eye before checking the hefty price tag and moving along. Sophia felt them watching her and making comments in Spanish. She wasn't exactly sure what they were saying, but she didn't need to be fluent to infer the snide tone being directed toward her.

Sophia looked around for Alejandro, hoping he'd translate what they were saying so she could then in turn tell them off before leaving, but he seemed to have disappeared. Maybe he'd gone to the bathroom.

Even if the clerks hadn't been bitches, she wouldn't have bought anything. The clothes were beautiful, but out of her price range, so she just bided her time looking at the racks until her companion reappeared.

Instead of Alejandro appearing, an older woman with her dark hair in a tight bun and dressed in a sky blue Chanel suit and pearls, marched straight toward her. The way her matching shoes click-clacked authoritatively off the shiny epoxy floor had the younger clerks scurrying to look busy as she approached. Reading her name tag prominently displayed on the right side of her chest, *Rolanda Romero, General Manager*, explained a lot.

"*Señora* Guzman," she said warmly as she grasped Sophia's palm between her two hands. "It is an honor to have you in our shop. I apologize if my staff didn't immediately make you feel welcome." She shot daggers at the younger women who were pretending not to eavesdrop as they folded clothes. "That will be addressed, I assure you."

Sophia furrowed her brows in confusion. "How did you know who I—?"

At that moment, Alejandro appeared, and things made sense. He'd tattled to the manager—on her behalf. She wanted to hug him.

With a polite smile, Sophia addressed the woman again. "Thank you. You have beautiful clothes."

She was about to apologize and say they were out of her price range, when it hit her that doing so would be an embarrassment to Ramon. She was the wife—at least on paper, of the most powerful man in Ensenada, and she needed to play the part. She wasn't about to damage Ramon's reputation in public, especially after what she'd done the night his associates slept at the estate.

Ramon may be a player and treating her coldly, and she may have enjoyed letting him know he wasn't the boss of her this morning, but she wouldn't disrespect him in public. She'd learned her lesson about that.

Not to mention how quickly she was able to leave the country possibly hinged on her playing the part of his doting wife.

"Thank you, we try our best." Rolanda seemed to be assessing Sophia's frame. "May I pick out some clothes I think would work for you?"

Shit. How was she going to get out of this? Sophia decided to just swallow her pride and rack up a bill on her charge card. Maybe she could sell the clothes on one of those resale websites once she got back to California to help recoup some of the costs.

Once she decided to not worry, she realized she was having fun being doted on. And the clothes... *oh, the clothes.* They were so beautiful and fit her body just right. Perhaps she'd keep an item or two.

She couldn't help it—there was a strut to her walk when she exited the boutique wearing a designer ensemble Rolanda had put together for her—one of the many new outfits she'd just purchased.

"It's in pesos," she reasoned to herself when she was given the total. There was no way she was going to think about the U.S. dollar conversion right now.

With her hands overflowing with bags and Alejandro carrying even more when they walked out, all she needed were oversized sunglasses to complete the diva look. Her knock-off Aviators would have to suffice, she thought with a giggle as she put them.

"Where to, *Señora*?" Alejandro asked once she was situated in the back of the Escalade.

Feeling this good, she knew who she needed to see.

"*Antigüedades Prestigiosas.* I think it's just the next block over. We could probably even walk."

"No, it's too far. Ramon wouldn't want that."

"He'd have a problem with me walking a block on a nice, sunny day?"

"If there were more men with us, probably not. But, since it's just me... and now that people know who you are, he wouldn't like it. *Señora* Guzman, he'd kill me—literally, if anything happened to you. If for nothing more than the sake of my family, let's just play it safe, okay?"

Surely, Alejandro was being dramatic. Ramon would never hurt him. Besides...

"Why would anyone want to hurt me?"

His face was serious when he looked at her through the rearview mirror. "There are many people who would like to do *Señor* Guzman harm. Doing something to you would cause him the most pain, so you are vulnerable."

Ramon had done a great job selling their marriage to everyone if even his inner circle believed someone hurting her could cause him the most harm.

"*Many* people?"

Just how many are we talking here? She realized, probably a lot if he had bodyguards everywhere he went and was always armed.

"He's a very powerful man. That makes him a target."

She tried to press Alejandro for more details, but he cut her off. "I've already said too much. Just know that you need to be careful and stick with me, okay?"

She nodded soberly, lost in thought on the short drive to Francisco and Juan Diego's store. Maybe they could tell her more about what they knew about her husband.

With a huge smile, she walked inside the chic, modern storefront. Once again, Alejandro made a call before coming inside.

"You know, for a place that's supposed to sell antiques, this place is pretty art deco," she quipped loudly when she noticed Juan Diego behind the counter looking at a piece of jewelry through a magnifying glass.

It seemed like he didn't recognize her when he looked up at her with a scowl. Then his indignant expression turned into a wide grin, and he quickly set the items down and came around the counter.

"*Ay, dios mio*, would you get a look at what just breezed through my door!" Calling over his shoulder, he yelled, "Francisco, come see who it is!"

He grabbed both her hands and looked her up and down. "You've been shopping—and without me, I might add. Look at you!" He noticed Alejandro standing quietly near the door. "And look at him... He's yummy with a capital Y. No wonder you went MIA on us."

"Well... that's a long story, actually. One I'd like to tell you over lunch. This is Alejandro. He works for Ramon."

Juan Diego raised one eyebrow. "And he's here with you because..."

"He's my driver. Ramon wouldn't let me go out without one."

Juan Diego squealed and squeezed her hands, noticing her wedding ring in the process.

Staring at her with wide eyes and his mouth dramatically opened wide, he then yelled at the top of his lungs as he continued staring at Sophia, "Francisco! Get out here! Now!"

Francisco appeared from the back, wiping his hands on a towel. "Good Lord, what is the problem, Juan?" He noticed Sophia and smiled broadly. "Hey, Soph. So good to see you. We were worried we'd never hear from you again after you left the hotel without saying goodbye."

With his arms folded, foot tapping, Juan Diego interrupted, "It seems our little Sophia has been a busy girl this week." He then grabbed her left hand and held it up to show Francisco. "Apparently, she's Mrs. Ramon Guzman."

Francisco's eyes grew wide. "Girrrrl, you need to tell us everything."

That would be tricky. The men had been nothing but kind to her, but she also knew they were terrible gossips. Her secret would *not* be safe with them. There was no way they'd be able to help themselves from spilling the tea over something as juicy as Ramon Guzman taking a fake wife.

Just like Ramon had said his housekeepers would.

Sophia was beginning to think being filthy rich might not be all it was cracked up to be. There was something to be said

Flashpoint

for being a middle-class nobody who no one cared about. Even if that sometimes included rude salespeople.

Although, she had to admit, she'd kind of loved the smug feeling she'd felt when the bitch salesclerks had to fawn all over her. Walking out of that shop in an outfit that probably cost more than they made in a week felt like payback for every mean girl encounter she'd ever had growing up.

If Kevin could see her now. *Ha! Mousy my ass, prick.*

Which led her back to her dilemma. What would she tell Juan Diego and Francisco?

Having Alejandro within earshot helped make up her mind. She'd stick with the story.

"We just..." She thought of Ramon's face and smiled. "Fell in love."

Juan Diego narrowed his eyes, his lips pursed.

"So, just like that... Ramon Guzman—the man who is notorious for never being seen with the same woman twice, meets you and suddenly decides the next day that marriage really is for him. That he's been wrong all these years?" He crossed his arms and shook his head. "No. I don't buy it."

"You shush," Francisco scolded. "When the right person comes along, it just hits you. You should know that."

Juan Diego scowled at her. "No, there's something else going on, and I'm going to get to the bottom of it."

"Okay, look," she said in a hushed tone. "I was detained at the airport, and we had to get married, or the chief of police would have thrown me in jail."

Juan Diego stared at her as he contemplated her story. Finally, he shook his head skeptically. "No, I don't believe that either. Your first story was better."

Sophia threw her arms to her sides. "I give up! Let's go to lunch!"

Francisco hugged her shoulders. "I wish we could, sweets. But we have a big client coming in. Maybe we could get together for cocktails later this week."

"That sounds fun. Text me when you're available."

Juan Diego scoffed. "So, you can ignore us some more?"

"What are you talking about?"

"I've been blowing up your phone ever since we found out you left without saying goodbye!"

She pulled her phone from her purse and opened her message app. "There's nothing from you." She waved the device at her friend then examined it closer. "All my saved messages are gone, too. I don't think my phone likes me being in Mexico."

That meant that she'd probably missed calls or texts from work and her family. That could also explain why she hadn't heard from Kevin lately either.

"I better call my mom," she murmured.

"You haven't told your mom?" Juan Diego practically shouted at her.

"Of course I have. What I meant was, I should call her in case she called today. She's busy planning a party for when Ramon and I are back in San Diego."

Hey, if you're going to lie—go big. At least she'd learned something from her ex.

"So, what did your parents think of you marrying a man you barely know?"

"They're happy if I'm happy."

Juan Diego continued eyeing her suspiciously, then suddenly his face softened. "You seem happy. I think being married to Ramon will be good for you. Lord knows you're just what the doctor ordered for him."

Sophia huffed out an indignant laugh. "What does that mean?"

"Nothing bad. Simmer down, *Señora.*" He emphasized the Spanish *Mrs.* "I just think you two are going to balance each other out. Maybe he'll provide you with the many adventures you deserve, and you're exactly the woman Ramon needs to settle down and have a family with."

"*Family*? Now who's the one who needs to simmer down?"

Having a family would require sex—and staying together. Neither of which were happening. But she couldn't exactly tell Juan Diego and Francisco that. To ward off any suspicion, she added, "I mean, we've only been married a few days. Let me have a little time to enjoy being a newlywed before you go having me get knocked up."

"But your babies..." Francisco sighed. "They're going to be beautiful."

She couldn't help but smile. They *would* have beautiful babies.

And suddenly, an image of a houseful of little Ramons and Sophias running around filled her head. She could imagine Ramon being wrapped around his little girls' fingers. Or their sons interrupting his workday to try to talk him into playing with them—kind of like she had the other day. And he'd oblige them—just like he had her—before she ruined it. And…

Woah. Woah. Woah.

Where the hell did all that come from? Juan Diego was right—she needed to simmer down.

Francisco handed her a business card. "Get a hold of us when you want to have drinks. Or feel free to stop by anytime."

Juan Diego jutted his bottom lip out. "Any other time, we'd love to have lunch. Just today is no *bueno*."

"I knew it was a longshot, just popping in like this, but I was literally a block away, so I had to try."

"Well, we're glad you did." Francisco hugged her, then Juan Diego stood before her, holding her hands as he looked at her sweetly.

"I'm happy for you, Soph. When I met you at the pool last week, I never in a million years could have predicted this, but I really do think you and Ramon are going to make each other very happy."

"Me too," she said with a smile.

And somehow, it didn't feel like a lie as she hugged him before leaving.

Walking back toward the Escalade, she said to Alejandro, "Let's go have lunch. There's a restaurant a few doors down from where we parked."

He stopped short on the sidewalk and turned to her—concern written all over his face. "Um...." It was obvious he had no idea how to handle the idea of the two of them having lunch together.

She rolled her eyes and shifted her weight. "Good grief, I think we both know it's not a date, Alejandro."

Still, he hemmed and hawed, which annoyed her.

Pushing past him, she huffed out, "Oh my god, we can sit at separate tables if you're that worried about it."

He jogged to catch up to her. "I'm sure it will be fine."

When they reached the restaurant's storefront, he once again paused before coming inside. "I just need to make a call."

Sophia gave him a fake smile as she opened the glass door. "You do that."

She had a feeling he'd been keeping Ramon apprised of everywhere she'd gone today anyway. The idea annoyed her, and she whirled back around when she heard him start talking. Marching toward him, she held out her hand. "Let me talk to him."

Reluctantly, he handed her the phone.

"Your spy and I are going to have lunch. Together—in a restaurant. Just the two of us. If you have a problem with that, you can take it up with me, because trust me, he does *not* want to even sit at the same table as me."

The deep chuckle on the other end disarmed her.

"He's not a spy—he's your driver. While I appreciate you letting me know, I don't have a problem in the least with him accompanying you to lunch. I'm sorry he doesn't want to sit with you, but have you considered maybe his hesitation about being seen with you in a restaurant has nothing to do with me and more to do with someone else in his life?"

Well, no, she hadn't. She just assumed it was because he thought Ramon would be upset.

"I, um…"

"Nothing about our marriage has been made public, Sophia, so right now, it's just word of mouth. And other than a few people you've been introduced to, no one knows what you look like. For all the gossips know, Alejandro is having lunch with another woman, and that has the potential to make life with his girlfriend quite miserable."

She hadn't even thought of that.

"So, should I eat alone?"

Again with his chuckle. "No, just request a table for three, I'll take care of the rest."

"Are you coming for lunch?" She knew her question had sounded hopeful, but she couldn't hide that she liked the idea of him joining her for lunch, much to the dismay of her better judgment.

While her tone had turned from being a brat to hopeful, his turned from amused to cold. "I'm in the middle of something with work."

"Oh," she said, unable to hide the disappointment in her voice. She didn't like being at odds with him. "Maybe I'll see you for dinner, then."

"I have a business dinner tonight."

She didn't know why that bothered her, but it did.

"You didn't mention that at breakfast," she said curtly.

"I didn't think I needed to."

Right. Why would he need to? They weren't *really* married—she'd been telling him that repeatedly.

Still...

"I don't know, common courtesy?" She didn't give him a chance to respond before she huffed, "Have a nice time." With that, she handed the phone back to Alejandro, muttering, "I'll see you inside."

The hostess seated her right away, and Alejandro soon followed. They ordered drinks, and the hostess appeared again to let them know Sophia's husband, *Señor* Guzman, had tried calling her cell, but she must have it in her purse because she hadn't answered, Unfortunately, he wouldn't be able to make it to lunch but would see her back at home.

"Very smooth," she said with a laugh once the hostess walked away.

"*Señor* Guzman thinks of everything."

Alejandro had said it as praise, but to Sophia, it almost felt like a warning. She wanted to press her companion for information, but needed to ease into it.

"I'm sorry that I didn't consider your reputation when I suggested we go to lunch."

He shrugged. "As you shouldn't. I'm an employee."

"No," she said with a knowing smile. "I mean, yes, you work for Ramon, but it's obvious that he thinks of you as much more than that. And vice versa. Everyone at the estate acts more like family than employees. You're very loyal to him."

"He takes good care of us."

She could understand how being treated well at work could instill loyalty to an employer, or maybe it was the fear of being fired.

"And you take good care of him."

"Their enchiladas are really good here," he said casually, changing the subject. She smiled at how easily he'd done it—something Sophia had no doubt he'd learned from his boss.

She set the menu down and studied him as she asked her next question.

"So, last week… when you had to come to the winery. Does that happen very often?"

He looked at her with a grin and took a bite of a chip, signaling he wasn't saying anything.

"The woman in the bar… the one Ramon was with…"

Flashpoint

"He wasn't *with* her," Alejandro interrupted. "He *met* with her; that's it. And he didn't even know it was going to be with *her* until she showed up."

Sophia smiled at her ability to get him to tell her more, and he muttered, "Goddammit," under his breath, then sat back in his seat with a thud and a scowl, his arms folded in front of him. The usually easy-going young man was mad at her. "I'm not talking about anything else, so don't bother asking."

She felt bad over how upset he was. "I won't," she said, picking up her glass of water and taking a sip before continuing, "And I promise, I won't say anything to Ramon."

He unfolded his arms, and his scowl lessened as he also reached for his water glass, too. "Well, I'm going to."

Of course he was.

Chapter Twenty-Two

Ramon

"Boss, we've got kind of a problem here," Alejandro's voice was calm on the other end of the phone, but hearing the words, knowing he was out with Sophia, made Ramon's heart race.

"What kind of a problem?"

"Well, it's kind of hard to explain. Your wife is going toe-to-toe with um... a dogcatcher."

Did Ramon hear him right?

"A dogcatcher?"

"Yeah. It'd probably be cleared up easily if you just came down here. The guy doesn't believe she's your wife, even though she's told him numerous times, and I even vouched for her."

"Why would a dogcatcher give a damn if she were my wife?"

"Because he's trying to round up a stray, and she won't let him. She wants to bring it home with her, and he won't let her. So, they're at a bit of an impasse. She tried using your name—said she was bringing the dog to your house, which impressed the guy... then he insisted that Ramon Guzman was single, and she was lying about being your wife."

So, Sophia wanted to be married to him when it suited her. Interesting.

"I'm on my way."

Flashpoint

Ramon hopped in the McLaren. If he was going to show up and save the day, he was going to do it in style. He pulled up the app to find the location of her phone—yes, he'd put a tracker on her phone, but only for her safety. His enemies wouldn't hesitate to kidnap her if the opportunity presented itself. He'd inject her with a tracker if he thought he could.

He expected a scene straight out of the American TV show *Cops* when he arrived—with lots of yelling and people acting belligerent. He should have known better. There's no way Alejandro would have let it get that out of hand, not to mention, that didn't seem like Sophia's style.

Instead, Sophia sat on the curb, petting a filthy dog that reminded him of Benji, while the uniformed animal control officer stood calmly at his truck, talking to Alejandro.

Ramon opened the car's dihedral door and slid out, fastening his suit button out of habit as he stood and walked toward his wife, only to unbutton it again when he crouched next to Sophia, still sitting on the curb.

"What's going on, *mi amor*?"

"I found this girl when we were on the way back to the car after lunch," she said as she affectionately scratched the dog's ears. The dog stared at her like she was a goddess. *Smart dog.* "She's really sweet and gentle, and she let me pet her, so I decided to take her home." She then glared toward where Alejandro and the animal control officer were standing. "But Alejandro wouldn't just go get the Escalade and leave me with her, so I had to go with him back to the

Cadillac. She was too skittish to follow me—I'm sure people have been cruel to her in the past when she tried that. When we got back to where she was, *he*," she waved her hand in disgust at the uniformed man, "was trying to wrangle her with his stupid pole-thing, even though I tried telling him I was taking her home with me. Alejandro even translated for me. We argued, then, when I told him I was your wife, he called me a liar, so Alejandro called you... and, well, here we are."

"Here we are," he agreed with a smile. He looked over at the dog who'd obviously been on the street a while. Under the matted fur, she was quite skinny. "You sure you want to bring that thing home? Consuela and Antonia are going to have a fit if she brings fleas into the house."

"I've already thought about that. I promise I'll give her a bath—outside—the second we get home."

"Why don't we just stop at a groomer's before even bringing her home?" he asked with a wink.

He felt the pang in his heart when she smiled softly at him. "Alejandro's right. You really do think of everything." His sassy little *nerdicita* had paid him a compliment.

"I try."

He stood and adjusted his custom suit jacket again, wondering how much this was going to cost him, although he was sure Alejandro had already tried to pay the man off.

"Let me see if I can get this resolved."

He approached the truck, holding out his hand. "Ramon Guzman," he said authoritatively.

If the man hadn't recognized him, Ramon was sure pulling up in the McLaren helped.

"*Señor* Guzman," the dog catcher said with a bright smile as he gripped Ramon's hand tightly. "It's such a pleasure to meet you, sir."

That was a good start.

"My wife says there seems to be some confusion about being able to bring the dog home? I'm sure it's just the language barrier—she's still learning Spanish, and this must just all be a misunderstanding. Yes?"

The flustered man didn't know how to respond.

Ramon smiled as he reached inside his jacket for his wallet, pulling out ten, one-hundred U.S. dollar bills. "This should cover the fees?"

The man held up his hand. "I couldn't possibly take your money, *señor*."

It was smart on the dogcatcher's part to want to appear as if he was just being helpful to a man known for being ruthless with his enemies, but Ramon found money just made things easier. The man would go home with probably an extra month's wages and a story about how friendly Ramon Guzman could be, Sophia would take the dirty dog home, and maybe, Ramon would get a real wife in the process.

Ramon looked at the name tag on the man's uniform and put the money in his hand. "Esteban, I insist. I'm sure there are licensing fees that go along with us just taking the dog home, and I appreciate you letting us bypass filling out all that paperwork. Alejandro will give you all the information you need for it."

Ramon looked at Alejandro, and his youngest lieutenant produced one of Ramon's business cards, making a point to turn it over before handing it to Esteban, while saying, "*Señora* Guzman's name is on the back." He flipped it back over and pointed to the information on the front. "You can mail the paperwork here," then released the card to the man.

"I'll take care of it," Esteban said dutifully. Ramon had no doubt the dog license would arrive by the end of the week.

"I appreciate that," Ramon said, again offering his hand, then turned back to Alejandro. "We need to take this dog to a groomer before bringing her home."

"My sister has a grooming salon," Esteban offered, and pulled out his phone. "I can call her and have her fit you in."

"That would be great, thank you."

Ramon walked back to Sophia, who stood when he approached.

"Is everything okay?"

"You are now the proud owner of…"

"Daisy," she supplied.

"Daisy?" He looked at the dog and nodded. "Daisy suits her. Alejandro is going to take her to the groomer…"

"I want to go, too," Sophia interrupted. "He can take me to the pet store, so I can buy supplies while we wait for her to get groomed."

He couldn't help but smile at her excitement.

"You might want to stop by a bakery and buy some pastries for the gardeners. They're not going to be happy about cleaning up after her."

"I'll clean up after her; it's not a problem."

He shook his head. "My wife will do no such thing."

She started to say, "I'm not..." but stopped short when he raised an eyebrow.

"You can't have it both ways, Sophia. Either you're my wife or you're not."

She looked at the ground and pushed a rock with her toe as she nodded her head in understanding. Using his index finger, he lifted her chin so she'd look at him.

"We'll continue this conversation at dinner."

"I thought you were going out?"

The corner of his mouth lifted as he glanced down at his beautiful wife. The one who'd sassed him this morning and turned around and rescued a dirty mutt from the streets. Daisy moved protectively closer to Sophia when Ramon lifted her chin. The little guard dog had just won the doggie lottery; she just didn't know it yet.

"My plans changed."

"I'm sorry. I didn't mean to ruin your evening."

"Don't be sorry." He leaned down and kissed her cheek softly, then whispered in her ear, "I look forward to dinner," before turning toward his car without another word.

A small grin escaped his lips when he heard her utter, "Me, too."

****

Sophia

The shopping spree for herself earlier in the day was nothing compared to what she did for Daisy at the pet store. The back of the Escalade overflowed with bags when they finally pulled up to the front door of the estate.

"Didn't you say you really didn't like to shop?" Alejandro grumbled as he tried to organize the bag handles while he took them out of the back and handed them to her. Holding the end of Daisy's leash in one hand meant she only had one free hand.

"I think I'm going to have to make a few trips..." she conceded with a giggle.

Sophia felt him before his hands stroked both her arms up and down, so she didn't jump at this touch.

"I can help," Ramon offered before kissing her cheek.

"That would be great," she sighed.

He knelt down and rubbed Daisy's neck, talking sweetly to the pup as he did.

"Look at you. You look like a brand-new dog! Are you going to be a spoiled girl here?" He looked up at the bags with the different store labels in Sophia and Alejandro's hands. "I think you *and* your mommy are going to be spoiled here."

"I'll pay you back," she said defensively.

"Sophia…" There was a warning in his tone. "We'll talk about this at dinner." He stood and looked at his watch. "Which is going to be in about forty minutes, so you should probably get Daisy settled."

"I need to take her to go to the bathroom before going inside."

He took the bags from her hand and gestured to the grounds. "You'll have to talk to Jorge tomorrow about where you want to put a dog run."

A dog run. It was funny how something so insignificant carried so much meaning.

She'd been thinking on the car ride back about where they could put in a doggie door and dog run and what that meant. It'd be put in here. At the Ensenada estate. Then she wondered what it was going to be like going back and forth between Mexico and San Diego and how Daisy would do in a helicopter.

Sophia knew that she wanted to be Mrs. Ramon Guzman—in every sense.

Alejandro's confirmation of Ramon's story that what she saw in the bar wasn't what she thought had helped her open that door. Then when Ramon helped her today with Daisy, no questions asked and not batting an eye about Sophia bringing a dog to the estate without even consulting with him first… well, that sealed the deal.

If he still wanted her.

It seemed like he did. He'd called her 'my love' in Spanish when he arrived to help her with animal control. And when he told her she needed to decide if she wanted to be his wife or not, he sort of implied he wanted her to be.

Sophia watched the gorgeous man laughing with Alejandro as they wrangled bags upon bags, along with numerous dog beds from the rear of the Cadillac. His smile was so sexy, his presence so commanding. She was in awe when she said in her head, "That's *my* husband."

She'd be a fool to not at least try to make this marriage real.

Flashpoint
Chapter Twenty-Three

Ramon

She'd looked beautiful when she'd left to go shopping that morning. When she stopped in the office suite earlier that morning, he'd wanted to bring her in his office, close the door, and fuck the sass out of her. But she was absolutely stunning when she walked into the dining room where he was already seated.

She'd changed into a champagne-colored dress that reminded him of what his mother would wear *under* her dress when he was growing up. The luxurious silk material next to Sophia's skin made his fingers itch to touch her—especially when he noticed her nipples standing at attention under his scrutiny. *Ay, dios mio*, she wasn't wearing a bra.

"Did you buy that today?"

She nodded with a smile as she glanced down at the silk material hugging her curves. "Do you like it?"

"I love it. You look beautiful."

"Thank you," she said as she sat to the right of where he was seated at the head of the table. "I'm glad you like it. I bought it in a few other colors too."

"With matching shoes, I hope?"

"Of course," she said with a smirk. "You think Mrs. Ramon Guzman would be seen without matching shoes?"

She was teasing, but in doing so, she'd also said a lot.

"*Mrs. Ramon Guzman.* I like the sound of that."

Sophia looked up at him through her lashes and replied softly, "I do, too."

He was out of his seat in an instant and kneeling next to her chair, holding her left hand—the one with his ring on her finger—between both of his as he searched her eyes. He wasn't sure what he was looking for... permission? Affirmation?

"Sophia." Her name on his lips was almost a plea.

She stroked the scruff on his jawline tenderly with the fingertips on her right hand—the tender look in her eyes seemed like adoration. Then she leaned over and ever so softly kissed his lips; her eyes fluttered closed as she did.

Her kiss was gentle, but it lit a firestorm in Ramon's chest that burned straight to his cock. He released her hand and snaked his fingers into her silky hair as he deepened the kiss. Her mouth tasted like toothpaste, but it was her lips—so fucking soft that he couldn't get enough of.

Her whimper was his undoing, and he broke the kiss and stood, then bent down and scooped her right off the dining room chair, similar to how he had the other night when he took her from the guest room bed. Only this time, he wasn't seeing red. The silky material of her dress was slippery, but he liked how it felt as he held her in his arms in a bridal carry.

She giggled and looped her hands around his neck while whispering, "Don't drop me."

"Not a chance," he growled as he exited the dining room, just as Consuela was wheeling the dinner cart in.

"We'll call down later for dinner," he told his housekeeper. She nodded while beaming her approval at the scene unfolding in front of her.

"Whenever you're ready, we'll bring it up."

It would be awhile before they'd be ready.

****

Sophia

Ramon carried her up the stairs like she weighed nothing, then marched straight to the bedroom, where he closed the door with his heel, and didn't put her down until he deposited her gently on the king-size bed.

"You are so beautiful, Sophia Guzman," he whispered reverently.

Guzman. He was back to calling her by her married last name. That made her heart happy.

Ramon hovered over her in his suit pants and button-down shirt, sleeves rolled up to the elbows. He'd managed to lose his shoes before getting on the bed. Meanwhile, she'd lost one of her new high heels on the staircase like Cinderella, and the other in the hallway outside the bedroom.

At least that's where she thought they'd fallen off, although she couldn't be positive. She'd been too focused on the feel of Ramon's muscular frame and masculine scent as he carried her like a bride.

She guessed it was fitting, since he had been carrying her to their bedroom to make her his wife in the biblical sense.

"You are so sexy, Ramon Guzman," she countered, her fingers toying at the short hair above his collar.

One corner of his mouth lifted. "You think I'm sexy?"

"Have you seen you? You're like a Greek god. People could write stories about how perfect you are."

He kissed below her ear, murmuring, "I don't care what anyone but you thinks," as he dragged his lips down her neck. He ran his hand from where it had been resting on her hip, over the silk fabric until he cupped her braless breast.

"Just so you know," he growled against her neck as he squeezed her mound of flesh in his palm. "You'll wear a bra anytime you wear something like this in front of anyone but me and the *abuelas*."

Sophia couldn't help but smile. She liked this possessive side of him.

"Are you jealous?" she teased.

He lifted his head to look her in the eye. "Jealous would imply I wanted something that wasn't mine. On the contrary, I'm simply protecting what's mine, *Señora* Guzman."

His proclamation made her belly do flip flops.

Still, she couldn't resist taunting, "Are you mine then, *Señor* Guzman?"

"Abso-fucking-lutely. For as long as you'll have me."

She caressed his cheek in response, and he lowered his mouth to hers. His tongue sought hers out and demanded she respond, which she happily did. Deepening the kiss, he pressed his hips against hers, his hard cock hitting the spot where she wanted him—naked. She could feel how wet she was for him.

Sophia fumbled with the buttons on his shirt, and Ramon rolled off her with a wink and stood. He kept his eyes on her as he finished unbuttoning his shirt and pulled it open to reveal his muscular chest and abs, then unbuckled his belt and slid his trousers and socks off. She sighed out loud—literally—at the sight of his body. Grinning in response, he knelt next to her on the bed and inched her dress higher up her thighs, taking his time to caress her skin as it became exposed. He dipped his head to lay deferential kisses on her flesh as he pushed her dress higher, and suddenly he was sprawled between her legs, mouthing the fabric of her panties. The heat of his breath against her pussy was erotic, and she adjusted her hips in invitation, which he didn't take her up on. Instead, he ran his tongue under the stitching of her underwear while his finger ran pressed against her slit over the material.

The tease was both tortuous and wonderful. Just when she thought she would burst with need, he tugged on the waistband to lower her panties. She lifted her bottom off the mattress to help him remove them. After dropping her underwear off the side of the bed, his face was back between her thighs, nipping at the skin as he moved his mouth closer to her pussy that was drenched with desire.

She wantonly tugged on his hair to guide him where she needed his mouth to be. Even as she did it, she recognized how unlike her that was. Then again, she'd never had a lover quite like Ramon Guzman. Besides, she justified, if she couldn't be unabashed with her husband, who could she be with?

His tongue found her magic button, and she arched her back off the bed while crying out in ecstasy. He expertly lapped her clit while he slipped a finger inside her slick pussy and began to move in and out in rhythm with his tongue.

"Oh my god, Ramon. Yes," she panted.

"Come for me, *mi mujer*." His deep voice vibrated against her skin, and she found it impossible not to do as he commanded when she translated in her head what he said.

My woman. He'd called her that before, but it meant so much more now that they were naked together.

Her whole body shuddered as the orgasm overtook her, and a long moan of Ramon's name escaped her lips. He continued his attention to her pussy until Sophia melted into the bed in post-orgasmic bliss. She felt one last swipe of his tongue along her slit before he kissed his way up her stomach. She could feel her belly rising and falling underneath his lips as she attempted to regain her breath.

"If I live to be a hundred, I will never get tired of watching you come," he murmured against her skin.

"Do you think you'll be able to make me come when you're a hundred years old?" she teased

"I'm damn well going to try." He gently bit her nipple as if to emphasize his point.

The idea of growing old with him filled her with a sense of peace.

She reached between them and gently stroked his hard cock. "Maybe we could just start with coming twice in one night."

"Oh, *mi amor*," he whispered as he pulled the dress over her head. "You'll have lost count by the time the sun comes up tomorrow."

Sophia had no doubt he'd make good on that.

****

Ramon

Her beautiful body lay naked before him, and his leaking cock begged him to fill her. First things first.

"Are you on birth control?" he asked before he removed his boxer briefs.

"I am. Which reminds me… I'm going to have to find a pharmacy to fill my prescription if we're going to be in Ensenada much longer."

"We'll do it tomorrow." He hesitated stripping. "I'm clean. I've never not used a condom, and I was tested at my annual checkup last month."

He'd never gone bareback—not once, even if his companion said she was clean and on the pill. No way was he taking a woman's word for it. Now, he had a wife that he actually trusted.

"But, I can still use a condom if you'd be more comfortable."

She shook her head. "No. I don't want that. I'm clean too. I was tested before I came to Mexico, after I found out my boyfriend had been cheating on me." Sophia cupped his face. "I don't want anything between us."

Fuuuuck. He couldn't get his *chones* off fast enough.

It occurred to him that when she said she didn't want anything between them, she meant more than just physically. She was probably including emotionally and spiritually, too. Unfortunately, the best he could give her right now was no condom barrier, and it would have to do until the time was right to bare his secrets; he needed to be sure she loved him and wouldn't leave if she learned the truth. But not right now—it was too soon.

However, he wasn't kidding when he said she was going to have lost count of her orgasms by morning. He wanted her sore, so there'd be no doubt as to who exactly she belonged to.

However, when he entered her warm heat for the first time without a condom… he knew he wasn't going to last long—at least this time. That was okay, he reasoned. He had all night to make good on his promise.

Chapter Twenty-Four

Ramon

They lay entwined in each other's arms; the total number of their orgasms too many to count, just like he'd promised.

"You definitely know what you're doing, Mr. Guzman," she purred as she stroked his spine with a featherlight touch.

"As do you, Mrs. Guzman."

"Do you think it will always be this good? Or is this just the honeymoon phase?"

"It will always be good. Not necessarily always like this, but sometimes it will be even better. And speaking of honeymoons… where do you want to go for ours?"

She let out a heavy sigh. "I need to see my family and let them know that I got married before we do anything else. For the record, they are not going to be happy."

"That you got married in general, or that you married me?"

"Both. They're going to be hurt that they weren't there. And not that I married you, personally. Just someone they'd never even met… Or heck, that *I* barely met."

"Well, I told you before, we can have a wedding. We *should* have a wedding and exchange vows in front of God and everyone."

"So, I know what I'm actually agreeing to next time?" she said with a laugh.

Something like that.

"Let's have it in San Diego; it's probably easier for my guests to travel to the U.S. than yours to Mexico. And that way you can invite whomever you'd like, although I would prefer it to be small, so security isn't overwhelmed."

She kissed his chest as she contemplated his words.

"I just wish I knew when I was going to be cleared for travel, so we could pick a date."

"Pick a date, and I'll make sure you're able to leave by then."

She scoffed, "Oh, you'll just 'make it happen?' What if I said next week?"

He shrugged. "Then I'll make it happen."

"So why haven't you 'made it happen' so I could go home?"

"I told you, *mi mujer*. I didn't want to."

Surprising, she accepted his answer without argument.

He felt her smile against his skin. "Okay. Maybe we could video chat with my parents tomorrow, and I can introduce them to their new son-in-law."

"So, we're really doing this," he said with a grin.

She jerked her head up. "Why? Have you changed your mind?"

Ramon tucked her hair behind her ear. "Not even for a second."

She stared at him as if she was unsure she believed him.

"Not. One. Second," he reiterated.

She laid her head back on his chest. "Good. Because I definitely want to keep doing what we did earlier."

"So, you're just using me for my sexual prowess?"

She didn't miss a beat. "And your money."

He chuckled. "I can live with that—as long as it means you're in my bed every night."

She lifted her head again. "You know I'm joking, right?"

"I do."

"But, help me understand something."

Ramon nodded, waiting for her to continue.

"What do you get out of this marriage? I mean, I get a rich, sexy, husband who's an amazing lover... but what do you get? I'm a nerdy software analyst. I'm not a model, or world traveled or sophisticated or come from a family with connections. Heck, I'm not even that sexually experienced. You could have any woman you wanted—why me?"

His captains had asked him that same thing, in a more polite, roundabout manner, of course. They were satisfied with, "She took my breath away—no one has ever done that," even as Luis scoffed and mumbled under his breath. But, Ramon doubted Sophia would accept that answer.

"The minute you turned me down at Francisco and Juan Diego's party, I knew you were different from any woman I'd ever met..."

She snorted. "Yeah, because no one had ever turned you down."

He shook his head, ignoring her comment as he continued, "When we kissed on the beach, I felt like I was under a spell. I couldn't stop thinking about you after you went back to your hotel room, and I couldn't wait until morning to see you again. Then we spent the day together, and you just became more amazing… I knew I had to have more of your time. Imagine my dismay when I learned you'd left for the airport without a word, and I'd had no idea why."

"I guess my credit card mix-up with the hotel was the universe's way of making things right."

Something like that. Or a man with more money than he'd ever be able to spend in ten lifetimes paying people off to get what he wanted, like he always did.

"Talking to Chief Villasenor that morning changed the course of my life. Yours too, I guess."

Notice that he didn't say *why* he'd talked to the chief. Semantics were important.

She nestled closer and sighed. "For the better."

He hoped she still thought that way once he told her the truth about his involvement with the cartel.

Chapter Twenty-Five

Sophia
She woke up feeling tender between her legs, but that only served to put a smile on her face as she recalled how she became that way.

Her sexy husband was nowhere to be found—his side of the bed was cold, indicating he'd been gone for a while. But there was a single red rose on his pillow with a handwritten note on personalized cardstock.

Our journey together begins today.
Adoringly,
Ramon

It was too soon to drop the 'L' word, she knew that, but couldn't help feeling a twinge of disappointment at his use of *adoringly* instead of *love*.

Patience, Soph. It will happen when it's supposed to.

Last night had been a good start, she thought with a grin as she took a full body stretch.

Sophia took extra care getting ready for breakfast that morning, curling her hair and putting on lipstick, mascara, and a smidgen of highlighter across her tanned cheekbones. She dabbed the perfume she'd brought with her on her wrists and behind her ears before slipping on the cute turquoise cotton summer dress she'd bought yesterday. One of the many choices that were now hanging in her closet—thanks to one of the *abuelas*.

After one last check in the mirror, she went down to the kitchen and was met with the three older women grinning ear to ear. Sophia was sure her and Ramon's activities last night had been the talk of the estate.

"*Buenos dias, señoras,*" she said brightly.

"*Buenos dias, Señora Guzman,*" they replied in unison.

"Did Ramon say if he was going to join me for breakfast?"

"*Sí.* He asked me to let him know when you came down. I think breakfast with you is his favorite part of the day."

That brought a smile to her face.

"I'll just pop in his office and let him know myself. But, let's have breakfast on the patio."

Sophia could tell by the looks on their faces that they weren't sure if Sophia 'popping in' to Ramon's office was a good idea.

Too bad, she thought as she practically skipped to the office wing of the estate.

She walked in to find Jesús' desk empty, so she stepped further inside until she could see Ramon sitting behind his desk. His brows were furrowed as he spoke rapid-fire Spanish at someone she couldn't see. She could tell by his low, controlled tone that he was pissed.

Knocking on the open door, she asked with a shy smile, "Is this a bad time?"

His furrowed brows dissolved, and he smiled brightly as he stood. "Good morning, mi amor."

"*Buenos dias, mi marido guapo,*" she replied with a grin.

That caused him to chuckle as he came around the desk and wrapped an arm around her. "You've been practicing."

"A little. I need to take a class."

Ramon kissed her hair and said, "When we get back to San Diego, we'll get you a tutor."

"Thank you for your note. It was nice to wake up to."

She heard a snicker and glanced at his office out of the corner of her eye—she'd never actually been inside the room. It was impressive, with a lot of dark, ornate wood, floor-to-ceiling bookshelves filled with books, and camel-colored leather furniture... that three men happened to be seated in, watching their exchange with amused expressions.

She knew Jesús, of course, and Miguel, another man who'd had dinner with them on their wedding night. She'd seen both around the estate. The third man was sitting in a wingback chair, and he was disarmingly handsome. She recognized him as one of the men who'd been with Ramon the night of Juan Diego and Francisco's party.

"Sophia, you know Jesús and Miguel, and this is my nephew, Dante."

She smiled at the two men she knew and reached for Dante's hand. "So nice to meet you. I can't wait to meet your wife—Ramon says she's also American?"

Dante's smile faltered briefly, but he quickly composed himself and instead of shaking her hand, he brought it to his lips.

"Nice to meet you, too, Sophia. My uncle has told me a lot about you, but he left out how beautiful you are."

"*Sobrino*," Ramon growled in warning as he pulled Sophia back against his side. "Stop flirting with my wife."

Dante's smirk and wink at her told Sophia he'd deliberately intended for Ramon's ire.

Ramon ignored his nephew's goading and turned his attention to Sophia. "Did you need someone, love?"

"I just wanted to see if you had time for breakfast."

"Of course." He then turned to the men in the room. "I think I've made my position clear. Do you have questions on how to proceed?"

They murmured their understanding.

"Then, I'm going to have breakfast with my wife."

Ramon put his hand on the small of Sophia's back and ushered her forward. She looked back and offered a little wave. "Good seeing you, Jesús and Miguel. Nice to meet you, Dante."

"See you soon, Sophia," Jesús replied, along with Miguel telling her it was good seeing her, too.

"The pleasure was all mine," Dante said, the left corner of his mouth turning up to reveal a dimple when Ramon shot daggers his way. He was obviously a well-loved nephew—she couldn't imagine anyone else brave enough to blatantly flirt with her right in front of her husband.

****

Ramon

He knew Dante was getting even for all the times that Ramon deliberately flirted with his wife, Bella, just to get a rise out of his nephew.

His phone dinged with a text before they even reached the foyer.

Dante: Payback's a bitch, isn't it?

Ramon fired back: **I now understand why you got so mad. I promise to never do it again.** Followed by another text: **But don't ever flirt with my wife again, or I'll break your kneecaps.**

He could hear Dante's laughter from the hallway.

Fucking *sobrino*. Even though Dante was his nephew, the man was only younger than him by six years. While Dante got away with a lot, he also knew when to show *el patrón* respect. Not to mention he was a financial genius. He was one of a few that Ramon trusted implicitly. Although, that wasn't to say he didn't still have a few of Dante's men on his payroll to keep him informed of what was going on at his nephew's estate. It was the nature of the business.

"Is Dante your brother's son?" Sophia asked as they stepped through the French doors.

"Yes, my oldest brother."

"Do he and Bella have any children?"

"Just one daughter—Madison. She has him wrapped around her finger."

She stopped walking. "Madison Guzman... Madison Guzman... Her story was all over the news. Wasn't she kidnapped and..." Her hands flew to her mouth. "I cried for days after they discovered her body. I had prayed so hard she'd be found alive."

The first test of how much he could trust his wife was about to commence. He put his hand on her back and ushered her along, murmuring close to her ear, "I'll let you in on a little secret. Your prayers worked. The story of her death was made up to keep her safe after she was rescued."

Tears streamed down his wife's face. "I can't believe she's alive. My friends and I went to Mass and everything to pray for her safe return. We were devastated when the news broke. Wait until I tell my friends, Tammy and Iva..."

He grabbed her hand and led her to a patio chair, then knelt beside her. "Sophia. You can never tell anyone. We still don't know who is responsible for her kidnapping. Her life would be in danger if our enemies thought she was still alive."

"It would just be my friends..."

"No one can know, Sophia. No. One. Her life depends on you keeping it a secret."

All the color drained from her face.

Flashpoint

"Alejandro wasn't being dramatic yesterday about me staying close to him," she whispered.

"No, baby. He wasn't. You must always be vigilante when you're out. And you can never leave here without a bodyguard. A bodyguard *you know*. I would never let you go with someone you didn't know."

She bit the side of her cheek, deep in thought. Finally, she looked at him with a sad smile. "We probably shouldn't have a real wedding... the less people who know about me the better. Don't you think?"

"We're having a wedding, Sophia. I don't care if it's just you, me, and a priest, but you're wearing a beautiful gown, and we are saying our vows in front of God. And then I'm taking you on a honeymoon and getting you pregnant, so I'm not too old to play with my kids."

He had no idea where the idea of having kids came from. He'd never even considered it before just then. But now that he'd said it out loud, he liked the idea.

Sophia shook her head. "We can't have children, Ramon. I couldn't risk something happening to my child. I was devastated about Madison, and I didn't even know her except for what I learned from the news. I would be destroyed if that were my baby."

"They will be *our* children, and I would move heaven and earth to make sure you and our *familia* would always be safe. Fortunately, I have the money to make that happen."

She cupped his cheek. "Let's just enjoy being married for a while before we decide on babies. Good grief—we only just decided to try this out last night."

"*You* just decided last night."

"Oh, I'm sorry," she sassed. "You have a *whole* three days head start. This is crazy to even be having this conversation. We haven't even known each other a week."

"You're right. But we shouldn't wait long. I'm an old man, Sophia."

The look she shot him was pure sex, and it went straight to his cock, which was magnified when she brushed her tits against him and whispered in his ear, "You were quite virile last night."

He kissed the spot right below her ear that made her break out in goosebumps before murmuring, "If you got pregnant tomorrow, I'd still be forty-nine when my first child was born."

She drew back to stare at him, her eyes wide. "You're forty-eight?"

Ramon chuckled. "I told you, baby. I'm an old man."

Sophia reached down to stroke his hard-on over his trousers. "You don't feel that old."

He met her lips in a chaste kiss, then moved to take his seat next to hers. "I can keep up, *mi amor*. Don't worry. No blue pills required."

She slid onto his lap and wrapped her arms around his neck while she kissed along his jaw, purring, "I'm not worried."

Ramon massaged her left tit in one hand while stroking her thigh just above her knee.

"If you're not sore from last night, I failed," he growled.

"I'm a little tender," she replied between kisses on his neck. "But nothing a little coconut oil couldn't fix."

"Maybe my tongue can help."

It's the least he could do after how much sex they'd had last night.

"I'm sure it would," Sophia said with a grin.

Ramon lifted her off his lap and onto the patio table, then moved to lower himself between her thighs.

"Are you crazy? Not here. Oh my god, poor Maribel would be scarred for life, not to mention I'd never be able to look her in the eye again."

While he didn't give a fuck—this was his house after all, it was the staff's job to be scarce if he was in a compromising situation, not the other way around. But he knew Sophia would never be able to relax and enjoy what he was about to do to her if they remained out in the open.

He stood and offered his hand to help her off the table, then tugged her into the pool house, making sure she saw him lock the door behind them.

"On the couch, panties off," he barked.

As she scrambled to obey, a slight smile escaped her lips, and she bit the corner of her mouth like she was trying to disguise it.

She leaned back against the arm rest with her legs closed and her feet on the cushions. Ramon pulled her knees apart and settled between her thighs with a devilish grin. Her pink center was already wet.

"Mmm, I think that my wife is excited about having her pussy licked…" he murmured against her slit, his breath hot on her pussy, but he was careful not to touch her yet.

"Mmm hmm," she whimpered her confession.

"Are you sure you're not too sore, baby?" he teased before darting his tongue along her folds then looking up at her.

"Ohhhh." Her hand went to the top of his head, and she flexed her fingers in his hair. "No, not too sore at all."

Ramon circled his tongue around her clit while slipping a finger inside her.

"Are you sure? Because I can stop." He lifted his head with a smirk.

"Please, no… don't stop." she panted.

Teasing time was over. He spread her pussy with his free hand and explored her folds with his tongue, moaning with approval when she lifted her hips to press against his mouth.

"Fuck, baby, you taste so good."

She whimpered in response, but Ramon could feel how wet she was getting.

"Do you like when I fuck you with my mouth, *mi amor*?"

She spread her legs a little wider as she arched her back off the sofa. "Oh my god, yesssss."

"This is my pussy. Mine." He increased the tempo with his fingers in her pussy and brought his other hand up to assist manipulating her clit while he continued talking dirty to her.

The more he talked, the wetter her pussy got. He rubbed her clit faster, and she started to chant, "Yes, oh god, yes," as her body went taut.

"That's it, baby. That's a good girl. Come all over my face."

Her back bowed off the couch while she moaned, "Ohhhh my god, yesssss," before her legs shuddered.

With a smile of satisfaction, he continued licking her clit until she pushed on his shoulders and rolled her legs to the side of him.

"Damn, Ramon," she panted. "That was... wow."

He lay next to her on the couch and wrapped his arms around her middle to draw her close to him.

"God, you're sexy," he murmured in her ear.

Sophia reached down and started unbuckling his belt, and he placed his hand on top of hers to still her. "Baby, aren't you sore?"

"Mmm mmm. I want to feel you inside me again."

He stood to remove his pants and underwear, then grabbed the jar of coconut oil from the basket on the counter with sunscreen and aloe. After slathering it onto his cock, he reached between her legs and spread the liquid around her opening.

It had seemed like a good idea, until his cock glided smoothly inside her. Too smoothly.

"Fuck, you feel good," he groaned as he slowly moved his cock in and out. She met him thrust for thrust; her fingertips tracing up and down his spine.

Then his sweet, little American nerd turned the tables on him.

"Oh yes, fuck me… Just like that."

"I love it when you fuck me with your big cock."

"Mmm, yes, fill my wet pussy with your fat cock."

And the one that sent him over the edge, when she dug her fingernails into his shoulders and breathlessly commanded, "I want you to cum deep inside my pussy."

He pumped in and out of her, until he gave one last, long thrust and released his seed as he roared, "Fuuuuck!"

She molded her hips to his and held onto his back as he spurted rope after rope of cum deep inside her, then collapsed onto his forearms. His brow was sweaty, but he burrowed his face into her neck anyway as he regained his breath.

"*Mi mujer*," he whispered reverently against her skin.

His.

If he was dreaming, he didn't want to wake up.

Chapter Twenty-Six

Sophia

"I can't do it this way," she said as they sat in the living room with the afternoon sun warming the room. She had her phone in hand with the videoconferencing app open, her finger hovering over the icon for her mother—a picture of her mom smiling brightly at Christmas last year, but she just couldn't bring herself to push the button.

Ramon didn't seem to know how to respond. "Okaaaay?"

She dropped the phone into her lap. "I can't tell them over the phone. I need to do it in person." She let out a long sigh and lifted her left hand. "But I can't wait until I'm allowed to leave Mexico. Who knows how long that will be?" She then lifted her right hand. "But I can't call them and act like everything is normal." Then her left again. "But I can't not call them, or they'll be worried to death, and I don't want to worry them."

"Sounds like we need to go see them in person."

"Yes, exactly! But how are we supposed to do that? Who knows when I'm going to be cleared to leave?"

He stood with authority. "Go pack a bag. It's time you saw our home in San Diego."

She remained on the couch, staring at him in confusion.

"What? I can't just pack a bag and leave, Ramon."

"Sure, you can. It's about a forty-five-minute flight by helicopter; we can be there before dinner."

She knew her mouth was gaping open as she stared at him.

"I can't just..."

"Yes, you can. Go pack. If it will make you feel better, I'll call Roberto and let him know we're leaving."

"Oh, so you can just call him and get me cleared to leave?"

"Yes."

"Just like that?"

"Yes."

Suddenly, she had a realization.

"You could have gotten me cleared without marrying you."

He stared at her for a beat, contemplating her accusation. Sophia could see his Adam's apple move as he swallowed hard.

"Yes. I could have. I'm the reason you were detained in the first place."

"What do you mean?" she whispered.

"I called in some favors, paid a few bribes... anything to keep you from getting on that plane. I explained to Roberto I might be in love with you and couldn't let you leave until I knew for sure."

"So, you lied."

"No. I never lied. Not about why."

Flashpoint

The realization of what he was saying dawned on her, making her even more conflicted about how she felt about him being the mastermind behind her being detained.

She stood and paced in front of him.

"So, let me get this straight. You had the hotel say my credit card was stolen in order for the chief of police to keep me from getting on a plane, then *married* me… all because you thought you might have a *crush* on me?"

Ramon rubbed the back of his neck. "Not exactly like that, but close enough. And it was way more than a crush, Sophia."

She stopped pacing and folded her arms across her chest.

"So, what'd you find out?"

He cocked his head as if confused, but she didn't say anything to help him understand. She just waited, letting him piece together what she was asking.

It was obvious when he realized what she wanted to know. A slow smile formed on his lips, and he closed the space between them to slide an arm around her waist.

"I'm definitely smitten. Absolutely no regrets."

Smitten? That's it? He's smitten?

It was soon for the 'L' word, she knew that. Yet. She couldn't help but feel disappointed; same as she had when she read his note. Besides, now she was mad.

Sort of.

She stepped out of his embrace.

"You manipulated this whole situation, Ramon."

"I know I did. But I'm not sorry that I did or that we're married—for real."

"I agreed to that under false pretenses."

He drew her back into his embrace. "Did you, though? Yes, you married me under false pretenses, but you came to my bed willingly, *mi amor*. You consummated the marriage, knowing full well that doing so took an annulment off the table."

"That was before I knew what you'd done."

He kissed her below her ear in the spot that always turned her to mush. "I know you want me to apologize, *mi mujer*, but I'm not going to. I have no regrets about marrying you and would do it all over again. Actually, I'm looking forward to doing it all over again in San Diego."

"You can't just manipulate me like that."

She felt the sigh run through his body. "Yes, you're right. But, in my defense, you put my back against the wall when you took off like you did. Desperate times called for desperate measures. And I was desperate, Sophia. I was frantic I would never see you again—that I'd missed my shot. I couldn't let that happen. I think you're going to discover, I'm a man used to getting his own way."

"I've kind of already figured that out."

He bent his knees, so he was eye level with her. "I'm glad you're my wife, Sophia, but if this means you've had a change of heart—I won't contest a divorce."

The idea of divorce sent a pang straight to her heart.

"You wouldn't fight for me?"

"Baby, I'd slay dragons for you if I thought you wanted to be married to me. But, I also lov—care enough about you to let you go if that's what you want."

She shook her head. "It's not what I want. I don't want a divorce. I just want you to promise that you'll be honest with me from now on."

He swallowed hard and nodded. "Go pack. I have my new in-laws to meet."

"What about Daisy? She's still pretty skittish, I don't think she'll do well in a helicopter. Heck, I'm not sure *I'm* going to do well in a helicopter."

"I'll have Alejandro bring her in the car with him. Have you ever been in a helicopter before?"

"No."

"Well, hopefully you don't get airsick. I'll make sure the pilot knows it's your first time."

And, once again, she was caught up in the whirlwind that was Ramon Guzman.

****

Ramon

As they approached his San Diego estate's helipad, Sophia turned to him with wide eyes and said through the sound system, "*This* is where you live?"

"It's where *we* live. Most of the time."

"How—?" She glanced at the pilot and stopped. Ramon could tell something was on her mind, but she didn't want to discuss it front of anyone. *Good girl.* He'd make a *patrón's* wife out of her yet.

They touched down and were met by two of his San Diego staff that lived on the property.

Lupita was Consuela's youngest sister. She and her husband, Hector lived full-time in a house near the property line. She was one of the housekeepers, and Hector was his head gardener. Blanca, a niece of Maribel's was his main cook and lived in an apartment in the staff's quarters. Ramon suspected there was something going on between her and Chachi, who had ridden with them from Ensenada. The huge smile she gave the bodyguard when he got out of the chopper seemed to confirm that.

Ramon had security that stayed at the estate around the clock, even when he wasn't there, but a lot of his detail traveled with him between Ensenada and San Diego. They'd be arriving by convoy soon, along with Daisy the dog.

"Welcome home, *Señor* Guzman," Lupita said in perfect English with a bright smile. The woman appeared to be the designated spokesman tonight, because she turned to Sophia and gushed, "We're so pleased to meet you, *Señora*. Anything you need, we'll be happy to provide."

"Yes, anything," Blanca added, then cast a shy smile at Chachi.

"Thank you. We're just about to head out for the evening, so we won't need anything tonight."

The women turned to go, but not without one last look from Blanca thrown Chachi's way.

Ramon tried to contain his smirk. If there wasn't something going on between those two yet, there would be soon. He kind of wanted to fuck with his bodyguard and remind him of the no-fraternization policy. The policy that was non-existent, but it'd be fun to see Chachi's face. Maybe having to sneak around would make it even more exciting for the young lovers.

Right now, he needed to prepare for meeting his new in-laws. Normally, he didn't give a fuck if people liked him, but he sensed it was important that these people approved of him.

"How much time do you need to get ready?"

"I texted my mom and said I'd be there for dinner, and I was bringing a guest. Dinner is at six-thirty sharp, so we should probably get there by six, and since there's no helipad in their subdivision, we need to leave in twenty minutes..."

He smirked and pointed to his 'garage,' which was more of a large warehouse that served as a hangar, garage, vehicle repair shop, and sleeping quarters for security staff. "Luckily, we've got a ride available to us."

"You have another McLaren in there?" she teased.

"No, but I do have a few Ferraris, a Bugatti, a couple of Aston Martins, and a Rolls, along with some others, and of course, plenty of Escalades."

"Seriously?" Her eyes grew bright as she grinned from ear to ear. "Oh, we have to take the Bugatti; my dad will flip."

He shook his head. "Sorry, baby. We need security with us."

Her face fell. He didn't like seeing her disappointed.

"We could have security meet us there, but that would mean two cars in your parents' driveway."

"That's okay. My mom will probably try to feed them though."

"They don't eat on duty."

"Unless they're out with me," she corrected, "and I make them go to lunch."

He chuckled. "Unless they're out with you…" then grabbed her hand. "Come on, I'll show you where the master wing is, and you can get ready. Tomorrow, I'll take you around so you can get a feel of the layout."

Ten minutes later, she reappeared with reapplied lipstick and her hair in a messy bun on top of her head. Ramon wanted to do nothing more than kiss the freshly applied color right off her lips but refrained himself, reasoning, they had all night after they left her parents.

Sophia gasped out loud when she walked into the garage behind him. His cars were lined up on either side of an extra-wide hallway for cars—as if they were on display. The paint gleamed off the varying body styles under the lights.

"Oh my… this is more than a few, Ramon," she murmured as she walked down the aisle, carefully observing his collection, then turned to him. "Do you have this many cars in Mexico?"

"No. Not even close. But I only spend about a quarter of my time in Ensenada. Dante really is the one who takes care of things there—although, since his daughter's… incident, he keeps his family in San Diego and travels back and forth. Fortunately, he has John to help him handle things here when he's gone."

"Let me guess, he has a helicopter, too?"

He winked with a smirk. "My old one."

"I don't know if I'll ever get used to this…"

"You will."

"Hopefully, my job will keep me grounded."

He felt his brows furrow. "You're keeping your job?"

"I like my job, Ramon. And I like working. I'd go crazy just sitting around being waited on hand and foot."

"But, your job is in San Francisco. I'd rather you found something where you could work from home. We can have one of the rooms renovated into an office for you—with your exact specifications."

"I'm sure I can continue telecommuting and just fly in quarterly for the meetings if I can't Zoom."

"And your apartment... We can send someone to box your things and turn in your keys."

"Maybe I should keep that..."

"No," he interrupted. "If you need to go to San Francisco, you're staying in a hotel with a security team. You can't be protected in your little apartment."

She cocked her head. "How do you know my apartment is little?"

Shit. He couldn't exactly tell her he'd run a thorough background check on her the day after they'd met.

"I just assumed, since San Francisco is such an expensive city."

She crossed her arms over her chest. "Ramon... remember what you promised, not five hours earlier?"

He felt his shoulders slump. "Fine. I had my men run a background check on you." He quickly added when he saw your eyes narrow. "Just to make sure you weren't sent by someone looking to take down Guzman Enterprises." He reached for her hand, which she reluctantly gave him, and he brought her knuckles to his lips. "You just seemed too good to be true, *mi amor*. I had to be sure."

"Your charm is not always going to work, you know."

He grinned and pulled her into his embrace. "Yes, it will."

He was banking on it.

****

Sophia

"You know, I think we should take a Mercedes instead."

"You do? Why? What's wrong with the Bugatti?"

He seemed insulted, like she was implying there was something wrong with his car.

"Oh, absolutely nothing. It's beautiful. I just think the first time meeting my family, we should probably arrive in something a little… Less flashy."

"We can do that. Let me tell Chachi and José."

Minutes later, the four of them were in route to her parents' house, and Sophia began to feel nervous. After texting her mom that she was bringing a guest, she had a feeling both her brothers, Liam and Greyson would be there, along with Liam's family. It'd be just like her mom to invite everyone. Unfortunately, her mother wouldn't know what to make of Ramon Guzman—or the fact that he'd married her daughter after barely meeting her.

Then was her dad.

Sophia closed her eyes at the idea of how he would react. Hopefully, the fact that they were having another wedding would soothe his ruffled feathers over not walking her down the aisle.

Not that there even was an aisle.

"I'm not sure what to tell my parents about our wedding," she said softly in the backseat. She had no idea how much his bodyguards knew about how their nuptials came to be.

"We can say we got married at the courthouse if you'd prefer. Or that Roberto came to the estate specifically to marry us."

"Yeah, let's say that he came to the estate. But, I'm still not sure how I'm going to explain getting married to you so quickly after meeting you."

"Well, we could tell them that the chief would only let you go if we were married, since I'd told him we were engaged in an attempt to help you. And that we fell in love in the meantime."

"We fell in love?"

She'd said it like she was teasing him, but deep down, she wanted him to admit it.

"You know what I mean. That we decided we liked being married."

"I think I'm just going to say that we fell head over heels in love and decided to be spontaneous when the chief was over visiting."

"I like that."

"And now, we're going to have an official ceremony in San Diego."

"Have you given any more thought to if you want a reception?"

"A small one. I definitely think we should try to keep it as quiet as possible."

Flashpoint

"And the other thing we talked about?"

She knew he was talking about babies. Even though they were talking softly, and the radio was playing in the car's front speakers, he didn't want to be overheard.

Sophia didn't know how to answer. Yes, she wanted kids, and she was thirty-four; she wasn't exactly getting any younger either. But Madison's kidnapping had affected her, and she was terrified it could happen to them. Especially since he told her the people responsible for it hadn't been caught yet.

"Let's just enjoy being newlyweds. Besides, I don't think my poor mother's heart could handle a new son-in-law *and* a new grandchild."

Turned out, she was wrong.

Chapter Twenty-Seven

Sophia
"I can't believe my mother asked if I was pregnant," she said with her hands on her face as she stood next to him as she got ready for bed in their marble bathroom that was bigger than some houses.

He dried his face and looked at her with a grin. "She seemed pretty disappointed you weren't."

Sophia dramatically slid her hands down her face, tugging on her chin while staring at him through the mirror. "Right?"

Ramon was shirtless in only a pair of pajama pants and was downright edible.

"I think your dad was glad though. He still seems to be on the fence about me."

"You just married his little girl, before he even got a chance to meet you and approve. How would you feel if our only daughter brought home some guy she married on vacation, who was closer to your age than hers?"

"Probably like I'd want to kick his ass. I'm betting if your dad hadn't known Chachi and José were right outside, he might have considered just that."

"So that's the real reason you brought them."

"No," he said with a chuckle, "but when both your brothers showed up, I was glad I had."

Flashpoint

"My brothers are pretty harmless, especially Liam—Jennifer and the kids have mellowed him out. The good news is my dad seemed excited about coming over for dinner and seeing your cars. That's a start. But if that garage full of cars doesn't win him over, you might as well forget it—nothing will."

"I know you're kidding, but I also have a feeling you're right. Hopefully, your mom will approve of the grounds for the wedding. It will be much easier to control security here."

"We're having the wedding here, babe. I suggested she come so she could see for herself how beautiful everything is, but even if she hates it, this is where I want to have the ceremony."

Wrapping his arms around her middle from behind, he dropped kisses on her bare shoulder. "Have I mentioned how happy I am you're here with me?"

"Um, no, I don't think you have."

He looked at her through the mirror's reflection with the corner of his mouth turned up and traced the skin between her boobs peeking out of her emerald green silk cami. "I've been a neglectful husband. I need to do something about that."

Sophia turned around and looped her arms around his neck. "Yes, you do."

With his hands at her waist, Ramon lifted her onto the black marble vanity, tugged her silk pajama shorts off, and then opened her legs to play with her pussy as he spoke.

Damn him and his deep voice and dirty talk. His amazing body didn't hurt either. She was already wet when he glided his index finger up and down her slit, something she knew he wouldn't pass up mentioning.

"I think my dirty, wet girl wants more attention..." He drew small circles around her clit. "Right here."

Sophia whimpered her agreement and fell back on her elbows as he continued stimulating her knot. Using his other hand, he slid two fingers inside her pussy. "Or maybe she needs it here."

"Both," she panted. "But I want your cock inside me."

Somewhere in the back of her mind, her sensibilities were shocked that she not only used the word *cock*, but also told her lover she wanted it inside her.

But this wasn't just a lover. This was her husband, and somehow, she felt safe expressing her dirty desires.

Ramon untied his pajama pants and dropped them to the floor. His naked cock jutted out, and he lined it up with her entrance, pushing inside as they both moaned in unison.

"Fuck, you feel good, baby."

Sophia mewled her agreement while wrapping her legs around his back.

Still manipulating her clit, he moved in a slow, steady rhythm in and out of her. His eyes never left her face, as he watched her orgasm build.

Flashpoint

She felt her body flush, and he increased his pace—both with his fingers and his thrusting, murmuring, "That's it. Be a good girl and come for me. Come on my cock, my little slut."

Sophia panted, her body tight, and her husband growled, "That's it. Come on my dick, you naughty girl. Come right. Fucking. Now."

His command was so primal, it was almost as if she had no choice but to obey. At least, that was what she told herself later.

Her body quivered from head to toe as the orgasm wracked through her. Ramon didn't give her any time to recover and fucked her hard with feral grunts, making her come again just as he let out a long groan and held her hips tight against his.

"Oh my god," she panted as she slumped her back onto the cool marble and put her hand to her forehead while staring at the ceiling. "I always thought multiple orgasms were a myth." She lifted her head and looked at him. "Not a myth."

He grinned down at her. "It was hot. My wife has a naughty side we need to keep exploring."

She could get on board with that.

Chapter Twenty-Eight

Ramon
Having his wife available to fuck multiple times a day was almost like a dream come true. Having her get bolder each time and share her dirty desires was like a fantasy come true.

Sophia was a natural submissive; she just hadn't realized it before meeting him. Either that, or she'd never been with a man worth submitting to. Luckily for her, Ramon had no problem being all-alpha, all the time.

During their play, he'd discovered that, in addition to liking to be fucked hard, dirty talk turned her on. The dirtier, the better—which was adorable because outside of the bedroom, he'd never heard her mutter more than *shoot*.

But what surprised him most, was their times of intimacy—when they were making love. That was a first for him, but there was no doubt Ramon loved her. He probably fell in love with her the first night on the beach. He just didn't know when he should express it, which seemed counterintuitive since they were already married. But nothing about their relationship had been conventional. There was also the matter of not being one hundred percent sure she felt the same way yet. He was a proud man—if he said it, and she didn't reciprocate the sentiment… he didn't know how his ego would recover. So, it was better to continue in their marital bliss and not rock the boat.

Flashpoint

Because that's exactly what they were in—marital bliss. There was no other way to describe it.

They'd been officially married a month, but their upcoming ceremony and reception was still ten days away. Sophia and her mom had been busy working out the arrangements, although Ramon asked to have the final say about who was coming onto the property—whether it was guests or someone working the event, they all had to be vetted. His lieutenants only grumbled a little about the extra work, but fortunately, the guest list was small.

Dante walked in Ramon's office to find him rubbing his temples after receiving a text from Sophia about a change with the catering staff.

"What's wrong, *Tío*?" he asked as he helped himself to Ramon's bar.

"Just wedding stuff."

His nephew handed him a tumbler of whiskey with a grin. "This is why you should *go* to parties, not *host* them," the younger man teased as he sat with a glass of scotch in his hand and proceeded to cross his ankles on Ramon's desk.

"I *know* you aren't disrespecting me like that," Ramon growled with one eyebrow raised as he glared at Dante's shoes.

Dante quickly removed his feet from the desk and sat up straighter.

"Have you made a decision about bringing Madison to the wedding?"

"Bella's still debating. She doesn't think it's a good idea, but Quinn said she could be there."

Ramon wasn't about to argue with Dante's wife. She was a force all her own.

"So, people will think she's Quinn's daughter? I'm sure John would love an opportunity to play the role of father, too. Fortunately, *El Rey* and his daughter aren't coming... No love triangles to worry about."

"Bella and I are staying out of John's love life—and Quinn's. I don't want to hear anything, see anything, know anything... nothing. My best friend's love life is his own."

Ramon chuckled. "That's probably for the best. Still, it's got to be hard trying to live under the radar—first with Bella, and now with Madison."

"It's not my ideal situation, but we'll make it work. Once Madi gets a little older, I think it will be easier."

"What are you going to do when she starts school?

"Fuck if I know. I'd say have tutors come in, but Bella won't hear of it. She says Madison needs to go to school. We've still got a couple of years to figure things out."

Ramon was certain that 'figuring things out' also included learning who ordered the little girl's kidnapping. Jacob, one of the men who'd rescued Madison, was convinced it was Los Zetas, as some of the men had Zeta tattoos. But chatter also indicated the Colombians had been in town, so the Colombians and Zetas could have been working together. Either way, they were going to get to the bottom of it, and when they did, there would be hell to pay.

Dante had vowed a scorched earth—Carthage style—to whomever was behind his daughter's abduction. Ramon had always been one hundred percent behind his nephew, but now that the idea of having a baby had entered his head—and Madison's abduction was creating a roadblock for his wife— he reaffirmed his commitment to finding and punishing whoever was responsible.

He needed to get through the wedding and moving Sophia's things from San Francisco, but then, he was taking the meeting with the Colombians in New Orleans to try to get to the bottom of things.

Chapter Twenty-Nine

Sophia
"Are you happy?" Her mother's face was solemn when she asked the question of Sophia, who was standing on a platform at the bridal shop for the final fitting of her wedding dress.

"Deliriously so."

Her mom's face softened with a smile. "Good. You seem happy, and Ramon obviously adores you."

She glanced down at her mother. "Why do I feel there's a *but* coming?"

"No, no buts. I just wonder why you rushed into this. That's so unlike you."

"Maybe that's exactly the reason I did. I was tired of living life on the sidelines. When I met Ramon... I don't know. It just felt like I was suddenly living life instead of watching it go by. He makes me feel brave."

"But why did you get married? He could make you feel all that dating."

"I don't know. He asked me, and I wanted to."

"I'm glad you're happy. That's all a mother could want. Well, and more grandchildren to spoil."

"Not you, too!"

Her mom cocked her head. "What does that mean?"

Dammit. "Nothing." But she knew what wouldn't fly. "It's just Ramon would like to start a family soon."

"And you don't want to? I always thought you wanted children."

"I do. But I want to enjoy being married, with just the two of us for a little while. He has the means to travel—I think I'd like to explore some places in the world first. Just him and I as we get to know each other better."

"You know… most people get to know each other *before* getting married."

"I know. But, that's not how it happened for us." Sophia spun around to showcase her dress, trying to steer the conversation back to why they were at the boutique. "Besides, look at how beautiful I am in this gown."

"That dress costs more than your brother's wedding."

"Well, Liam didn't marry a multi-millionaire, Mom. I'm marrying a man with a private jet and ten houses spread throughout the world. I can't exactly walk down the aisle wearing something from the clearance rack."

"I don't see why not. If he loves you, he won't care what you're wearing."

Yeah, but he doesn't love me yet. Not that Sophia could say that out loud.

"I know he wouldn't care. But I want to look beautiful," *and make him proud to be waiting for me at the end of the aisle.* "He said I didn't have a budget."

"So, if he has so much money, why are you still working?"

So many questions, woman!

"Because I like working, and my job is being super flexible with me, so I don't quit; there's no reason not to keep working. Ramon wants me to just invest my salary into my brokerage account, for now."

"That's good—let you build up a nest egg in case..."

Sophia interrupted her. "In case what? Do you not like my husband? Where is all this coming from?"

"No, that's not it. I *do* like him—and he adores you, that much is obvious. Your dad and I just don't know anything about him. Where did he grow up? How did he make his money—is it inherited, or is it self-made? What does he do? How old is he?" Her mom splayed her hands in a questioning manner. "You show up to our house married to a man we know nothing about, that *you* know nothing about, and are planning another wedding to him that's going to have more security than Prince Harry and Meghan Markle's. Why?" She sat on one of the provided purple velvet couches. "It's been a lot to process. This just isn't the Sophia I know and raised."

"I'm still me, Mom. I fell in love with a man, and the pieces fell into place. I'm thirty-four years old; I can decide what's best for me."

"I know you can, honey." She gave the placating smile that Sophia had come to despise, growing up. "I'm sure we just need to spend more time with Ramon and get to know him better."

"Well, you're coming for dinner, tomorrow—that's a start."

Flashpoint

"Yes, we're looking forward to it. What can we bring?"

"Nothing. We have a fantastic cook who will take care of everything."

"Well, how about a bottle of wine, then?"

Sophia knew her mother thought it was bad manners to show up to someone's home empty-handed—an etiquette lesson she instilled in all her children. And one that Sophia took to heart, so she nodded her head. "Wine would be great." With a grin, she added, "Now, can we get back to the reason we're here?"

"Oh, honey..." Her mother put her hand to her heart. "I'm so sorry. Of course. The dress is stunning, and you're breathtaking in it."

Exactly the look she was going for.

****

Ramon

"I need to make sure all the cars are available to drive tonight," he told Gabriel, his head of security, on the phone that morning.

"In-laws coming over again?" the other man said with a chuckle.

"Yep. If driving my cars is what it takes to win over my father-in-law's approval, that's a small price to pay."

"Until he wrecks one."

"Even then, totally worth it. Happy wife, happy life, right? And her parents are important to her."

"I don't know… Rumor is she stares at you like you hung the moon."

"You gossiping again?" he said with amusement. Ramon liked the idea of her looking at him adoringly.

"Never. You know us security guys. We're the silent, stoic types."

"That's not how I heard some of you were described at the club last weekend."

"Don't you have a wedding you're supposed to be planning? How do you have time to be gossiping?"

"I am the wizard, my friend. I know and see all."

Gabe's loud laugh came through the line. "I'll make sure the cars are ready by this afternoon. Do you want to go over the security plan for the wedding again?"

"I'm about to have breakfast with Sophia, so let's put that on hold."

"I'll wait to hear from you, then. Have a good morning."

He was about to spend time with his bride—a good morning was a given.

Chapter Thirty

Ramon

"It was a beautiful wedding, *Tío*." Dante had stopped in the morning after the ceremony for a few last-minute instructions before Ramon headed out on his honeymoon. He was planning on being *unavailable* for the next ten days and wanted to make sure everything was going to run smoothly in his absence. He'd decided to take the Colombians' meeting the week after he returned. He also wanted to ensure his homes in Europe were ready for their arrival.

Earlier this week, while talking in bed, he and Sophia had decided to visit *their* properties in Greece, Italy, and Portugal on their honeymoon.

"I'm going to fuck you in every room of every house," he warned in her ear when they'd finalized their plans.

She pulled back to look at him with a smug grin. "Oh, then maybe we should include another stop? Didn't you say we have a house in the Dominican Republic, too?"

"You are so fucking perfect," he growled before tugging her underneath him to stare into her eyes. "I can't believe I was lucky enough to find you."

She caressed his cheek while looking back at him. "It does feel like fate wanted us to meet." She gave him a wry smile while shaking her head. "But then, you... well, you took it out of fate's hands and handled the rest."

"I wouldn't leave being with you up to chance, fate, or anything else."

"No, that's definitely not your style."

Their wedding had gone smoothly, and Dante was right—it had been beautiful. But his bride… She had taken his breath away when she appeared at the end of the aisle on the patio. The backdrop for their nuptials had been the Pacific Ocean—but the view was nothing compared to how stunning Sophia had been.

And she'd been charming and gracious, making sure to chat with all their guests even though Juan Diego and Francisco had wanted to occupy all her time.

"We will have a spa day the next time I'm in Ensenada, I promise."

"And when will that be?" Juan Diego had demanded. "And don't say, *soon*, because that's not going to cut it. I want a date."

"Let me get back from our honeymoon, and I promise, I will call you and set something up."

"And you better be okay with sharing her," the man warned Ramon.

"I promise I will share her."

But right now, he was going to have her all to himself for ten days straight—no interruptions, distractions, or worries. Just her and him. He couldn't get her on their jet soon enough.

Flashpoint

****

Sophia

While there were still some things she was getting used to about being wealthy, she had no problem adjusting to traveling in a private jet.

"How am I ever supposed to fly commercial again?" she lamented as she melted into her butter-soft leather seat across from his.

"Well, if it's a short flight, I've found first class can still be tolerable and makes a lot more economic sense."

"I know, but even just using the private terminal... no crowds, people waiting around to help you... I definitely could get used to that." She surveyed their surroundings. "And this."

Ramon chuckled. "Wait until I take you back to the bedroom."

She gave him a sly smile. "Twelve hours is a long time. I'm sure I'll need a nap at some point."

"You won't be napping, *mi mujer*."

Her toes curled like they always did when he growled in his alpha voice. It always turned her on when he took charge.

"I don't know. I'm kind of tired..."

She'd said it to be impish and tease him, but his face changed from sexy Mr. In-Charge to concerned husband in an instant, and he grabbed her hands.

"Are you feeling okay? I knew you were doing too much, taking on the wedding planning without hiring someone."

"No, silly. I was just being sassy."

"Oh." He sat up straight with a grin, then warned, "Sassy girls get punished."

She practically purred her reply, "That's what I'm hoping for."

Without a word, he threw her over his shoulder as he stood and marched down the aisle to the bedroom in the back.

Good thing they'd just reached cruising altitude.

****

Ramon

They'd just sat down for a late dinner at an outdoor café in Lisbon when his phone rang. He pulled it from his pocket and looked down to find Dante calling.

Ramon had given explicit instructions that he wasn't to be bothered during his honeymoon—and since he still had two more days before that was over, he knew something big must be going on.

"*Sobrino*—is everything okay?"

Sophia's eyes widened with worry as she took a sip of wine and listened to Ramon's end of the conversation.

Dante's voice held concern. "Is Sophia with you?"

Ramon glanced across the table. "Yes," then stood, prepared to take the call away from where she couldn't overhear his conversation.

"Are you sure?"

What an odd question.

"I'm looking right at her beautiful face. What's going on?"

She smiled brightly at him as he winked at her while excusing himself to the sidewalk, out of earshot.

"The Ritz Carlton in New Orleans just phoned Jesús. It seems *your wife* is there, trying to check in early."

"*Early*? I'd say two weeks is a little early," he said with a laugh. "The CIA needs better informants, so their information is updated."

The Colombians originally wanted the meeting right after he returned from his honeymoon, but Ramon put them off in case he and Sophia decided to stay a few more days.

"Yeah, that's actually what tipped the hotel off that something could be wrong, and why they called Jesús, since he was the one who made your reservation."

"So, who was it? Do we know yet?"

"Not yet. The Ritz's security is sending over still photos from the video."

"Don't out her, whoever it is, at least not yet. I want to see what she does. I'll make sure to switch rooms though—last minute after we arrive, and we'll still need to have a team come in and sweep for bugs."

"That's a given with the Colombians. I still don't know why you're taking this meeting. We just need to destroy them and not look back. They're still crippled from when Edward and his team blew up their operation in Cartagena."

"The one you were a part of without my authorization?" Ramon reminded him.

"I've already paid my penance..."

"I know you have." It was water under the bridge as far as Ramon was concerned. "And I know you think the Colombians were behind Madison's... ordeal, but I think we need to dig deeper. They might let something slip when I meet with them."

"When *we* meet with them."

"Sorry, *Sobrino*. This is too personal for you—you're sitting this one out."

"Like hell, I am."

"We'll discuss it when I'm back home, but yes, you are. That's an order—am I clear?"

"*Simon*," Dante said gruffly.

"I'll be back in California in a few days. Hopefully, we'll have photos of my alleged wife by then."

"Enjoy the rest of your time." Without another word, the younger man clicked off.

Ramon knew he was pissed, which furthered his point—Dante was too close to this to be involved. His judgment would be clouded. They needed to go into this meeting with

Flashpoint

their wits about them—*especially* now that the CIA was trying to get their claws into things.

"Is everything okay?" Sophia asked when he sat back down.

"Well, yes and no. Apparently, someone was trying to impersonate you at my hotel in New Orleans. Seems they didn't get the memo that the dates had been changed. Fortunately, the hotel caught it."

"Why would someone want to impersonate *me*?"

"Lots of reasons, but I think in this instance, they were trying to gain access to my room so they could plant spying devices." He chuckled. "Unfortunately, they were a little early."

She stared back at him, shaking her head. "How do you do it? Isn't it exhausting having a target on your back all the time? I mean, you worry about things that, until I met you, I thought only existed in the movies. How do you know who to trust?"

"Well, fortunately, the people closest to me have been in my inner circle a long time and have proven their loyalty time and time again. Still, they all are still scrutinized and monitored for anything I would deem a threat, but so far, they've taken good care of me. Doesn't necessarily mean I let my guard down—you're the only one I can truly relax with. Dante is a close second."

She reached for his hand across the table. "I like that you can relax with me."

He brought her knuckles to his mouth. "Me, too."

Later that night as they lay wrapped in each other's embrace with the moonlight reflecting off her hair, she whispered, "This past week has been like a dream come true. I never knew I could feel so happy." She kissed his chest softly. "Thank you."

"I've loved every minute with you. I can't tell you how much I've loved showing you Europe and seeing it through your eyes. It was like experiencing it for the first time again. We definitely need to schedule more time here."

"I don't care where we are, as long as I'm with you."

Fuck me. This woman—his wife—never ceased to amaze him.

"I'm not going anywhere, *mi amor.*"

"I was thinking... Maybe when we get back... About me maybe going off the pill? I mean, who knows how long it could take for the hormones to get out of my system so I could get pregnant..."

Except for softly stroking her hair, Ramon lay perfectly still, afraid to spook her and make her change her mind. She lifted her head to look at his face. "What do you think?"

He stared down at her angelic face. "I think I would love to put my baby in your belly. But are you sure that's what you want? You had your doubts before."

She put her head back on his chest. "Never surer."

"You're not scared... because of what happened with Madison?"

"Of course I'm scared. But I trust you when you tell me you'll take care of us and keep us safe."

He flipped her over onto her back and hovered over her to stare into her eyes.

"I will, I promise. I will never let anything harm you—or our future children. You mean the world to me."

"You mean the world to me, too. I love you, Ramon. I want to have a family with you."

I love you. The words he'd been too much of a chicken shit—or ego maniac, he wasn't sure which—to utter, but had felt in his soul. And his beautiful, brave wife just said them without hesitation.

"God, I love you, too, Sophia Leigh Castle Guzman. So fucking much it scares me."

He leaned down and captured her lips with his, taking his time to explore her mouth with his tongue while pressing his growing erection against her.

"We should probably practice making a baby..."

"If we're doing this again," she murmured against his lips. "And believe me, I *want* to do this again, we're going to have to use the coconut oil this time."

They'd used almost whole jar in the last seven days. Granted, he'd been heavy handed with his pours, but they'd had *a lot* of sex. This would make it the fifth time *today*. Before marrying her, he had sex maybe an average of five times a *month*. Sophia wasn't the only one who appreciated the oil.

Instead of letting him retrieve it off the nightstand, she sat up and got it herself, then pushed his shoulder so he collapsed on his back, where she straddled him at the waist.

With a glint in her eye, she slowly unscrewed the top while watching his face.

"You sexy bitch," he growled.

She just smirked and scooted down so her bare pussy was against his thigh, then proceeded to drizzle the lubricant on his cock, that was jutting straight in the air—he could still smell her pussy on it from their last round.

With his dick sufficiently greased up, his wife-turned-sex-kitten slowly stroked his shaft—starting at the base and working up, then circled his head with her thumb before going back down. She took extra care to press the vein along the underside of his shaft. He watched, mesmerized, as her hands stroked him, then let out a low moan.

"Fuuuuck, that feels good."

She continued looking at his face as she worked his cock, only pausing when she poured more oil on him.

With one hand, she reached down to caress his balls that were also nice and slippery.

"Baby, you need to stop, or you're going to make me come."

"But, I want you to come."

"You don't want me to fuck you?"

"I'm pretty sure I owe you one or ten," she said with a wink and a smirk.

Flashpoint

Ramon leaned his head back on the pillow, closed his eyes, and let his hot wife finish her amazing hand job.

Life was fucking good. *It's good to be king.*

Chapter Thirty-One

Sophia

"I should probably go to San Francisco and pack my apartment," Sophia said at breakfast the day after they returned from their honeymoon.

Not that she needed anything—she'd bought new, designer everything, right down to underwear—even yoga pants. Which, after wearing them for an afternoon, decided she wouldn't do that again. She couldn't tell a difference between her usual fifteen-dollar ones and the one-hundred-dollar ones she'd bought at the high-end fashion boutiques in San Diego that she'd always wanted to shop in but could never afford. Now, the store owners were sending her texts to let her know about new arrivals.

Still, she didn't like leaving things unfinished, and her abandoned apartment hung over head.

"I should also pop into work while I'm there."

"Do you want me to go with you?"

"No, I'll be fine. I should only be gone a few days."

"I'll have Jesús make your travel arrangements—when do you want to leave?"

"I was thinking tomorrow?"

He nodded his head. "I'll send Alejandro and Chachi with you." She opened her mouth to protest and quickly closed it when she saw him looking back at her with a set jaw and raised eyebrows. He wasn't going to change his mind. He reached across the table and squeezed her hand. "Try not to be more than one night, *mi amor*. I don't think I'll be able to sleep without you next to me."

Later that morning, she sat poolside and did some work—including emailing her boss to let him know she'd be in the day after tomorrow. She also sent an email to HR, letting them know her name change and new address, as well as her new 'in case of emergency' contact. She left her parents as the beneficiary for her life insurance and 401k, should something happen to her. Ramon didn't need her money—but the modest totals in her accounts would make a difference to her parents.

Jesús stopped by with her itinerary. They were flying commercial—first class, tomorrow morning. "I've arranged for a team of movers to be at your apartment at one o'clock."

"I don't think movers are really necessary. I don't have much I need to move, other than my clothes and a few personal things—and I can just ship whatever I can't fit in suitcases to bring back with me. The big stuff, like my furniture, I'll donate—along with my linens and dishes."

"The movers will take care of all that. You'll just need to point and tell them what's going where."

"I'm capable of packing my apartment, you know. It's not that big."

"Sorry, Señora. Boss' orders."

She glanced down at the sheet he'd handed her. "We're staying at the *Fairmont*? Why?"

The Fairmont was the most expensive hotel in the San Francisco area—by far. He looked at her with a smirk, like it was obvious being rich was still something she was getting used to.

But the price wasn't why she was concerned.

"It's nowhere near my apartment or my job."

"You'll have a driver."

"Have you ever experienced San Francisco traffic?"

"I imagine it's a lot like LA's."

"Isn't there anything closer that Ramon would approve of?"

"He wants you staying at the best. Not only do higher-end hotels tend to be more willing to cooperate with our security team, but they just tend to be safer in general. And their staff are usually extra nosy and keep an eye on things."

"I just realized... my car. I'm going to need to drive it down here."

Jesús smiled and took a deep breath, like she was trying his patience. Apparently, he thought her Volkswagen didn't exactly belong in Ramon's garage. But she bought Olaf—named for the white exterior—brand new when she landed her job in San Francisco—her first grownup job. He was coming to San Diego with her; she didn't care who she had to fight.

Her determination must have shown on her face, because Jesús sighed under his breath before saying with a polite smile, "I'll arrange to have it shipped."

"I'm capable of driving it..."

This time his sigh was loud and deliberate. "Señora, we both know your husband would never approve of that. In fact, if I even mentioned it, I think he would fire me on the spot. So, for the sake of my job and sanity, would you please just accept that you're married to a billionaire now, and while yes, you are more than capable, there are just some things you can no longer do—either because of appearances or safety, or both."

Billionaire? Like, with a capital B? She guessed it didn't really make a difference—multi-millionaire, billionaire... it was all still more money than she'd ever dreamed of.

"I know, Jesús. I'm trying. Be patient; it's all still new to me."

His shoulders relaxed, as if he just realized she wasn't purposefully being difficult. "Of course, Señora."

"I'll be ready to go tomorrow morning bright and early. Thank you for making all the arrangements. I hope you don't think I'm ungrateful for everything you've done, because I'm not. I really do appreciate it."

His smile was genuine this time. "*Claro que sí.* Anytime."

****

Ramon

Dante video-called him as he finished packing an overnight bag. Sophia had left an hour before, and Ramon was scheduled to be on the next plane to San Francisco. No fucking way was he sleeping without her.

"The Ritz security sent still photos from their video footage. It looks like Raquel Torres."

"Jesus, is the U.S. government in a hiring freeze? They can't even send a new agent—one we haven't seen before?" Ramon huffed in disbelief.

"Who knows what the method to their madness is. But Bella thinks Raquel has convinced someone that she's an expert on us—well, particularly you."

"They seriously believe because I fucked her one night, that makes her an expert? I knew who she was the whole time and gave her a bunch of bullshit intel. She should have been fired; that's how worthless the information was. Not given more assignments with me."

Dante chuckled. "Well, you must have done something right… she came back for more."

Ramon laughed at the innuendo. "She left satisfied—I'm not a barbarian."

"Maybe you should have been. This almost feels personal. Crazy chicks are dangerous enough, but crazy chicks with a badge and gun? Keep your guard up."

All the more reason he needed to get to his wife. Not that he didn't trust Chachi and Alejandro to keep her safe—he'd just feel better if he were with her, too.

Flashpoint

"I'll talk to you tomorrow night when I get back from San Francisco. Sophia left this morning to pack her apartment, so I'm on the next plane out to surprise her."

"I never thought I'd see the day..."

He glared at his nephew through the screen. "What do you mean?"

"You are over the moon for this woman."

"Well, no shit. She's my wife."

"Something else I never thought I'd see."

Ramon's brow furrowed deeper, and Dante quickly backpedaled.

"Not that I'm not happy about it. I am. I think she's the best thing to ever happen to you. Just... the way you always talked... I thought you'd be a bachelor forever. Then you shock us all and marry Sophia two days after meeting her."

"I just knew she was the one for me."

"You two are perfect for each other. I'm happy for you, *Tío*. We'll talk when you get back—we need to discuss strategy for New Orleans."

"I haven't changed my mind about you going, *Sobrino*. But we'll talk."

With that, he ended the call and rushed out the door to make his plane and surprise his wife. He hoped Sophia would be as happy to see him as he was going to be to see her.

Chapter Thirty-Two

Sophia

They made it to her apartment faster than normal. Alejandro was much more skilled at maneuvering through traffic than she was.

"You guys don't have to come up. It's a pretty small space."

Alejandro cocked his head and looked back at her from the driver's seat like she should know better.

She shrugged and put her hand on the door handle. "Don't say I didn't warn you."

They walked into her little apartment, and he teased, "You weren't kidding."

She hadn't been there in almost two months and looked at it through their eyes. Her closet in San Diego was bigger than the entire space. Now granted, her closet was obscene and only about an eighth full, but still… The apartment was spotless, with little clutter—it had to be. A small area would amplify any mess. The shabby chic furniture gave the place a homey feel, and she'd always felt comfortable here. Best of all—it was *hers*. All by herself. No one helped her get the place, and she hadn't relied on anyone to keep it.

Chachi set the bags he was carrying down and asked, "How can we help?"

In addition to the two empty suitcases she'd brought, Jesús had sent her two companions—she refused to call them

Flashpoint

bodyguards—with two empty suitcases each for her to also fill. Well, they had been empty except their weapons they had to check. But they'd quickly retrieved them as soon as their bags arrived. She was impressed at how discreetly they'd tucked the guns in their waistbands right at the luggage carousel—and no one had been the wiser.

When she realized that their empty luggage was intended for her to fill, she simply smiled. Jesús was Ramon's right-hand man for a reason—the guy thought of everything, anticipated everything, and never missed a beat. Sophia had no idea how much Ramon paid him, but she'd venture a guess that it was a lot. Her husband had no trouble paying what he felt something, or someone, was worth—and Jesús seemed invaluable.

"There's nothing for you to do. No offense, but I don't want you helping me with my drawers and closet, and the movers are supposed to be bringing boxes for things like dishes and linens, so..." She looked around the tiny apartment that was cramped by the two big men. "Make yourselves at home. I have magazines on the coffee table, and the TV remote is right there." She pointed to the remote in the little pocket on the side of the couch.

She'd managed to empty her closet—filling two black garbage bags of clothes for Goodwill, so she still had two suitcases left for the contents of her drawers. She looked at her cute bedding and felt a twinge of sadness. She'd felt so decadent when she bought it earlier this year with her bonus money. She earned it, she'd reasoned at the time to justify the expense. Now, she was just supposed to donate it to Goodwill without a second thought.

This was the end of an era in her life, and it seemed to be happening too fast. While she was excited about what came next with Ramon, there was a tiny seed in her gut reminding her that her new, opulent lifestyle had nothing to do with her accomplishments, only her husband's. That's what prompted her to pack her bedding in one of the remaining empty suitcases. She somehow wanted to hold on to who she used to be, even if it was just for a little while—until she was ready to let go, on *her* schedule.

There was a knock on the door, and she glanced at her Fitbit. The movers were early.

She moved to open the door, but Chachi politely stood in front of her with a smile. "I'll get it."

It took everything in her not to roll her eyes, but she was successful, returning his polite smile with one of her own.

It wasn't the movers on the other side of the door—it was her husband. She let out a squeal. "Oh my god!" and skirted by Chachi to throw her arms around Ramon's neck, stand on her tiptoes, and plant kisses on his face, murmuring, "What. Are. You. Doing. Here?" between each kiss.

His hands came around her waist, and he smiled brightly. "I came to be with you." Then chuckled, "Are you glad to see me?"

She dropped to her flat feet. "Nope."

That elicited loud laughter from him, and he ushered her inside and closed the door. "Well then, I think I'd like to see my welcome if you had been happy to see me."

Sophia hugged him around the middle and rested her face on his chest. "Of course I'm happy to see you, silly."

"So, this is your place…"

****

Ramon

Her little studio apartment was exactly how he imagined it would be—small, but charming with modest décor she probably bought at Target, Pottery Barn, or from a thrift store and refurbished. There were open suitcases on the floor and full canvas bags on her dinette set chairs, and with Alejandro and Chachi seated on her loveseat and only chair, the only place for him was to lean against her tiny kitchen counter.

Alejandro stood, quickly followed by Chachi. "If you don't need our help, we're going to wait outside."

When the door closed behind them, Ramon took her in his embrace and kissed her tenderly on the mouth.

"I'm so glad you're here," she whispered when he broke the kiss and leaned his forehead against hers.

"I didn't want to be away from you, even for a night. And, as you've so eloquently reminded me in the past, I am the boss, so… here I am."

"I'm sure you have a ton of work to catch up on, after being gone for ten days. I know even I'm behind, and my job isn't nearly as important as yours."

"My laptop is in the car with Gabriel and Jorge. I can get some work done at the hotel. But I'll worry about that later." He looked around her space. "I'm here now. How can I help?"

"There's not much left that I can do before the movers get here. I'm assuming they'll have boxes for the things I can't bring on the plane. I was originally planning to ship the rest, but I think I can just put the boxes in my Jetta and bring them down that way."

"What time are the movers coming?"

"Not until one."

"You want to go to lunch? Show me around your city?"

"We can grab a bite at the deli down the street, but I want to be back when they get here so I can supervise and show them what I want done." She stroked his jawline with the back of her fingertips and laid a feather light kiss on his neck. "But I'll be happy to show you around tonight."

"It's a date." Ramon reached for her hand and motioned toward the door. "Let's go get lunch."

****

Sophia

"Which cart do you want the sofa on?" the burly man in the coveralls asked.

The movers had been taking boxes to her car and to the truck going to Goodwill on different wheeled carts all afternoon.

Obviously, the loveseat wouldn't fit in her car, but he just needed to hear her say it to cover his bases.

She sighed. "Goodwill, I guess."

Ramon took her hand and pulled her to his side. "What's the matter, *mi amor*?"

She shrugged, feeling a little ashamed at being so melancholy and worried Ramon would misinterpret her mixed feelings as not wanting to be with him. "This apartment—and everything in it—represents my whole adult life, and I'm just giving it all away."

"You don't have to give anything away, baby. Well, except the mattress. If you want to bring everything down to San Diego, we can set your new office up with your furniture."

"Even my dishes?"

"If you want."

The fact that he wasn't expecting her to get rid of everything somehow made her see things in a different light, and she felt lighter.

She thought about it for a second as she looked around, then shook her head. "No, I'm sure this will all be a great find for someone who needs it more than I do."

She opened the suitcase with her bedding ensemble and pulled it out, her arms overflowing with the fabric as she placed it in an empty cardboard box. "Here, this should go on the donation cart, too."

Ramon stroked her arm. "Are you sure, baby? We can take anything you want back."

"I'm sure. I don't need it anymore."

His smile was tender, and he pulled her to his side and kissed her temple. "Tell you what. Why don't you redecorate the houses however you want them. Make them *ours*."

"I'd love that, but I really am behind with work..."

"Hire an interior decorator. I didn't mean for you to take care of everything." He whispered in her ear, "I don't know if you've realized this yet, but we're rich. We can afford that."

It suddenly occurred to her that keeping her job was, well, stupid. But, she needed to do something.

"Does Guzman Enterprises have a charitable foundation?"

"No."

"Do you want one? That I can run?"

A slow smile spread across his face. "I would love that. We'll have to have a lot of business meetings though, so you can keep me apprised of what's going on. And we'll need to be naked."

She shook her head at him with a grin. "Do you take all your meetings like that?"

"Only with my wife."

Flashpoint

"I'm going to want a salary and goals that you want me to meet. I don't want this to just be some fluffy thing to keep me occupied."

"You're going to want a salary? How much? I'm assuming benefits too."

She shrugged. "I'm not sure how much. I'll have to research what other foundation managers make."

He wrapped an arm around her waist and growled in her ear, "How are your negotiation skills?"

She cupped his growing erection in her palm. "They seem like they're pretty good."

"Let's put them to the test."

Chapter Thirty-Three

Ramon
He fucked his wife on the little counter in her kitchen after she negotiated a five-hundred-thousand-dollar salary. He'd wanted to give her two million, and she countered with a hundred thousand.

"Sweetheart... I don't think you understand how contract negotiations work..."

"I do. I just can't imagine I'll need that much, considering all my expenses are already taken care of."

"Take the salary, baby."

She shook her head, and they eventually settled on half a million, but only after she convinced him in a way only she could.

He'd never doubt her ability to negotiate again. Although, it was unusual to negotiate for lower than his original offer.

They left the nearly empty apartment, and Sophia took him to all her favorite places in San Francisco before they headed back to the hotel. The four bodyguards kept a respectful distance, but maintained a sharp lookout, not that he anticipated any problems, but it was good to be prepared.

They continued their ritual of getting ready for bed and talking about their day—even though they'd been together the entire day.

"As excited as I am about getting started with the foundation," she said as she rubbed lotion on her elbows, "I'm dreading having to give my notice tomorrow. They've been so willing to work with me; I kind of feel like a jerk bailing on them like this."

He dried his face with one of the hotel's hand towels. "So, agree to finish your project but tell them you're not taking on any new ones, if that will make you feel better."

She froze and looked at him through the mirror. "That's actually a great idea. How did you get to be so smart?"

He felt the corner of his mouth lift. "You may find this hard to believe, but I'm not just another pretty face. I actually have a few degrees from some prestigious schools tucked in a drawer somewhere."

"Where did you go to school?"

"I got my undergrad degree in Business Administration from the University of Michigan, and my MBA from Colombia."

"Aren't you fancy," she teased. "I just went to Stanford for a computer science degree."

"I know."

She narrowed her eyes at him. "How do you know?"

"I ran a background check on you, baby, remember?"

"It had where I went to school?"

He shot her a look. "Sophia. Come on. Of course it did; it had everything. High school, middle school, first job... given how many people are trying to infiltrate my inner circle, my guys are very thorough. You were too good to be true, *mi amor*. I had to be sure."

She sighed. "I get it. I probably should have run one on you, too."

Ramon tried not to flinch at the idea.

He paid a lot of money to have his digital footprint as small as possible, but when Madison was kidnapped, that opened the whole organization up to internet speculation.

Fortunately, no rogue keyboard warriors got a wild hair in their ass to try to investigate his business or him. That would have been unfortunate for whomever attempted such a suicide mission—something he suspected most people understood. The cartel didn't play by the rules—and they had the means to bankroll hunting people down and eliminating them with no remorse. Still, there were the gossip sites that speculated that Guzman Enterprises was just a cartel front, but they offered no proof, so Dante convinced Ramon they were relatively harmless and didn't need to be dealt with.

He might come to regret that decision.

Chapter Thirty-Four

Sophia
She left her boss' office feeling a lot lighter than when she'd originally gone in. He'd been gracious about accepting her resignation, especially when she said she would finish her current project for him.

"You have a job here, anytime, Sophia," he'd said at the doorway of his office when he walked her out.

"I appreciate that, Garrett. I've loved working here."

"Just send me an email outlining what we talked about, so we can make it official with HR."

"I will. Thank you again for everything."

She turned to leave and had taken less than three steps when Kevin popped out of a nearby cubicle.

"You're quitting?"

"Yes, after I complete this project."

"Why?"

"I'm going to start and oversee my husband's charitable foundation."

He stared at her for a beat. "Then it is true. I mean, I guess I knew when you quit answering my texts altogether. Although I was a little surprised that you didn't even respond when I offered you congratulations. The Sophia I knew would never have ignored someone's best wishes."

She furrowed her brows in confusion. "I never got any texts from you. The last time I heard from you was…" She paused, trying to remember exactly when she received a text from Kevin. It was the morning she was at the airport.

"Sophia, I've been texting you almost every day since... the night you, um, left. Apologizing, begging you to take me back. Every day."

He pulled his phone from his pocket and showed her the pages and pages of texts he'd sent—all with no response.

"Send me one, now."

He did, but it never showed up on her phone.

"Did you block me?" he asked in disbelief.

"No, of course not."

She looked for him in her contacts, but he was nowhere to be found. Her wheels turning. When the chief had taken her phone at the airport, and she didn't get it back for a few days... all her messages had been gone. She'd just assumed it was because she was in Mexico, and her phone carrier didn't like that, making things go wonky. Maybe that wasn't really the case.

He looked over her shoulder at her phone screen and huffed a mirthless laugh. "I guess that's to be expected when you're married to the leader of the cartel. I should probably be thankful I've only been blocked on your phone, nothing worse."

"What are you talking about?"

"The Guzman cartel, Sophia. The little girl who was killed? You remember. You're married to the biggest drug lord in Mexico—although I'm still trying to figure out how *that* could have happened."

That couldn't be true. Ramon was the president of Guzman Enterprises... not the cartel. That was ludicrous.

Memories of when Madison was kidnapped... how she, Iva, and Tammy became obsessed with the case—reading everything they could and talking about it whenever they got together. How they even went to Mass to pray for her safe return and mourned her death as if she were a friend. Some of the articles had alluded to the reason she was kidnapped was revenge from a rival cartel—that her father was some high-ranking cartel member.

How could she have forgotten that?

Because she'd *met* Dante, Madison's father. There was no way he was involved in the drug trade. And Ramon. He was head of the family business, and the family business wasn't drugs. It wasn't possible.

She felt the color drain from her face, and the room began to spin.

Kevin, who had dated Sophia for over three years, knew by her expression that he'd struck a nerve. "Good luck with your blood money *charity*. I'm not exactly sure how you're going to reconcile that with your conscience."

She blurted out the first thing that came to mind, from one of her favorite YouTube videos—a little girl scolding her dad. "Worry about yourself, Kevin," then turned on her heel to escape.

"I still love you, Soph," he called after her as she hurried past the rows of cubicles. "You can come back to me. I'll help you."

Fuck you, Kevin. I don't need your 'help.'

"Asshole," she muttered under her breath as she pushed open the glass door to the brick courtyard with the fountain in front. Alejandro and Chachi had been sitting on the wall next to the water feature and immediately stood when she made her hasty exit from the building.

The two men escorted her to the waiting car, and she realized... she might have been fooling herself.

Juan Diego's comments about not asking what Ramon did for a living... bodyguards wherever she went... the obscene wealth... servants sworn to secrecy...

What had she done? She'd just quit her job to go to work for her *mobster* husband?

And I gave away my furniture!

Alejandro looked at her through the rearview mirror. "Everything okay, *Señora?*"

She mustered up as genuine a smile as she could. "Everything's fine. Thanks."

****

Ramon

The second she stepped through the airport's sliding doors he knew something was wrong. Her posture was ramrod straight, and she refused to look at him as they maneuvered through the airline's first-class line.

"Everything go okay?"

"Yeah. It went fine. I think I'm going to call Garrett tomorrow though. I may have been a little hasty about quitting. A foundation seems like a big undertaking."

She had been excited last night when she chatted nonstop about which projects she wanted to start first, and which ones she wanted to tackle down the road.

"What's wrong, *mi amor*? Last night, you couldn't wait to get started.

"Nothing. I just think starting your foundation might not be for me."

He watched her face closely, trying to figure out what was going on. Other than refusing to look at him, she wasn't giving anything away.

"Huh. Why the change of heart?"

She glanced at his men behind them in line. "Let's talk about this when we get home."

He wasn't waiting the three hours it would take before they were back at the estate. She'd told him her girlfriends weren't able to get away to see her on such short notice, but they'd probably be coming down for a visit soon.

"Did you see anyone else today besides Garrett?"

She finally glanced at him, except it was with complete contempt. He may have preferred her not looking at him.

"As a matter of fact, I saw Kevin. He's been trying to reach me, yet for some reason, his messages haven't come through on my phone."

There it is. She'd figured out Ramon had fucked with her phone and essentially erased her ex-boyfriend from existence.

Sorry, not sorry.

Ramon hadn't needed Kevin messing with her head—not when he was trying to convince her to stay married to him.

"Did you show him your ring?" he asked with a grin, like he was unaffected by her open hostility toward him.

"No."

One word. Then she went back to ignoring him.

Well, shit.

"Sophia, I'm sorry, but I—"

She cut him off, hissing, "I told you I didn't want to talk about it now."

"Okay," he said in his most contrite voice. He knew he would have to serve his penance and act remorseful—although he'd do it again without a second thought. Still, that attitude wouldn't get him back in his wife's good graces.

They made it through security and waited in the terminal to board. She still wasn't speaking to him.

"Lupita sent me a picture of Daisy…" he said, flashing his phone screen at her. There was no way she'd be able to resist seeing pictures of her dog.

Flashpoint

She gave him a wary look but took his phone anyway and glanced down with a smile at her scruffy dog looking back at her.

Her mouth tightened, and she handed him back his phone. "Why didn't she send it to me? Is she not on the list of approved people I can receive texts from? Like I'm a goddamn child."

The fact that she swore didn't bode well for him. She had to be *really* mad at him.

"I can explain."

"Ramon." Her voice was eerily calm. "Unless you want me to make a huge scene right here in the airport, I suggest you drop it until we get home like I asked."

"You're right. I'm sorry."

They sat in silence for a few more minutes, and he heard her mutter, "And for the record, there's no explaining this."

****

Sophia

"Look, Sophia, I'm sorry that I had your phone hacked to have that asshat removed and blocked. I saw what he'd written—I didn't want him fucking with your head anymore."

She'd walked in their bedroom first, followed quickly by Ramon. Their wing was empty except them; away from where anyone would overhear the two of them arguing unless that person was eavesdropping.

She whirled around. "You *saw* what he'd written? You read my *private* messages? How would you like it if I did that to you, Ramon? Probably not very well since you're a goddamn drug lord."

If she was hoping for a shocked reaction, then admission of guilt, she was sorely disappointed, because that's not at all what happened.

He cocked his head and chuckled. The bastard actually chuckled. "Did you just say I'm a drug lord? Like... Viagra, Prozac, Amoxicillin...?"

"Don't play cute, Ramon."

"I'm sorry, *mi amor*, I just don't know where this is coming from—well, I have an idea where it's coming from, but no idea what the basis of this accusation is."

"Don't *mi amor* me. I remember now when Madison was kidnapped—all the newspapers said the Guzmans were being targeted by *rival* drug cartels. You don't have *rival* drug cartels unless you're also one."

Again, he laughed. "And what newspapers were these, Sophia? TMZ? The Enquirer? The Weekly World News? No reputable publication has suggested such a thing—because they know I'd sue the pants off them, and win."

"Your brother was murdered, and your grandniece was abducted... This isn't normal—even for rich people."

"You think Jeff Bezos doesn't worry about being abducted? Or his mistress? Of course he does; it's just not something that's advertised—but I guarantee he takes precautions just like I do."

"How have you made so much money, Ramon?"

"I told you, Guzman Enterprises is a conglomerate—just like Warren Buffet; we own many, many businesses. I can show you the books, and you can see for yourself."

She tried to remain skeptical, but he was making it hard. He was so assured and confident, not a trace of worry, and he had an answer for everything.

Part of her was relieved, but there was a tiny sliver in her brain that still wondered.

When he cautiously approached her and tucked her hair behind her ear, she didn't pull away.

"I love you, my little American nerd. You have to trust me."

"Why? You obviously don't trust me—reading my messages and hacking my phone. You can't do that, Ramon. You crossed the line."

He sighed. "You're right—I did. I'm sorry. In my defense, although you're not going to think it's much of a defense, I took your phone to put a tracker on it." She opened her mouth to let him have it, but he held his hand up so he could continue, "*Not* to keep tabs on you because I don't trust you, but if something happened to you... that would help me find you. I promise I haven't looked at where you've gone, and I won't unless in an emergency." He stared in her eyes, and she could feel the emotion in his words. "Sophia, I would put a tracker in your big toe if you'd let me. When Madison disappeared, I watched Dante wracked with grief and climbing the walls because he was helpless to find her. I didn't fully understand how he could love someone so much—until I met you. I would die if something happened to you, *mi amor*. I'm sorry that I didn't tell you—but I'm not sorry that I did it."

"You promised you'd be honest with me."

"I know. I'm sorry. I'm just trying to keep you safe."

"You can't do that by lying to me. Is there anything else I need to know, Ramon?"

He swallowed hard then shook his head. She realized that was one of his tells.

And yet, she chose to ignore it. She did love him and *wanted* to believe him. Maybe if she wanted it hard enough, it'd be true.

Chapter Thirty-Five

Ramon

Sophia seemed to have forgiven him... again, and life was back to normal. While it weighed on him to lie to her about the cartel, he just couldn't bring himself to be truthful. The risk was too great.

He couldn't lose her.

If that meant keeping her in the dark, that's what he'd do.

Ramon was already seated at breakfast when she arrived the next morning. Instead of taking her normal seat, she came around to the back of his chair and slid her hands along the front of his chest while she whispered, "Good morning, *mi querido*," in his ear.

He covered her hand with his and smiled. "Good morning, *mi amor*," then tugged on her wrist to bring her around his chair and onto his lap.

"I'm sorry I was asleep when you came to bed last night."

"I'm sorry I've been neglectful this week. We've been wrapping up preparations for the New Orleans meeting tomorrow."

"What time are you leaving?"

"We're flying on Dante's jet."

"We? Is Dante going, too?"

Dante had acquiesced and allowed John, his lifelong friend and second-in-command, to take his place, along with

Jacob—the man who led Madison's rescue. Jacob had been transitioning out of the mercenary business and was a partner in some of Guzman Enterprises' legitimate pot dispensaries east of the Mississippi but had agreed to attend as a favor to Dante. Well, probably more accurately, Dante's wife—who Jacob had worked with when they were both in the CIA.

Ramon felt confident going into tomorrow's meeting.

"No, it will be me and John, and we're meeting an associate who lives in New Orleans before the meeting."

"What's it about? You've been planning it since I met you."

"It's with a Colombian agency who wants to supply us with product. But, we're not sure if they can deliver. Not to mention, Dante suspects they were involved with the kidnapping of Madison. So rather than make a deal with them, he wants their organization destroyed."

"Oh my gosh. That sounds… complicated. You can't do business with them if Dante feels that strongly about it."

"Well, Dante acknowledges we don't know for certain if it was the Colombian business or another business in Mexico trying to take our market share. Part of the reason I'm taking the meeting is to see if they acknowledge any responsibility."

"Where are you staying again? Will you be able to get out and do some sightseeing?"

"At the Ritz. Probably the most sightseeing I'll be doing is in the back of a car. We've got the meeting tomorrow, and then a breakfast meeting the next day about some of our pot dispensaries, then I'll be home in time for a late lunch with you."

"Can you take a long breakfast with me today?" she cooed seductively before kissing along his jawline. "You came to bed so late last night... and, my Fitbit says I'm ovulating."

"You want to try to make a baby?"

She opened a few of his top buttons and slipped her hand inside his shirt. "Well, or at least practice."

****

Sophia

With a grin, he stood with her in his arms, murmuring, "I would love to practice," before setting her feet on the ground.

He took her hand, and they walked toward the house, running into Blanca wheeling their cart of breakfast out to them.

"We'll have that brought upstairs later," he told the cook with a smile.

"Of course, Mr. Guzman."

"I feel bad. She went to all that trouble to make us breakfast..."

"Don't feel bad; trust me—there are plenty of people on this property who are happy we're missing it. It won't go to waste, that's for sure. Besides, that's what Blanca gets paid—a lot of money—for."

That helped ease her guilt.

So did the feel of his arms as they wrapped around her the minute he closed the bedroom door.

He kissed her bare shoulders and gestured to the turquoise and chartreuse sundress with the spaghetti straps she wore, braless. "Did you wear this just for me?"

Sophia lifted the hem to reveal she wasn't wearing any panties either.

"Maaaaybe."

Ramon pulled her against him, staring down at her. "Have I told you today how much I fucking adore you?" he asked with a crooked grin.

"No, you haven't."

"I should probably just show you then..."

He lowered his mouth to hers, and she let out a contented sigh, gripping his shirt front in her fists when he slanted his mouth to deepen the kiss.

She felt the zipper on the back of her sundress lower, then the fabric slid down her body to pool at her feet. He stepped back and stared at her, naked before him.

"Oh, *mi amor*. You are so beautiful."

Had any other man swept his eyes from her face, down her body to her feet, and up again, Sophia would have instinctively tried to cover herself. But with Ramon, she

Flashpoint

basked in his lustful gaze, feeling empowered. He left her with no doubt about how much he wanted her.

Closing the gap between them, she reached down to finish unbuttoning his shirt that she'd started at the breakfast table, then untucked it from his pants to pull it open and expose his gorgeous core. Planting soft kisses on his chest, Sophia gently raked her nails down his six-pack to his waistband and unbuckled his belt—impressing herself that she managed to do it as well as unbutton his slacks with just one hand.

He took a small step away from her and toed off his shoes, then unzipped his pants and dropped them to the floor, tugging his socks off after stepping out of the discarded pants.

Now they were both naked, and she turned and pulled back the comforter of their already-made bed, then let out a nervous giggle as she scampered between the sheets.

Ramon was right behind and pulled her to him—their naked skin touching felt like heaven. She'd never felt safer or more content than when he held her.

"I can't believe I'm about to actually *try* to get pregnant," she whispered out loud. "I feel like I've spent half my life doing the exact opposite."

She didn't know what his soft smile meant.

"I love you, Sophia Leigh Castle Guzman."

"I love you, too, Ramon Esteban Guzman."

Hovering over her body, he kissed the spot right below her ear—*the* spot, then dragged his lips down her goosebump-covered neck and chest until he reached her stiff nipples.

He swirled his tongue along one pink peak, slipping his arm underneath her back to draw her body closer to his mouth as he sucked her flesh into his mouth—causing her to moan out loud. He released her with a *pop!* then alternated to her other boob, repeating the process.

Sophia loved his mouth on her body. He always seemed to know exactly how to drive her wild—whichever body part he attended to.

His cock was situated between her thighs, and she moved her hips to draw him to her entrance. She was already wet and ready for him.

"Please, Ramon," she whimpered. "I need to feel you inside me."

He alternated boobs again, suckling her into his mouth as he gently thrust his cock inside her pussy, causing her to let out a small gasp of pleasure.

"Oh my god, baby," she moaned. "You feel so good."

Cupping her face in his hands, he stared into her eyes, then brought his lips down on hers. Sophia weaved her hands around his back and clung to him while she pressed her hips up.

He broke the kiss and stared down at her face. "Fuuuck, Soph."

Flashpoint

With slow, gentle thrusts, he began moving in and out of her, burrowing his face into her neck—his massive frame enveloping her.

Sophia pressed her hips up, seeking friction on her clit.

Ramon, always in tune with her needs, sat back on his knees and manipulated her nub while he continued his rhythm in and out of her pussy.

Her body went flush, and she tensed her stomach in anticipation of the orgasm that was about to erupt through her.

"Oh my god," she panted. "Oh my god, don't stop, Ramon. Please, don't stop."

Ramon doubled down on his manipulation of her clit, and she arched her back off the bed, letting out a long, "Ohhhh," before her body convulsed.

He held her hips tight and fucked her with abandon, grunting out a long moan as his orgasm quickly followed hers, then collapsed on top of her—taking care not to crush her.

"Holy hell, *mi amor*," he panted with his face in the pillow.

"Yeah," she agreed, her chest heaving.

He rolled off to the side of her, and she felt something cold on her hip. Instinctively, she reached down and realized it was his cum.

On her hip. And on the sheets.

He hadn't cum in her.

"Um, I don't know how they make babies in Mexico," she quipped, trying to mask her disappointment about why he would have done that. "But here in the U.S., you actually have to come inside the woman to get her pregnant."

"I didn't come in you?"

She took his hand and placed it on her hip.

"Oh, babe. Let me get a towel. I'll be right back."

She lay looking at the ceiling. Disappointed, especially since he was leaving in the morning. They could try again tonight, provided he came to bed early enough.

The hormones probably aren't even out of my system, she told herself. Yet, it still bothered her that he hadn't tried. Was it an honest mistake, or did he pull out on purpose?

****

Ramon

He took his time in the bathroom retrieving a towel, using the restroom and washing his hands first. He gripped the vanity and took a deep breath while staring down at the marble design, then looked up at himself in the mirror.

He'd meant to pull out and come on her inner thigh and the outside of her pussy, so she'd think it'd just dribbled out of her, but, obviously, his aim was fucking off.

It wasn't that he didn't want a baby with her. He did. Hell, he was the one who'd suggested it in the first place. But there was this nagging feeling that things between them were going to unravel—she was somehow going to find out he'd been lying about Guzman Enterprises' role in the drug trade, and she would leave him.

And he'd have a kid out there that he'd never know.

The pang he felt at the idea of losing her was bad enough, but if they were to throw a child in the mix... well, that was a recipe for him doing things he didn't want to do.

So, he pulled out rather than risk it.

Ramon could tell she was disappointed, and he hated letting her down, but they needed to remain childless until she knew the truth.

He sighed. Which needed to happen soon if he was going to be a father before fifty.

Chapter Thirty-Six

Sophia
"I've never been to New Orleans before," she said as they stood outside the Escalade.

Hint. Hint.

Gabriel was already in the driver's seat, and Chachi had just put their overnight bags in the back, and Ramon kissed her lips with a grin. "I promise I will take you, soon. Jacob and his wife live there, so I'm sure they'd love to get together sometime."

"Soon, like when? And are we going to stay at the Ritz? Because I've never stayed there either."

He laughed and planted a kiss on her forehead before turning toward the open car door. "Yes, *mi amor*. We'll stay there—or we can stay wherever you want."

"Have a safe trip. I'll see you... tomorrow?"

He was seated in the backseat with his hand on the door to pull it closed, but paused to say, "Tomorrow. We'll have a late lunch. I'll call you tonight."

She couldn't resist giving him one last kiss and leaned in to wrap her arms around his neck as she did. She pulled away, but Ramon held the back of her head while looking into her eyes.

"I love you, *mi mujer*. I'll see you soon."

Sooner than he thinks, she thought while fighting back a grin. She couldn't wait to see his face when she surprised him later.

She had her flight already booked. Now all she needed to do was sneak out of the estate without Alejandro finding out she was gone. Probably easier said than done—but she had a plan.

****

Ramon

"Boss... I don't know how to tell you this. Sophia isn't here. I can't find her anywhere."

He stared at the woman across the lobby from him. "Well, that's because I'm looking right at her."

Ramon heard his youngest lieutenant utter, "Fuuuck."

Yeah, *fuck* was right. Actually, no, *fuck* didn't even come close to summing up this shitstorm.

"Obviously, we've got some issues with security that will need to be straightened out when I get back."

He'd been intentionally vague—enough that they'd all be worried about job security and busting their asses before he even got home—more so than normal. Get them all in the mindset for all the changes that were about to go down.

He was pissed—security should have caught her leaving, but he also knew his little *nerdicita* could be quite resourceful.

Still. So could his enemies. There'd been a breakdown somewhere, and it better be caught and dealt with—preferably before he returned to San Diego, but it would be fixed upon his return.

He stared at Sophia standing in line for the front desk in her cream designer suit, pink scarf, and matching pink shoes. Her hair was down and styled, and she looked like something straight out of the pages of a fashion magazine. She was utterly breathtaking and received more than a few second glances from passersby.

That's my wife, he thought with a wry smile.

And her timing couldn't have been worse... He groaned internally when he saw who was walking toward him. He knew what he had to do—hopefully, Sophia loved him enough to be able to forgive him.

*

Hours earlier, Ramon, John, and Jacob had met at a café down the street from the hotel. Until today, he hadn't seen either man since Madison had gone missing.

"Jacob. Retirement seems to be treating you well. Or is it marriage that has you looking so happy?"

"I think it's marriage since I can't seem to stop working—much to the chagrin of my wife," the former fixer said with a laugh.

"Yes, I imagine your line of work isn't something you can just decide one day to be done with and not go back the next."

"No. But Marcus seems to be the perfect man to replace me. He has a lot more field experience than I ever did and has brought some important connections to the table."

Ramon had a hard time believing *anyone* had more experience or connections than Jacob. He was the man you called when no one else could do the job—and he always delivered. Of course, he was richer than sin because of it, but it was well-earned.

John had been busy looking at his phone with furrowed brows, like he had been the entire plane ride—when he wasn't furiously typing on it with a scowl.

"Everything okay, John?"

"Yeah," he said, schooling his expression before looking up.

"Are you still seeing Layla Hernandez?" Ramon asked.

"Occasionally."

"That's good—keep her happy. We don't need El Rey declaring fucking war over his slighted daughter. Especially when we're gearing up for another war."

"That might be hard to do when he's carrying a torch for someone else," Jacob said with a grin before taking a sip of his drink.

"I told you—we're just friends," John snarled at the other man.

"Yeah, sure. Keep telling yourself that, buddy."

Ramon chimed in, "I don't know who this other woman is that you're 'just friends' with, but Layla better not know about her—and you better just stay friends. For everyone's sake."

Ramon knew exactly who the other woman was—Quinn, Bella's assistant. Rumor was he'd been in love with her since the initial interview where he'd been instrumental in making sure Bella hired her. Quinn had been invaluable to Bella who was very pregnant with Madison when Quinn came on board.

"Not a problem."

Somehow, Ramon wasn't convinced, but that was a problem for another day. Today, they needed to focus on the Colombian cartel, and what they were going to do about them.

"You obviously need to hear them out," Jacob said when they started discussing strategy. "I know what Dante thinks, and I'm still working with my sources to see if the Zetas have somehow teamed up with the Colombians, but there has been zero chatter to substantiate that idea. And if they have, it doesn't make sense for them to ask for a meeting to try to work with you."

"Unless they're planning on double-crossing us," John chimed in before glancing down at his phone again.

Ramon replied, "If that's the case, we need to have the organization sealed tight."

"You need to keep that new bride of yours out of sight." Jacob warned. "Kudos to you so far, there has been minimal talk about your marriage. And I haven't been able to find pictures of her anywhere yet."

"Well, that's a start, but we thought Dante had done a good job keeping Madison and Bella hidden, and look what happened."

Jacob took another drink before responding, "That's why I'm still convinced it was the Zetas. Mexicans talk with other Mexicans... Word could have easily—and innocuously—crossed state lines for the Zetas to learn about her."

"We definitely learned some things—the hard way, unfortunately."

"I hear the staff appreciated the raises, though," John said with a smirk without looking up from his phone.

John wasn't considered 'staff' and received no such raise to his already hefty payouts. He had been Dante's best friend since boarding school, and the two were like brothers. He knew Dante trusted him implicitly, but it was harder for Ramon to do the same since he wasn't blood.

But blood or not, Dante had made sure his friend reaped the benefits of being in the cartel. He was richer than most men could even dream of. Far more than he would have ever achieved as a computer engineer—what he was doing before Dante tapped him to work for him.

Most of Ramon's bitching about John to Dante had been for show to keep his nephew on his toes. Ramon knew John's worth to the organization, and through the years, had grown to rely on him as well.

Today being a prime example.

The three men arrived at the South Americans' hotel suite, flanked by their bodyguards. Four waited outside with the Colombians' bodyguards, while Chachi and Gabriel went inside with them, standing watch at the door while they sat in the living room to conduct business.

It had all been very civilized, and the other four other cartel members had shown respect to the Mexicans—acknowledging the Sinaloans' power and position throughout Mexico, the U.S., and other parts of the world. Still, Ramon's gut told him he didn't want to do business with these men. While the Guzman cartel was far from sainthood, these men seemed to have no code of honor whatsoever.

When Martin, their leader, suggested, "Let's have a drink at the bar in the lobby," Ramon's hackles immediately went up. Why the bar downstairs instead of here?

He cast a glance at Jacob, whose side-eyed look back seemed to indicate he was thinking the same thing. It was John who voiced the question.

"I thought we'd all enjoy a change of scenery and perhaps an opportunity to get something to eat," Martin replied with a polite smile. "Besides, I wasn't sure if you'd take a drink here if I offered it."

No, probably not. And Ramon could fucking use one. He was sure Jacob and John felt the same.

"Why don't we meet you there in thirty minutes? Give us a chance to get checked in and situated." Although, Jesús had already taken care to make sure they were checked in, their bags delivered, and their rooms swept for surveillance equipment. He then stationed more of their men outside to keep watch, so no one went in or out. What Ramon wanted was a chance to debrief with Jacob and John before heading to the lobby bar to meet with the other group.

When they were back in Ramon's suite, Jacob—without even hearing what the other two men were thinking—suggested, "I think you're going to want to consider that offer. Or at the very least, leave them dangling on the hook while you get all your loose ends shored up. If you turn them down, they're going to team up with the Zetas..."

"If they haven't already," John snorted.

"If they haven't already," Jacob acknowledged. "But I'm skeptical they have. They're still weak from when we paid them a visit in Cartagena and blew their operation to shit. You either need to hold your nose and make a deal with them, or you need to cripple them again before they make a deal with the Zetas."

"If they haven't already," John added again.

Ramon grimaced. They'd gone to war before when Enrique was still alive. It was ugly and something Ramon had been trying to avoid. He didn't like doing business with no code of honor, but turning them down meant they'd team up with the Zetas—who always looked for an opportunity to encroach on their territory. He had a feeling it would get a lot uglier before it got better. Except this time, he now had Sophia to worry about.

"Let's go have that drink."

*

The Colombians were already seated when the trio arrived, bodyguards still in tow, but relatively discreet. His men were good at that when they needed to be, and Ramon appreciated it.

When the waitress brought their round of drinks, Martin raised his glass and offered a toast. "To a budding new partnership."

The three Mexicans gave a half-hearted, "Cheers," then clinked glasses with the rest of the table.

"Your new bride, Ramon. She's enchanting, no?"

Ramon was sure to keep his expression neutral. He couldn't let Martin know that Sophia was a point of vulnerability for him. He picked up his glass with a casual grin and replied, "I like to think so," before taking a drink.

"I met her this afternoon when she was having lunch in the hotel's restaurant. She was waiting for you to arrive so she could surprise you. Did it work?"

He had no idea what the fuck was going on but went along with it, not wanting to show weakness. "She's full of surprises."

"You're a smart man—sending your wife to the spa for a week. Was your mistress in town?"

He knew not to clench his jaw. That was a sure tell that Martin had struck a nerve, and Ramon knew it. Instead, he clenched his fists tight under the table as Jacob chimed in, laughing, "Just be careful not to send them all to the same spa at the same time," then cast a look at Ramon that said, *Cool it. We'll get this figured out.*

Ramon felt his phone buzzing in his pocket and reached inside his jacket while the other men were in discussion about various ways they kept their mistresses hidden from their wives. He knew Jacob was full of shit with his contributions to the conversation—that man worshipped the ground Taren walked on.

Nonchalantly glancing down at the screen, he saw he had three texts from Alejandro. Knowing he was the one in charge of the San Diego estate where Sophia was, Ramon opened them.

Alejandro: I need to talk to you.
Alejandro: It's important.
Alejandro: It's about Sophia.

Ramon looked up at the table. "Excuse me one second," he said as he stood. "I'll be right back."

John and Jacob gave him questioning looks, but quickly turned back to whatever inane topic the group had moved on to.

As soon as he stepped out the bar's door, before he even had a chance to hit the button for Alejandro's number, he saw her breeze through the revolving door.

His first instinct was to smile—how could he not? She was there—obviously to surprise him like he'd done to her in San Francisco, and she was fucking stunning.

His first thought was that Martin had really met Sophia at lunch. But that didn't make sense. He and John didn't arrive until this afternoon, and they'd taken Dante's plane. There's no way she could have gotten here before him. And she had a bag in her hand—she was obviously just arriving.

He saw more of Martin's men milling about the lobby, much like Ramon's men were. Then he saw faces he recognized from Juan and Francisco's party—and they were CIA. Ramon had a good idea who his 'wife' was that Martin had met. Thankfully, it wasn't Sophia.

Unfortunately, his real wife's sudden appearance put him in a bind. He couldn't go talk to her as she stood in line, so he'd have to discreetly send Chachi.

But first, he needed to call Alejandro and find out how the hell Sophia was in New Orleans and no one told him she was coming.

Chapter Thirty-Seven

Sophia

Her plan of saying she was doing a Zoom meeting in the pool house, then working on a project all afternoon and didn't wish to be disturbed, seemed to work.

She'd timed it after the guards passed through and slipped out the secret back gate that she was sure she wasn't supposed to know about, to meet her Uber down the road and take her to the airport.

Now, here she was in New Orleans. At the Ritz, no less, about to surprise her sexy husband and try for another round of baby making.

She'd packed sexy lingerie in the event she'd be able to surprise him, but didn't count on it. Especially knowing how many men Ramon had taken for security—although that may have contributed to how easily she was able to sneak off the estate unescorted.

He would probably scold her for doing so, but she planned on using seduction as a means of earning his forgiveness. She looked forward to doing a little submissive groveling.

Sophia couldn't contain her joy at the idea of Ramon's face when he saw her. It must have been contagious because people automatically smiled at her when they walked past.

She glanced around the grand lobby. It was beautiful—a far cry from the hotels she used to stay at. How she ended up at the same hotel as Ramon in Ensenada… it was kismet, she decided. Kevin cheating, the Mexican resort having a flash sale, meeting Juan Diego and Francisco at the pool, and being invited to their party… The universe knew they belonged together and made sure to make that happen. Hopefully, the universe was also on her side about a baby.

She was so lost in her daydream of a happy family, she almost didn't recognize him across the lobby, smiling down at the woman he had his arm around. It was the same woman from Mexico. Raquel. The two turned and walked into the bar with their arms around each other. There was no way she was his 'enemy' like he'd insisted, and there was no misunderstanding they were together—not the way she ran her hand up and down his back while his hand was firmly around her waist as they walked inside.

She looked around with tears in her eyes to see if everyone witnessed her humiliation and was staring at her. Of course they weren't—they were going about their happy lives oblivious to the fact that the bottom had just dropped out of her world. She picked up the weekender bag at her feet and with an embarrassed smile as she wiped the tears from her eyes, stepped out of line, and made a beeline to the front door.

****

Ramon

Chachi: She's not here, Ramon. We've looked everywhere.

Ramon: Well, obviously you haven't looked everywhere if you haven't fucking found her. FIND HER. Get with security and watch camera footage.

Chachi: Gabriel is already in their office doing that.

The fact that his head of security was already on that made him feel a little better. Although not much, since right now, he wanted to put a bullet in Raquel Torres' brain. Personally.

What he ought to do is rat her out as being CIA to the Colombians and let the two groups battle it out while he went to look for his wife.

Because fuck this shit.

He hadn't told Jacob or John anything about Sophia being at the hotel since sitting back down in the bar with his 'wife.' Instead, he texted furiously for his security team to find her and discreetly take her to his room. Still, he got a text from Jacob that said: **They'll find her.**

How the man knew everything about everybody, everywhere was beyond Ramon—but that's why Jacob was paid the big bucks.

Ramon replied: **They fucking better.**

Jacob: Go. Do what you need to do. We'll keep Raquel under control.

Ramon: I'll check in soon.

He stood. "Will you gentlemen keep my wife company? I need to make a phone call." He took a dramatic pause and smiled at Martin, like they shared a secret. He wanted the man to think he was doing Ramon a favor by keeping Raquel busy while he talked to his mistress.

He directed his attention toward Raquel, "Darling, try not to be too enchanting while I'm gone. I don't want Martin trying to steal you away from me."

That's *exactly* what he'd like. What a perfect excuse for the scorched earth he was about to leave behind while he looked for his wife.

*

"She's fucking gone, Dante. I have men at the airport looking for her. Jacob has people looking in New Orleans. I tried tracking her phone, but I was a goddamn dumbass and told her I'd put in a tracker on it in a moment when I was attempting to be honest with her as, well… as honest as I could be at the time."

Ramon heard the clicking of Dante's keyboard on the other end of the phone.

"She just withdrew twenty grand about an hour ago from a bank not far from the Ritz."

"She's getting ready to run."

"Well, for a little while anyway. Twenty grand isn't going to last her forever. She'll have to resurface soon enough."

"*Sobrino,* one fucking night wouldn't be soon enough. We need to find her."

"I'll keep monitoring her credit cards. Most places require a credit card deposit even if she pays cash. Same for rental cars. And we'll keep a close eye on the fly lists."

Ramon knew Dante was doing what he could, but it wasn't enough.

He hung up the phone and paced his hotel suite like a caged tiger. Jacob and John arrived to update him about what transpired after he left the bar. As much as he didn't give a fuck about the Colombians or the CIA at the moment, he knew he needed to handle that shit. He was the goddamn Guzman patrón—there were a lot of people depending on him to not fuck this up and go to war before they were ready.

"Most of Martin's men left at the same time we did. But he's still at the bar—with Raquel, and she's supplying him with plenty of alcohol, cleavage shots, and lingering touches."

"I hadn't figured out her angle. I thought she was just trying to bug our rooms—this makes a lot more sense. If Martin thinks she's my wife, he's going to let her get close to him. Especially if he thinks he's pulling one over on me and fucking her behind my back." He sat contemplating his next move. "I need photographs of them together in the bar, and, if possible, going into his hotel room together."

Jacob smiled. "Already on it."

Of course he was.

John asked, "Any news on Sophia?"

"Nothing yet."

"We'll find her."

Everybody kept telling him that, but so far, they had been empty words.

"I hope so. For everyone's sake."

Chapter Thirty-Eight

Sophia
She had slid into the cab outside the Ritz just as the tears had started to fall.

"Where to, ma'am?"

She had no fucking idea. She had no desire to stay in New Orleans, but she certainly couldn't go back to San Diego, and he'd easily find her in San Francisco. She thought for a hot minute about calling Francisco and Juan Diego, but knew someone in Ensenada would rat her out.

"Can you take me to the nearest bank?"

She was about to make a large withdrawal of cash and live off the grid for a while. At least until she was done licking her wounds and ready pick up the pieces and move on. If she used her credit cards, Ramon would find her, and she wasn't emotionally strong enough to have it out with him yet.

She'd have attorneys deal with that while she found a place to hole up. Although, the last time she attempted to go into hiding to put herself back together, look where it got her.

Married to a bigger liar than she'd been running from.

Did she have *naïve fool* stamped across her forehead? Why did she keep ending up with cheaters?

The cab pulled up to the bank, and Sophia asked the cabbie to wait while she went inside. She came back outside fifteen minutes later, and twenty thousand dollars richer. That would buy her a plane ticket and lodging for a month—

easily, where she could mend her broken heart and heal her pride.

Although, the way she felt right now, she doubted she'd ever be ready to face the world again. Not in a year, let alone a month.

I should have taken out more money.

The cab driver dropped her off at the airport, and Sophia stood looking at the board of departures, debating where to go. It was such an odd feeling... on one hand, she had her pick of the world, and on the other, her world had completely fallen apart.

Maybe she should just go hide out at her mom and dad's, or her brother's.

She was in line to buy her ticket back to San Diego, when she thought about having to explain to her family why she wasn't staying at the estate, and quickly stepped back out of line to return to the departure board. She knew she had to look like a kook who didn't know what she was doing—getting in and out of the line, with her tear-streaked faced and red eyes, but she was beyond caring.

Another cruel joke that just an hour before, she'd felt beautiful, sexy, and filled with joy about surprising Ramon.

I get it, God. You want me to be single and childless. Point taken and received—loud and clear.

Sophia decided she'd take the next plane out that she could get a seat on—it didn't matter where it was going. She studied the list of cities for a minute before deciding, *Boston, Massachusetts... ready or not, here I come.*

****

Ramon

"What the fuck do you mean, *she's there?*" he snarled at Alejandro through the phone.

He'd been going out of his mind for the last four hours looking for her. When Dante let him know she'd withdrawn twenty thousand in cash, he thought for sure it would take some time to find her.

"She just pulled up in a rideshare, got out with a bunch of shopping bags, and said she'd gone shopping and went inside like nothing was wrong."

"*What?*"

"Are you sure it was her that you saw at the hotel, Boss?"

"I fucking know my own goddamn wife."

Don't I?

Shit. Now, he was questioning if he'd somehow conjured her up in his mind.

No, that was bullshit. He *knew* Sophia. It was her in line at the front desk.

"Is she wearing a cream suit with pink shoes and a pink scarf?"

There was a pause, like Alejandro was looking. "Yeah."

She was at the hotel. What the fuck was going on?

He put his hand over the mouthpiece of the phone to address Gabriel. "We're leaving. Now. Let the pilot know we're en route to the airport, and we'll be headed back to San Diego," then switched back to his lieutenant in San Diego. "I'll be home by midnight. Do *not* tell anyone I'm coming."

"What do I do in the meantime?"

"What would you normally do?"

The younger man huffed out a frustrated laugh. "I don't know. You've never had a wife before, Ramon. This is all new territory."

That was true.

"Well, if *I* were in charge of security, and the woman I was supposed to be guarding snuck out without a bodyguard, I'd probably let her know I was mad. Respectfully, of course. I mean, she is still my wife..."

Alejandro sighed. "I'll see if she's downstairs and talk to her."

Under different circumstances, Ramon would probably put her over his knee for pulling a stunt like taking off to go shopping without a bodyguard—and he'd enjoy it. But what happened today wasn't that simple. He knew she'd been at the hotel in New Orleans—probably to surprise him, and that she'd probably seen him with Raquel and took off, making a pit stop at First National Bank of Louisiana and withdrawing twenty thousand dollars. He'd assumed she'd taken the money so she could disappear, but now she was back in San Diego like she'd never left.

So the question was, what had twenty thousand dollars bought his beautiful bride, and was she now a threat? *Hell hath no fury like a woman scorned.*

He slid into the back of the rented car and headed to the private airport.

I guess I'll find out soon enough.

Chapter Thirty-Nine

Sophia
When the man identified himself as a special agent while she waited in the terminal and asked her to come with him, her first thought was, "Here we go again."

Except Ramon didn't come to her rescue this time. Far from it.

At first, she was confused as they laid photographs of Ramon with Raquel on the table, thinking, *No shit, assholes. I was there.* But then she wondered why the government would care in the first place that her husband was having an affair.

Then they put more photographs of him with other women in front of her. Except, she could tell they were older, from before she knew him; there was no grey at his temples.

Why would the government want to rat my husband out to me, and why do they want me to think he's doing more than what he's already doing?

"I'm just curious," she said, crossing her arms. "Why are you showing me all these photos? Has the CIA teamed up with Joey Greco for an episode of Cheaters? I don't get it."

"We just want to make sure you understand what kind of man your husband is, because we need your help."

****

Ramon

Sophia jumped a mile high when she walked out of the closet in her pajamas and found him standing in the bedroom right after midnight.

With her hand on her heart, she gasped, "Oh my God. You scared me!" then scurried away from the closet and got under the covers. "I thought you weren't coming home until tomorrow."

"I couldn't sleep alone, baby. Aren't you happy to see me?"

Her nervous giggle was obviously fake, her smile forced. "Of course! I'm just surprised, that's all."

He slowly loosened his tie, keeping his eyes on her. He liked that she was nervous; surprising her by showing up tonight had given him the upper hand—he needed that, especially since he had no idea what she was up to.

Ramon sat next to her on the bed and leaned in to kiss her below her ear—the spot that usually turned her to putty in his hand. Her body was tense, but she murmured a robotic, "Mmm."

He smiled. She wasn't very good at this. So, he stepped it up a notch by crooning in her ear, "I thought I'd come home so we could try to make that baby tonight—while you're still ovulating."

He could hear her breath catch in her throat and wondered how she would play this. Not once since she'd agreed to stay married to him had she not been enthusiastic about having sex. She had to know he'd be suspicious if she started now.

"I, um…"

Ramon kissed down her neck and massaged her breast over her nightshirt. "You what, baby?" he murmured against her skin.

"I'm just really tired, Ramon."

"I understand," he said, pulling away to softly stare at her. She would be a horrible poker player. He could see the pulse in her neck throbbing, and she couldn't stop fidgeting.

Tucking a strand of hair behind her ear, he continued, "Flying to and from New Orleans in one day takes a lot out of someone. I get it. I'm tired, too."

"I—I don't know what you mean?"

He traced her bottom lip with his thumb while his other hand went to the back of her neck. His hold was gentle—he'd never hurt her—but he wanted to exert his dominance.

"I saw you, Sophia. In the lobby at the Ritz—and I know you saw me, too, with Raquel." He squeezed her neck gently while tugging her lip down with the pad of his thumb. "What I can't figure out is… what did twenty thousand dollars buy you, and why are you still here—in my bed, like nothing is wrong?"

She refused to answer him, tears welling up in her eyes.

"I assumed you wanted one last fuck… but, now you're saying you're too tired." He squeezed again. "So, tell me, *mi mujer*. Because I'm just *dying* to know."

Flashpoint

"I can't believe I ever trusted you," she whispered then pushed on his chest to try to get away from him. He didn't budge but did release his hold on her.

"We seem to have a lot in common tonight."

"You *saw* me?" Her bottom lip trembled, and she repeated, "You saw me. And you didn't even care enough about me to..." Her face crumpled as she let out a strangled sob and pulled the covers up to hide her face.

Seeing her fall apart in front of him made him feel like he'd been kicked in the nuts, but he persisted. He had to know. "What did you buy with twenty thousand dollars, Sophia?"

She brought the covers down and stared at him—tears still streaming down her face. "That's what you care about? The money?"

"Answer me."

She pushed him aside and scrambled to put both feet on the ground at the same time. When she stormed into the closet, he thought she was packing her things, but she came out a moment later with a wad of money in her hand and threw it at him.

"Here's your stupid money, Ramon. Go spend it on your girlfriend."

Fuuuuck.

Then she went back into the closet and really started packing her things.

So, he'd been wrong about what she used the money for—it'd been for nothing, apparently. But it didn't explain why she took it out in the first place, or why she was here pretending nothing was wrong.

But her reaction confirmed she felt betrayed—and with good reason. And that she did love him.

He'd played this all fucking wrong.

Quietly entering the closet, he found her pulling things out of drawers and stuffing them into a suitcase, sniffling and occasionally wiping the tears from her eyes.

Ramon came up behind her and reached for her wrist. "Stop. *Mi amor*, just stop."

Her shoulders slumped as she leaned against him momentarily, then she gave her head a little shake, stiffened her spine, and resumed packing, let out a sniffling, "No. I'm through being a fool."

Holding her by her shoulders, he turned her around so she'd look at him.

"My beautiful, Sophia... You are many, many things—but a fool isn't one of them. You're beautiful and sexy, kind and wonderfully innocent, and brilliant all rolled into one. And I fucking hit the jackpot when I married you."

She brushed the back of her hand under her nose and huffed out a humorless laugh, "Yeah, that's why you decided to have an affair and not care that I knew."

"Sophia... do you know who Raquel is, baby? She's a government agent. She showed up today pretending to be my wife—without my prior knowledge. And since I was meeting with my enemies, who I don't want knowing about you—for your safety, I went along with it. I'd rather them have her in their sights than you."

Her eyes grew wide. "She's with the CIA?"

"She is." He sighed. It was time to bite the bullet. "There's a lot I need to tell you. But you need to know this... you showing up today complicated things—immensely. But, baby, I was so fucking happy to see you when you first walked through those lobby doors. It killed me that I couldn't go up and kiss you as you stood in line." He leaned down and tested the waters, kissing her chastely on the lips. "You're the woman I love, Sophia. I don't want anyone else."

Her eyes welled with tears again, and Ramon pulled her close, kissing her hair as he whispered, "Don't cry, *mi amor*. Please, don't cry."

He continued holding her close while her little shoulders shook as she kept crying. Finally, he felt her body shudder after she took a deep breath, and he whispered, "There's some things I haven't been honest with you about..."

She took a step back and brought her finger to her lips, then pointed to a shopping bag on the floor. He glanced inside and found CIA-grade bugs in a handy container for easy transport.

Well, at least that explained why she hadn't been on any airline's roster back to San Diego. Had she duped him from the beginning?

"I guess I'm the one who feels like a fool, now."

****

Sophia

She grabbed his hand and walked out of the closet. "Can we take a drive? Just you and me?"

He nodded solemnly, not saying a word nor releasing her hand until he opened the car door on the Mercedes in the warehouse of a garage.

"Everything okay, Boss?" Gabriel asked as he appeared from a side room. "You need an escort?"

"No, I'm just taking my wife out for a drive. I think we'll be okay."

"I'll stay close to my phone, just in case you need us."

Sophia reflected on the night they'd ended up at the winery. How many men had shown up at the drop of a hat to protect him. Then contemplated everything else she knew—trying to see the big picture through a neutral lens. The security, bodyguards, extravagant wealth... it all made sense, especially after what the CIA had shown her. Maybe in the back of her mind she'd always known but just didn't want to admit it. Ramon's wealth and power had been part of what drew her to him. Perhaps she hadn't really wanted to know how he'd acquired it.

But, the signs were all there from the beginning, if she would have been willing to look. On the first night she met him, Juan Diego and Francisco had flat out said that she shouldn't ask what he did for a living because it was better not to know. That should have been Red Flag Number One.

Raquel Torres should have been Red Flag Number Two. And she's an agent? Why hadn't the men told her that on the plane ride back to San Diego when they fed her all the information about him being with the bombshell beauty?

Another thing that hadn't made sense was why the CIA was trying to make her hate Ramon. She'd sat on their private plane as they showed her picture after picture of him with glamourous women. Some of them had not been PG rated, and she'd wondered how they'd gotten the photos in the first place. Were there any of her with Ramon?

Then there were the stories of all the destruction the Ensenada cartel caused—the photos of dead bodies, the bales of seized drugs, and stacks of money. Daniel Day, the man who identified himself as the lead agent, tried to make it seem as if Sophia would be a patriot if she bugged the estate and assisted the government in bringing Ramon and the rest of the cartel down.

She'd been confused and upset when she got off the plane in San Diego and had every intention of helping the CIA, but as she got closer to home, she realized that's exactly how she thought of the estate—*home*. She'd grown to care for everyone working and living there—even the asshole who owned it. Could she betray all of them?

Sophia had been devastated at seeing Ramon with Raquel, but when she had a chance to step away from all the information the agents had piled on about his infidelity and illegal dealings—it was amazing how much they knew about it—something in her gut told her there was more to the story. So, instead of going home and planting the bugs right away, she stowed them in her closet in the bag she'd used to bring them inside without suspicion.

She'd hoped that a good night's rest would bring some clarity about what she should do. Then Ramon showed up out of the blue and dropped the bombshell that he'd seen her in New Orleans. Not only that, but he also knew about the money she'd withdrawn.

When he told her he needed to explain some things, he'd seemed so genuine. She had to at least hear what he had to say, or she'd regret it for the rest of her life.

"Don't be fooled," the agent had told her before she left the airport. "He's a master manipulator." Yet, all she could think as she looked at the balding man was, *Takes one to know one.*

"Was any of it ever real for you?" Ramon asked quietly as he slipped the car into first gear and pulled out of the garage.

"How can you ask me that? Of course it was real."

His huffed laugh let her know he didn't believe her.

"Kudos to you," he snarled as he downshifted into second gear when he made the turn out of the driveway gate,

Flashpoint

followed quickly by third and fourth gears as he accelerated through the streets. "You had me and my entire team fooled." He looked at her with disdain. "Obviously, since I fucking married you."

Sophia turned in her seat to glare at him.

"Don't try gaslighting me, Ramon. This is *your* doing, not mine. I'm not the one lying and cheating. That's all you, buddy. So, don't you dare try to manipulate me into thinking this is *my* fault. That I somehow don't love you because you cheated on me."

He looked over at her with raised eyebrows.

"Are you fucking kidding me? You're calling *me* the liar? That's rich, coming from a goddamn federal agent living in *my* house, Sophia. *My. Fucking. House.* You've known who I am all along, but I don't have a clue who you really are. And spare me with the cheating bullshit. You know damn well that Raquel was a setup, nothing more. I'm not interested in that woman—or any other woman, and you fucking know it. So save the victim act, sweetheart."

Her anger dissipated into confusion, and she shook her head with her eyes closed.

"Wait, you think I'm an agent?"

He looked between her and the road. "That would explain a lot."

"Explain what, exactly? That I'm an idiot for trying to surprise you today, and instead caught you with your mistress?"

His knuckles whitened as he gripped the steering wheel tighter. "She's not my fucking mistress. Quit calling her that."

"Oh, I'm sorry. Would you prefer lov-ah?"

Ramon took a hard right into an empty parking lot and screeched to a stop before throwing the car in park and turning to her with a scowl. He was scary as hell when he was angry. She should probably tone down trying to push his buttons.

"You have a lot of explaining to do, *wife*. I suggest you start talking, while I still have an iota of feeling left for you and care whether you live or die."

She felt her eyes widen and leaned to the other side of her seat. "So, it is true. Everything they said..."

He narrowed his eyes and cocked his head. "Who's *they*?"

"The CIA agents who picked me up at the airport this afternoon and flew me hom—back here, to San Diego."

"Picked you up? At the airport...?"

"After seeing you with Raquel. I left, got some money, and was planning to stay in Boston for a while. They pulled me away while I waited to board."

Sophia watched his face as his mind raced as he tried to piece together what she was telling him. "That's why you had the money," he said softly, then leaned his head back in his seat and uttered, "Fuuuck."

"I think you were about to explain some things in the closet. Before I showed you the presents the government gave me?"

He stared at her for a beat before nodding in defeat.

"What do you want to know?"

"Everything."

Chapter Forty

Ramon
"Who were you going to see in Boston?"

The idea of Sophia meeting up with an old boyfriend had his gut churning.

"What? No one. I don't know anyone in Boston. It was the first flight out of New Orleans, that's why I picked it."

That soothed his green-eyed monster, somewhat. Although, he didn't like the idea of her being alone with federal agents. But, one of them hitting on her was probably the least of what he should be worried about them doing or saying to her.

"So, what did they tell you?"

"Just what I asked you about in San Francisco, and you swore wasn't true." She didn't release him from her stare. "You lied to me. Right to my face, after promising you wouldn't." Sophia twisted her hands in her lap. Her expression was sad when she glanced back up at him. "And that you're a playboy—which I guess in my heart, I probably already knew."

"*Was* a playboy," he corrected. "You've been the only woman since the night I met you. Anything they told you to the contrary is bullshit."

"What about the other stuff, Ramon? You're *head* of the cartel? You have people killed? You smuggle people and drugs?"

He pinched the bridge of his nose and sighed, "Yes."

There, it was out in the open.

Before she could say anything, he grabbed her hand and held it between his. "But, we've been acquiring legal businesses ever since I took over, and Dante said almost fifty percent of Guzman Enterprises' dealings are legitimate now."

She pulled her hand away. "So you're only half a psychopath?"

"A psychopath? Good grief, what bullshit did they feed you, *mi mujer*? I'm a businessman—a ruthless one, but I'm not a psychopath. I get no joy from hurting people."

"But you do hurt them."

He chose his words carefully.

"The drug business isn't rainbows and sunshine, Sophia. It's ugly and dirty, and unfortunately, I'm a major player in the game. I would love to sit here and tell you that I will give it all up for you and become completely legal, but that's not going to happen. I would if I could, but if I want to keep me and my men alive, and our families—including you, I can't. I'm in too deep, *mi amor*."

Her bottom lip trembled. "I don't think I can be with you, Ramon. I can't live like that."

"You've been living like that," he pointed out.

"That was before I knew you were a criminal."

He leaned over the console to get in her personal space. "So knowing the truth about me... that means you no longer love me? You can just flip that switch," He snapped his fingers. "Just like that?"

"Of course not. But this has made me question everything about us, Ramon. I didn't know the real you—I only knew what you allowed me to see."

He moved closer, his mouth inches from hers as he pleaded with his eyes. "You're the only person who knows the real me, Sophia. I've never trusted anyone enough before to let my guard down to do that."

She snorted and turned her face. "You didn't trust me enough to be honest with me."

He reached for her hand to plead his case, but she clenched her fist and drew it tight to her stomach.

"Only about what I do. I was afraid to lose you. But I was always honest about how I feel about you. About my hopes and dreams for a future with you—for a family."

"I could never have a family with you, Ramon."

Her words were like a knife to his heart, and he slumped back in his seat.

"We need to go back, Ramon."

He didn't want to agree. He wanted to shake her and make her love him again. Make her see that he would do anything for her. Anything.

Except the one that would probably convince her to stay.

Maybe if it was just him he'd be sentencing to death, he'd consider risking it. But it was the entire organization—

including Sophia. He'd learn to live the rest of his life with a broken heart if it meant she would be remain safe.

He put the car back into drive, foregoing his seatbelt, because how he felt at that moment... fuck it. Dying in a car crash would be better than living without her.

"For what it's worth, Sophia," he murmured as they pulled into the drive. "I was never unfaithful to you. Never even considered it."

"For what it's worth, I think I believe you."

"So, what now, *mi nerdicita?*"

She took a deep breath. "I'm not sure. Maybe I can get my job back in San Francisco."

"I'll make sure you're financially taken care of."

"I told you in the beginning, Ramon. I don't want your money. And I certainly don't want it now."

He pulled in the garage and shut the car off, then turned to face her again. "You realize that half my money comes from legitimate business dealings, don't you?"

He could see that she was in a moral dilemma. She opened her mouth to speak but just stuttered out, "I—um—" before he interrupted her.

"Why don't you still start the foundation and run it, like we originally discussed?"

"You'd still want me to do that?"

He smiled. "Yeah, Soph. You had some great ideas that I was on board with, and I know you'd use the money for what it was intended. If I can't get you to do it, it's not happening.

I don't trust anyone else with that kind of money—other than Dante, and he has no time for something like that."

"I can't believe you'd still want me involved."

"My feelings for you haven't changed, Sophia."

"But, I brought bugs in your home... and not the dog kind." She brought her hands to her mouth. "What am I going to do about Daisy? I can't take her to my parents, and it wouldn't be fair to coup her up in an apartment."

"The dog can stay here until you find a house. You can come by anytime to visit her. Your status here isn't going to change; you're still my wife—until you're not. Then you'll still be someone we trust."

"I almost betrayed you, Ramon."

"But you didn't."

Because you still fucking love me, goddammit! He just needed to help her realize it.

As long as he kept her involved in his life, he knew he still had a chance to win her back. He just needed her to see there was more good in him than bad—that he was worth loving, warts and all. Having her run his foundation that he was going to overfund the shit out of would be a good place to start.

Chapter Forty-One

Sophia

Ramon made her take the twenty thousand she'd withdrawn that day, over her objection.

"Consider it an advance," he'd said when he put the money in her hand and closed her fingers around the stack of bills.

She felt her eyes tear up. "Why are you being so kind to me?"

The corner of his mouth turned up in a wry smile. "Because you're my wife, and I love you, and I want you to be happy."

Sophia had serious doubts if she could be happy without him. If he would have fought her one tiny bit about leaving, she may have stayed. Instead, he practically rolled out the red carpet to show her the door.

It wasn't because he wanted her to go, she believed that. He thought *she* wanted to go, and he wasn't going to stand in her way.

But she found herself wishing he would.

Yet, she was too proud to do it herself and say she wanted to stay. The truth was, she didn't know if she could accept his illegal activities, but her heart was breaking at the thought of not being with him.

Hopefully being away from him and the estate would provide her some much-needed perspective.

One thing she knew she'd never regret though was not betraying him to the CIA. Fuck them for trying to make her hate him.

With tears streaming down her face, she left the estate in Olaf at one a.m. with the understanding she'd be by later in the week for more of her things and to visit Daisy.

His genteel smile didn't reach his eyes. "I'll try to be off the property when you come."

"You don't have to do that."

He considered her words thoughtfully, then politely disagreed. "I think I do. For my sake. I can't watch you leave me."

Please ask me to stay, she implored silently.

But he didn't… instead, he walked her closer to her car door.

"I think I already know the answer, but I'm going to ask anyway."

She held her breath in anticipation of what was to follow.

"I'd like you to have a security detail. Just a small team."

"No one knows what I look like, remember?"

"The CIA does. They're not going to like it when they realize you double-crossed them."

"You think they'd try to hurt me? I'm a U.S. citizen."

"Dante's wife was a CIA *agent*, and they tried to kill her."

She should have listened to that little voice the first night she met him that warned she'd be in over her head with him. His admission about the CIA's hit on Bella was just further confirmation she was naïve and didn't have a clue about his world.

"A *small* team would probably be okay. Would you mind waiting until I found a little place though? I don't want my parents to have to deal with that."

"Keep in contact with Jesús, so he knows what's going on."

She nodded, frozen in her spot—unable to will herself to get in Olaf and leave.

Ramon made the decision for her. Leaning down, he softly kissed her cheek, and whispered, "Take care of yourself, Sophia Castle," then opened her car door. With a sad smile, he gently closed it and lifted his hand to signal goodbye as she started the engine.

Sophia had no idea how she made it to her parents in one piece; the tears had been blinding when she left the driveway—the uncontrollable sobbing started before she reached the main road.

She'd never felt so much grief nor been filled with such helplessness to make the pain stop. A part of her died when he closed the door of her Jetta.

Their marriage was over.

****

Ramon

He met with his captains the next day about what to do with the bugs Sophia had left. They'd decided they would plant them in Ramon's office and provide bullshit information to set the Colombians up. They then put the wheels in motion with the Colombians.

"I'm glad we didn't shut that down at our meeting with them in New Orleans," John remarked in Dante's San Diego office. That was where the real business was being conducted for the time being while his office was under surveillance.

Ramon had always tried to play ball whenever the CIA came knocking. They had an unspoken arrangement. Under the radar, the Guzman cartel would keep things in check in Sinaloa and other areas they controlled. No headless bodies hanging off bridges or shooting up unarmed tourist caravans to make a statement. That was his predecessor's idea of control, and was precisely why the CIA had him killed. And why no one in the organization tried to prevent it. Although, Ramon had held it over Dante's head that his future wife had been the CIA's assassin, and her killing Enrique hadn't been officially authorized by Ramon.

But what the CIA had done with Sophia had been unforgiveable, and he would have no problem fucking with them.

When you mess with the bull, you get the horns. And Ramon was in the mood to gore some motherfuckers to teach them that lesson.

Other than the bullshit he spewed for the CIA's benefit, he didn't speak to anyone for days... just barked out orders and drank himself stupid every night in order to get any sleep. He didn't know if he wanted to cry, hit something, or go scoop Sophia up and not let her go until she promised to come back. He was the walking definition of miserable and didn't know how to fix it.

He even moved her dog into his goddamn bedroom. Daisy slept at the side of his bed and became his constant companion during the day—following him around the house and sitting at his side to get her ears scratched on a regular basis. Even though the staff took good care of the pup, he knew she missed Sophia as much as he did. He thought maybe she associated Ramon with Sophia.

Even the damn dog knows we're supposed to be together.

On the tenth day after she'd left him, Jesús stood tentatively in his office doorway. Ramon still did work there—just nothing on the phone or out loud that wasn't staged.

"What is it?" he growled from his desk.

"I was wondering if you wanted to grab some lunch."

They'd established anytime Jesús talked to him about food, that was code that they needed to speak outside of listening ears.

Sitting on the patio with Daisy at Ramon's feet, his lieutenant winced when he said, "You asked me to let you know when she was coming to get her things. Apparently, she's found a little bungalow on the beach and is moving in this weekend."

That made Ramon sit up straighter—she was staying in San Diego—that was a good thing, and more important, she was coming here, and he knew about it in advance.

Still, he tried to maintain a nonchalant attitude. "I suppose she's going to take Daisy."

"She said she wanted to."

Ramon had grown attached to having the furry girl around but liked the idea of Daisy keeping Sophia company.

"And security?"

"Dante pulled some strings. We rented the place across the street from her. She knows the guys are going to be there and has agreed to let them set up cameras on her porch and back door."

At least she wasn't fighting him on making sure she was safe. He thought the revelation about the CIA trying to kill Bella had hit her hard. Realizing the government guys in their off-the-rack suits weren't really as trustworthy as they'd wanted her to think probably had been a bit of a shock for her.

The shit those assholes did was no better than what any cartel in the world did—they just had the American people fooled into thinking what they did was for the greater good.

Yeah, the greater good of the rich fuckers who actually ran the country. What they did wasn't for the average Joe's benefit—although their control of the media that made the citizens believe otherwise was to be admired. There was no way Ramon's organization could compete with that.

But shit was about to go down with the Colombians in the next few days, so he was relieved that she'd be protected. And he could get rid of those damn bugs in his office.

"When is she coming?"

"This evening, around six-thirty."

"Tell Blanca I'd like to have dinner for two on the balcony off my bedroom at six-forty, and let Sophia know I'd like to see her to discuss some things."

"Consider it done."

Ramon smiled at Jesús, something he knew he hadn't done in ten days. The prospect of seeing her made him fucking ecstatic, although he remembered telling her he'd be gone when she came by for her things.

He'd been true to his word and not sought her out when she visited Daisy, but probably only because she'd come unannounced, and Jesús wouldn't tell him until after she'd left. Something Ramon both appreciated and resented.

Still, he'd left her alone like he said he would, so she couldn't hold wanting to see her tonight against him.

If anything, she needed to hold *him* against *her*.

****

Sophia

Miserable couldn't begin to describe her. She didn't eat or get out of bed for three days after she arrived at her parents' house. The only thing she did was check her phone and bawl all over again because he hadn't called or texted.

It wasn't until the fourth day, when her mother asked her about her dog, did the guilt of not seeing Daisy bother her enough to compel her to shower and get dressed to visit the pup. Although the idea of *innocently* running into Ramon may have also played a role in her decision.

The first time she pulled through the guard gates unannounced, she'd felt a rush of excitement about the fantasy of him coming outside when he heard she was there, followed by a pit in her stomach about how he might treat her if he did.

The idea of him treating her indifferently, or worse, with disdain made her sick to her stomach.

He'd all but said he didn't want to see her again the night she left, so she wasn't surprised not to cross paths with him, although, if she were being honest with herself, she had felt disappointment every time she left the estate after visiting Daisy without so much as a glimpse of him.

It was probably for the best. She was sure he was already over her and had moved on. Meanwhile, she'd lost seven pounds from not being able to eat and cried herself to sleep every night in the full-size bed in her old bedroom at her parents' house.

Besides, if Ramon did talk to her when she visited, it'd probably be about signing divorce papers. Something she knew was inevitable but had no energy to even contemplate yet.

When Jesús met her in the driveway when she pulled up to the estate and said Ramon wanted to talk to her, her heart lodged in her throat.

He'd already had the papers drawn up. She just knew it.

It was strange walking through the front door as a guest and not a resident of the house. Everything looked and smelled the same, and she was reminded how happy she'd been living there.

"He's upstairs—on the balcony in the bedroom. He's expecting you, so go on up."

Sophia trudged up the stairs, both excited about seeing Ramon, and dreading what he wanted to talk to her about.

She knocked on the open bedroom door and called out, "Hello?" then heard Daisy bark and the jingle of her tags as she ran into the bedroom from the balcony and barreled into Sophia, barking excitedly.

Kneeling with a laugh at her dog's enthusiasm, she hugged Daisy's neck and said, "I've missed you, too, girl."

"Hey," came his deep voice, and she looked up to find him inside the threshold.

She swallowed hard and stood on shaky knees while trying to find her voice. "Hi," she managed to reply in a soft voice.

He was as handsome as ever, dressed in a dark grey suit and crisp, white shirt that was open at the collar. Yet, he had circles under his eyes, and his hair somehow seemed greyer at the temples. And they stood in *their* bedroom—except it wasn't hers anymore—she no longer belonged there.

"How've you been?" she asked.

One corner of his mouth lifted in a sardonic smile. "I've been better."

"Yeah, I know the feeling."

He stood to the side of the balcony door and motioned toward outside with his head. "Do you have time to have dinner with me and go over some things?"

Her mouth went dry at the thought of what he wanted to go over, and all she could do was nod in response.

She caught the scent of his cologne when she walked by him and quickly brushed a tear from her eye as she made her way to the table set up outside.

"Was that Daisy's bed next to your side of the bed?" she asked him as he held out her chair for her.

"Yeah. She's been sleeping in there with me."

"Why?"

He sat, and the dog immediately went to his side.

Traitor.

He reached down to rub her head, not looking at the dog, but staring straight at Sophia when he said, "She made me feel like a part of you was still here."

Her stomach did a flip at his admission.

"It looks like she fell in love with you, too."

He jerked his head up and leveled her with his stare.

"It's going to be hard to let her go."

Sophia knew he was no longer talking about Daisy.

"Maybe we can schedule time for me to bring her by."

"Like a playdate?" he said with a smirk.

"Something like that."

"Can *we* have a playdate?"

She hadn't expected that. Was he flirting with her? She stammered as she tried to figure out a response.

Throwing caution to the wind, she darted her tongue along her bottom lip and said with a coy smile, "Maybe, depends on what we'd play."

Ramon raised one eyebrow and seemed like he was about to respond when Blanca announced her arrival, carrying a tray with two salads.

The cook must have sensed the sexual tension between the two as they stared at each other; she hastily put the cold plates down in front of them and said, "Just call down when you're ready for the main course. I'm going to take Daisy—it's her dinner time."

Sophia glanced at the woman and murmured her thanks, cognizant of Ramon's intense gaze still on her as Blanca and Daisy left the room.

She needed to change the subject—and the mood, or before she knew it, she would be in his lap kissing him.

"So, did anything ever come of the 'gifts' from the CIA?"

He knew what she was doing and smiled as he put his napkin in his lap.

"My office is bugged, and they are learning all kinds of things."

She felt no remorse over double-crossing the agents. They'd lied to her and tried to take advantage of her naivety. Fuck them.

Whoa! Where did that come from?

Being here, at the estate, with Ramon, she realized she was bitter, and surprisingly, not at her husband. But at the government agents who'd taken it from her. She'd been blissful in her ignorance—even trying to have a baby with the man she loved. Now, it was gone. All of it.

"We're sorry you're having to learn this way," Agent Dirtbag Day had told her on the plane. Except, they weren't sorry. Not in the least. They'd just wanted her to do their dirty work for them. She knew that now. "It's better to know who he really is, though."

Sophia knew who he was. Maybe not what he *did*—but there was no doubt she knew the real Ramon. She realized that now. Unfortunately, now she also knew he was head of the cartel, and he'd confirmed it. There was no way to unring that bell.

But sitting across from him tonight, she had to admit, she wished she could. She missed him so much.

Maybe that's why she didn't pull away when he reached across the table for her hand.

"Thank you for not betraying me, Sophia."

She felt the tears spring up at the thought of even considering it for a second.

"Thank you for being honest with me."

He let out a small snort and looked her in the eye. "I liked it better before I was."

She returned his stare, silent even though she was sure her thoughts of, *Yeah, me too,* was probably written all over her face.

His gaze became too intense for her, and she broke eye contact as she took a sip of wine. "I appreciate you trusting me with the foundation. I promise to make you proud."

He smiled softly. "I'm looking forward to hearing your plans."

They sat in silence for a moment, and she blurted out, "Thank you for taking such good care of Daisy."

"She's been a much-needed companion, but I'm sure she will be happy to be back with you. I hear you got a bungalow on the beach not far from here."

"I'm just renting it," she said, trying to dismiss it like it wasn't a big deal. "But it will be nice having her with me."

"I'm glad you're staying close to me."

"I'm not—" She stopped. Was that what she was doing? Maybe subconsciously she was trying to remain near him. With a shrug and a smile, she corrected herself. "I guess I am pretty close—I hadn't considered that when my agent showed it to me. But the good thing is it'll make it easier if I need to come here to have things signed for the foundation."

"Hopefully, you'll have lots of things for me to sign, then, and will have to see me a lot."

In typical Ramon fashion, he wasn't even trying to be subtle. It was as sexy as it was unnerving. She again tried to steer the conversation back to something innocuous.

"I was going to talk to you about a budget and how you wanted me to handle the start-up fees."

"Whatever you need. I can write a check for you tonight. You tell me how much, and it's yours."

"Are you always this easy to work with?"

"Nope. But for you, I'd do anything."

"Anything?"

He gave a sad smile. "*Almost* anything." Picking up his knife and fork, he prompted her to tell him more about her plans for the foundation.

They spent the rest of dinner with Sophia excitedly explaining her vision. He never offered his input unless she asked, which she did—often. He was a brilliant businessman, and she knew she could learn a lot from him.

Of course, his genius only served to make him more attractive.

She glanced at her Fitbit and gasped at the time.

"I can't believe it's already midnight," she said as she stood from the table. "I took up your whole night—I'm so sorry."

He stood and reached for her hand. "I'm not."

She didn't step away when he closed the distance between them, nor did she try to remove her hand from his soft hold.

With his other hand, he tucked her hair behind her ear, his eyes never leaving her face.

"Tonight was the best night I've had in far too long," he whispered, then bent to plant a chaste kiss on her lips.

She should have let him end the kiss and walk her to the door, so she could be on her way. Instead, she stood on her tiptoes and pressed her lips firmer against his.

That was all the encouragement he needed to wrap his arms around her and deepen the kiss. His hand moved up her back until his fingers were entwined in her hair, holding her in place as he ravaged her mouth with his. There was pent-up passion and pain in this kiss. An unspoken question of what the two of them doing this meant hung in the air.

She didn't want to think about tomorrow. She just cared about what was happening in that moment... as she was unbuttoning his white shirt at a frantic pace, needing to feel his naked skin against hers.

He scooped her up and carried her into the dark bedroom, the only light was from the soft balcony lights through the window. Sophia appreciated the night hiding what she was doing. She knew she should feel ashamed but being with Ramon felt too right. She still loved him with every fiber in her being, and she found herself voicing just that when she was completely naked under his body.

"I love you so much."

He drew a quick intake of breath and pulled her against him, kissing her hair, her cheeks, her eyes, and finally her mouth.

"I've been so miserable without you, Sophia. I need you like I need air, *mi amor*. You can't leave me again. I'll die."

It occurred to her that he thought this meant they were getting back together.

Maybe it was selfish on her part, but she didn't argue. She needed him to hold her and make love to her tonight. She'd worry about the repercussions tomorrow.

Chapter Forty-Two

Ramon

He woke up later than his normal pre-dawn time after sleeping like the dead. He assumed it was because he'd slept like shit for the past ten nights and was finally able to relax. His wife was home with him where she belonged.

Or maybe it was because he'd stayed up until the early morning hours making love to her until they were both exhausted. Either way, he fell asleep finally feeling whole again. Sophia was back in his arms.

His contentment proved to be short-lived though, when he realized she was no longer in his bed.

Ramon willed himself not to panic and showered and got dressed before leaving the bedroom. She was probably just downstairs having coffee and waiting for him to wake up so they could have breakfast together like they always did.

Except, she wasn't anywhere to be found downstairs—inside or out. And her Volkswagen was no longer parked in front of the estate.

He went back upstairs to see if she'd left a note that he'd missed in his haste to find her.

There it was, on his nightstand.

Ramon,

I loved seeing you last night and spending the night together. Maybe we can do it again, soon?

Love,

Sophia

Was she fucking for real? *Maybe they can do it again soon?* Like it had been a casual hookup that *maybe* they'd repeat if both their schedules allowed?

Oh. Hell. No. That wasn't going to fly with him. He needed to set her straight.

He bounded down the stairs, out the front door, and marched straight to the garage where he grabbed the first set of keys he could find.

The engine on the Ferrari had roared to life when his phone dinged with a text from Dante.

Let her come to you. She'll be back. Just be patient.

He jabbed the phone icon on his screen with his index finger, then gripped the phone so tight as he held it against his ear, it was a wonder it didn't snap in two.

The humor in his nephew's tone when he answered came through the line.

"Good morning, *Tío!*"

"One, how did you know she was here, and two, how the fuck can you tell me to be patient and let her come to me?"

Dante chuckled. "You're not the only one with spies."

That was good to know for future reference.

"You better start talking, *Sobrino*."

"Okay, okay. Maybe not *spies*, but *someone* saw her sneaking away this morning and knew you wouldn't take it well, so they called me for advice."

"Some motherfucker has a lot of explaining to do if they saw her leaving and called *you* instead of coming upstairs to get *me*."

"He didn't know what to do, so I told him to wait until you came downstairs. Apparently, you looked like you were about to murder someone as you headed to the garage, so I got another call—this time asking me to intervene. You can't go looking for her in your frame of mind—it's not going to end the way you want it to if you do."

"How do you know I'm going to find her? Maybe I'm going out for coffee."

"Because I would have done the same thing. And you would have tried to talk some sense into me, like I'm trying to do for you."

Goddamn Dante. Ever since the blowup in his office when his nephew thought Ramon had kidnapped his future wife and threatened Ramon's life, the two of them had become closer. It helped that Dante had been contrite as fuck afterward, but Ramon had also gotten a glimpse of the depths the man would go to for the people he loved, and he respected the hell out of that.

He shifted into drive and pulled out of the garage. "I'm going over there."

"You're the boss. I think you need to let her come back on her own terms, but that's just my opinion. What do I know?"

"Like you did with Bella?" Ramon scoffed.

"Bella is different, and you know it. She knew from the start what she was signing up for. A whole lot of shit just got dropped in this poor girl's lap—and not by you, I might add. She's got a lot to process. Give her time."

"Fuck that. So she can realize she's better off without me?"

"I don't believe that. I'm a betting man, and I like your odds. I've seen the way she looks at you."

"That was before when she thought…" He knew better than to finish that sentence on an unsecured line.

The engine revved as he downshifted to take a turn—and was certain the noise carried over the phone.

"If you insist on doing this, I hope you're smart about it. Don't go in like a fucking wrecking ball."

"I'll leave the *wrecking ball* at home. Say hi to Miley for me," Ramon grumbled before tossing his phone into the passenger seat.

Like he didn't know better than to go in half-cocked.

He slowed the Ferrari as he approached her parents' house. Her car was in the drive, so at least he knew where she was. As Ramon sat in the street without pulling in behind the

Flashpoint

Jetta, Dante's words to let her come back on her own terms echoed in his head.

It wasn't in his nature to not be in control, and he didn't like it one fucking bit.

Still, what would he say to her if he went to the door? Or what if her parents answered and wouldn't let him see her? Then what would he do? She'd obviously known what she was doing when she snuck out this morning and left him a note. What had it said? *I hope we can do this again, soon.*

That meant that there would be a next time—if he didn't fuck it up.

He sighed in resignation, then slowly pressed the gas, and drove away.

Okay, my little wife, I'll be patient. For now.

****

Sophia

She heard the engine when it was up the block before he even turned on her street. There was no mistaking the sound of a Ferrari-Maserati V8 engine.

Sophia should have known he'd show up there after she snuck out before he woke up, doing the walk of shame to the Volkswagen as his security looked on from the guard house.

She'd waved to Alejandro as she drove off. He'd waved back, but there had been a look of panic in his eyes, like he didn't know if he should be allowing her to leave unescorted.

Hell, *Sophia* didn't even know if she should be leaving like she had. Being cocooned in Ramon's embrace after he'd tenderly made love to her all night had felt like heaven. But the longer she lay in his arms, listening to his soft breathing as he slept, the more she felt like a fraud.

He was a criminal. Could she love a man on the wrong side of the law?

Scratch that—there was no doubt she loved him; the million-dollar question, or in this case, the billion-dollar question, was whether she could be with him knowing what he did.

Until she'd reconciled her heart with her head, or vice versa, she needed to keep things light between them. No moving back in yet.

One thing she did know was that there was no way she could stay away from him right now. But leaving in the morning was the best she could offer.

She took a deep breath, preparing herself for how she would tell him just that on her parents' front step, when she heard the engine rev as he drove off.

Sophia frowned. What was that about? Had he just been checking to see where she'd gone? Where else would she have gone?

Maybe he just wanted to make sure I made it home safely. She knew her being without security had been a source of stress for him. Staying with her parents, she hadn't been that worried, but when she moved into the bungalow,

Flashpoint

she knew she'd be jumpy since she'd just double-crossed the CIA, especially after what she learned about Dante's wife. Which was why she didn't buck Dante when he'd called to ask her about renting the house across the street for a full-time security detail, or why she'd agreed to the cameras—as long as they were on the *outside*.

She was married to a dangerous man who had dangerous enemies and, whether she liked it or not, she needed to acknowledge what it all meant—and that included someone watching out for her safety.

Chapter Forty-Three

Ramon

He wondered how long he'd have to wait until he heard from Sophia again. Turned out—not long. She sent him a text that afternoon.

Sophia: I didn't get my things—or my dog yesterday—the whole reason I came over. LOL! I start moving in today. Can I come by this afternoon to grab a load?

Ramon: You're welcome here anytime, you know that.

Sophia: I'll be there later then.

She appeared at noon wearing a high ponytail, dressed in a peach-colored t-shirt, grey yoga pants, and black sneakers, and looking far more refreshed than she had yesterday. The shadows under her eyes were gone, her easy smile was back, and she just looked... brighter, confirming what Ramon already knew: he was good for her.

"Hey," he said as he walked down the front steps to greet her when she got out of her car.

Her smile was genuine when she replied, "Hey, yourself. You're looking as sexy as ever."

He was unsure about leaning down and kissing her cheek, but he did anyway. She returned the kiss—on his lips.

"I was disappointed we didn't get to have breakfast together this morning," he told her, hinting at being unhappy to find her gone.

"I know, I'm sorry. I'm still trying to figure things out." She squeezed his hand. "Thank you for being patient while I do."

"*Mi amor*, I'm not going to lie. I don't like it. But what choice do I have?"

"You don't," she said with a cocky grin. "And one more thing—no pet names right now."

It seemed to him that she held all the cards right now—and she knew it and would take full advantage of her position.

"You're on a roll with your demands."

Enjoy it while it lasts, my love.

****

Sophia

She was dating her boss—who she just happened to be legally married to; that was the only way to describe their relationship right now.

They saw each other several times a week for dinner. On the nights they weren't having dinner, they met during the day—under the guise of him wanting to stay informed about the foundation. She knew it was bogus because they somehow always ended up naked.

During one meeting, she'd told him some astronomical number for expenses just to see his reaction. He didn't bat an eye—simply smiled at her from across his desk before coming around and pulling her into his lap on the leather couch in the meeting area of his office.

Sophia didn't complain. She found her job incredibly worthwhile and being with Ramon regularly was the best fringe benefit she could ask for.

It'd been almost six weeks since they'd started sleeping together again, and she knew it was only a matter of time before he asked her to move back to the estate.

She also knew she'd probably say yes. There was no way she could be without him. But she still struggled with reconciling Ramon being the cartel boss with her conscience. However, all the good the foundation would do helped.

She liked to try to equate it to Pope Leo X selling indulgences to rich sinners back in the 1500s. If the pope could do it... maybe her husband could too.

They had dinner one evening together at the estate, and he pulled out a large gift bag. Even though it was a bag, the way the tissue paper overflowed from the top told her that it'd been professionally assembled.

"What is this?" she asked with a smile.

"Open it."

Inside was a neutral-colored Prada bag, and she gasped out loud. "Ramon... it's beautiful."

"The sales lady said it should go with everything, so you'll be able to get a lot of use out of it."

"I love it. But you shouldn't have."

"Yeah, Soph. I should have. I wanted to get you something nice to show you how much I appreciate all the hard work you've been doing for the foundation."

"It's generous," she murmured as she ran her hand along the pristine stitching. "Thank you."

"Just promise me you'll use it and not stick it in your closet."

"I promise."

Keeping that promise wouldn't be a hardship.

The next afternoon, while Sophia worked from her little office in her bungalow rental, she stared out the window at the ocean and cried at how beautiful the view was.

What the hell is this all about? she wondered with a small laugh as she wiped her eyes. Then she realized—she should have gotten her period over a week ago.

Another wave of emotions washed over her as she considered what being pregnant would mean, and she found herself conflicted over whether she hoped she was or wasn't.

Don't jump to conclusions, Sophia, she chided herself. *You need to find out for sure and go from there.*

Now, how would she get out of the house alone to buy a pregnancy test?

It must have been serendipity because there wasn't the usual security overlap at shift change—instead, no one appeared to be across the street. Something that *never* happened. Maybe they thought she was having dinner with Ramon again.

Sophia didn't look the gift horse in the mouth. She grabbed her new Prada bag, phone, and keys and hurried to where Olaf was parked in the garage. With any luck, she'd be back from the drugstore before the next shift of guys arrived, so they wouldn't rat her out to Ramon.

She'd promised him that she would always travel with bodyguards, and she'd been true to her word, for the most part. It got a little suffocating on occasion, and she'd told him more than once that she felt like it was an invasion of her privacy. The last time she'd said it, it'd been when she was lying in bed talking to him on the phone.

"They're not reporting to me where you go. You're free to travel anywhere you want. Just take them with you."

"What if I want to have dinner with my friends?"

"They're not going to sit with you, Sophia. Have dinner with your friends. They'll either be seated at a table with a line of sight for you, or if you'd prefer, have them wait outside."

"What if I want to go to a club?" She knew he wouldn't like that idea but wanted to see what he'd say.

He was silent for a moment, then said quietly, "Do you want to go to a club?"

"No, not necessarily. But what if it's one of my friend's birthdays or something?"

"It'd be your call where you wanted them to wait—inside or out."

She'd rolled her eyes even though he couldn't see her. "Please, you'd *say* they'd wait outside, but you'd send spies in to report my every move."

"*Mi amor*, it's not your moves that anyone is concerned with. It's other people's."

"You can't call me that, remember? We agreed. No pet names."

"So many rules," he dramatically lamented. "Will you just hurry up and come back to me? I don't do well with all these conditions."

Now she was in line at the pharmacy to purchase a pregnancy test. Maybe she'd be going back to him sooner than he thought.

She'd planned on resuming taking the pill again once she got her period. Silly her for thinking since she was no longer ovulating, that it'd take awhile for the hormones to get out of her system, and she'd be okay.

I'm sure it's just a false alarm. My hormones are probably all out of whack. I'll bet my period starts the minute after I take the test.

She paid for her purchase and was lost in thought when a woman dressed in a business suit approached her in the parking lot before she reached the Jetta.

"Excuse me, I just love your Prada bag. Is that from their new line?"

Sophia smiled. "I think so. My—" she paused a second then continued, "husband bought it for me."

"It's so stylish. I'd sleep with the thing!"

She laughed at the idea, not noticing the van that had pulled up behind them until it was too late.

Chapter Forty-Four

Ramon

"What the fuck do you mean, *she's not there, and you don't know where she is?* How could that even be possible—since that's your *job*?"

Gabriel stood in his office after his meeting with *El Rey* ended. The Guzmans' association with Miguel Hernandez went back decades, to when their father had been running the cartel. Although Miguel was known as *El Rey*—The King, it probably had more to do with the fact that he was old school and well-respected than his actual power. His operation was somewhat on the small side.

Still, Ramon preferred to keep things between them harmonious, often going out of his way to appease the older man.

Much to the chagrin of John Turner, Dante's right-hand man, who was charged with making sure Miguel's daughter, Layla had a good time whenever she visited San Diego.

Layla was a beautiful woman, but she was also a spoiled brat, who was under the impression her father yielded a lot more power than he did.

Ramon knew John was getting tired of the situation, but he needed his captain to hang in there until they figured out who had kidnapped Madison. No sense creating another enemy right now if they didn't need to.

They had enough of those to go around these days. Fortunately, the CIA had taken his bullshit information supplied by his bugged office and had dealt with the Colombians for him.

That still left the Zetas and the CIA themselves, along with a few groups who popped up here and there when they attempted a power grab. Those were always quashed and dealt with swiftly and effectively because their organization was a fucking well-oiled machine.

Except now he was being told his wife was nowhere to be found, and his head of security had no idea where she was.

"There was confusion because the day shift usually escorts her to the estate on Wednesdays to have dinner with you, so the night shift came here instead of the bungalow. No one had told them about your meeting with *El Rey*, so by the time they went to the bungalow, she was gone. Camera footage showed her leaving right after five."

"Why in *the fuck* would the day shift leave before their relief arrived?"

"I'm still trying to figure that out."

Heads were going to roll.

"You all better pray she's fine and this is just a big misunderstanding."

"I'm sorry, Ramon. I've got Julian hacking the traffic cameras to see if we can locate her path and where she might be."

Flashpoint

Gabriel looked genuinely upset. His team rarely fucked up, so Ramon knew he was taking it personally.

"Has anyone tried calling her?"

"Yeah, it goes straight to voicemail."

Just then, Ramon's phone dinged with an incoming text. He glanced down, saw it was from Sophia, and let out a sigh of relief. "It's from her."

Sophia: **Baby, I'm sorry, but I need to take a break from us. I'll be in touch soon. When I have things figured out.**

What the fuck? Why was she doing this now? Things had been going great between them—and everything had been on her terms.

He fired back: **I don't understand? Why? What's wrong?**

Sophia: Darling, I'll explain everything. But, later. Just give me time. Please, my love.

Ramon looked up at Gabe. "Sophia's been kidnapped."

"What? What did her text say? Are they asking for ransom?"

"No, not yet. I'm sure whoever took her is trying to get a head start so we don't go looking for her."

"What did her text say?"

"Nothing—and everything."

His wife was pretty smart, he'd give her that. Thinking to call him a pet name *three* fucking times after she'd insisted on no pet names was brilliant.

As he called up the tracking app on his phone to locate hers—hopefully before it was shut off, he instructed, "Get everyone here, now. And call Jacob."

Gabriel was out the door without another word, and Jesús appeared in his office doorway. "What can I do?"

"Help Gabe with phone calls, send someone to the bungalow to pick up Daisy, and close the door."

He didn't need the whole house hear him lose his shit.

****

Sophia

The man pointing a gun at her, took her phone once she sent the last text to Ramon, and slipped it in his pocket.

"Make sure you shut it off," advised a man in a suit who'd just walked in the room.

She recognized him from the plane ride back from New Orleans. He'd been one of the agents who'd escorted her from the terminal and to the private jet that flew her to San Diego.

So it was the CIA who was behind this—that was good to know.

"What is going on? Why have you kidnapped me?"

She'd been echoing that question since the men pulled her in the van and sped away.

At first, she was met with, "Shut up." Then it escalated to, "Shut the fuck up." It wasn't until she received a few blows to her face and head that made her ears ring that she complied with their requests. She even texted Ramon that she needed a break when they'd demanded it. She didn't need a matching handprint on the other side of her face.

Still, she'd added a little touch to her message that she hoped he'd understand.

Now that the agent she recognized had appeared, she reiterated her question.

He bent down and examined her face, holding her chin as he tsked. "Why did they strike you?"

"Because I asked what was going on."

The back of his hand seemed to come out of nowhere, sending her and her chair backward onto the ground with a clatter. "And yet, you fucking asked it again?"

She lay on the floor, not moving as she fought the panic welling up in her throat.

The agent pushed her sprawled legs out of the way with his foot before walking past her, instructing the man, "Make sure her phone is delivered to El Paso. Turn it on once you get about an hour out of town."

"What about her?" the other man asked, tilting his head to where she still lay on the ground.

"We have plans for her," the agent said ominously. "They'll be here for her soon."

Ramon, please find me.

****

Ramon

His office had become a war room. His captains and most trusted lieutenants sat at different desks, examining data they'd collected, when Dante said, "Her phone's gone mobile."

"Her purse is still in the East Village though," John added, looking at the computer screen with the dots on the maps representing the trackers.

"I think the phone is a decoy, or bait for a trap," Ramon said. "I say we focus on the purse's location but send the helicopter after the phone, just in case." He glanced at the blinking dots. "Hell is going to rain down on whoever did this."

"Can I make a suggestion, *Tío*? Instead of intercepting her phone, why don't we follow it and see where it leads? It might help us figure out what their motive is."

"But what if Sophia is with the phone?"

"I think all the more reason for not putting the helicopter down in the middle of a deserted highway. You don't want to risk her getting hurt. Or killed."

Ramon would never forgive himself if that happened.

"Okay, but do not lose a visual."

"I think for stealth, we might consider switching the helicopter to a plane," Jacob suggested after having barely walked through the door. "And you're going to need a team on the ground once they reach their destination. I would suggest having a car pick up their trail on the road. They're

Flashpoint

on the highway headed east, so my money's on them passing through El Centro. I can have a group ready to go by the time they get there."

"Good idea," John agreed.

"But you're right—I think she's with the purse," Jacob said. "Nice move with that, by the way."

"It was easy enough to do. Hell, Prada does it themselves with their anti-theft devices sewn in the liner. I just had that taken out and put the latest tracker in its place."

"That's brilliant," Dante said, shaking his head.

"I wish I could take credit, but it was Gabriel's idea. I was just going to buy the off-brand purses with the trackers already installed, when Gabe suggestion doing that instead."

"That's actually perfect," Jacob commented. "I mean, what woman isn't going to use a designer purse? Taren loves her Dooney & Burke bags. I'm going to have to do that, too."

"Bella would kick my ass if I did something like that without telling her."

"Yeah, I know. Sophia probably would have been pissed if she knew, too. Except, in this case… I'm glad I did it," Ramon said, then defensively added, "But I wouldn't have used it except in an emergency situation like this."

"So, what's the plan for the purse location?" Jacob asked as he took a seat next to John.

"We've got eyes on it," Dante told him. "We're trying to develop an alternative strategy to Ramon going in with guns blazing."

Jacob chuckled, "That's probably a good idea. Any sign of her?"

Fuck those guys—it'd be the perfect plan if he could guarantee she wouldn't get hurt in the process.

John replied, "No, not yet. The good news is we've been able to monitor who's left the location—another reason I think the phone is a trap or a decoy. She wasn't seen leaving."

"Unless..."

Ramon glared at Dante, challenging him to finish his thought. His nephew shut his mouth.

"So, based on who you've seen leave—who do you think is behind this? The Zetas? The Colombians? CIA? All of the above?"

"Hard to say. I guess we'll know more when we move in. Which," Ramon scowled at the people on the opposite side of the desk, "we need to fucking do soon."

"I think we should wait and see where the phone ends up," his nephew, Luis, suggested.

"Fuck that. I'm not waiting."

Dante, who understood what Ramon was going through better than most, agreed. "We need to breach the house, then we'll know if we should put the chopper down on the car or let it keep going."

"Yeah, but if the house gets breached, the operation is going to be blown anyway. That's why I say we wait," Luis argued.

Ramon rubbed his eyes with his index finger and thumb.

"I don't give a shit about anything but getting her back safely. Sophia unharmed is Priority Number One."

"Okay," Jacob said, scrubbing the stubble on his jawline. "Let's do it simultaneously. Keep the helicopter in the air, and when they're in a remote part of I-8, make the move on the vehicle and the house."

Ramon was out of his seat. "Let's go."

Jacob looked at him skeptically. "I think you should stay—"

"Fuck that and fuck you if you think I'm not going to get my wife back."

Jacob looked at him with a smirk. "Then Dante oughta stay behind, since he's next in line. The last thing your organization needs right now is a power void."

Ramon couldn't argue with that. "I agree."

Besides, Dante had Madison and Bella to think about.

"Can I make a suggestion? I think you're going to want professionals for this. Marcus came down from LA with a small crew he had working a job there."

"Is his crew any good?" Ramon needed to make sure Sophia would be rescued unharmed.

"They were with me the night we found Maddie."

That was good enough for Ramon.

Chapter Forty-Five

Sophia
"Hey, Donny," her new guard called to the agent in the suit, the one who'd knocked her to the floor.

Donny poked his head in the door. "Yeah?"

"She's got a pregnancy test in her purse."

A sinister smile formed on the man's lips, and he sneered at Sophia, "Do you have a little Guzman heir in the oven?"

"No. It's for our housekeeper. She asked me to buy it for her."

Donny grabbed a handful of Sophia's hair and dragged her to the bathroom. "Let's just make sure about that."

The asshole made her pee on the stick while he watched, refusing to turn around when she wiped or when she stood to pull her pants up.

"Do you mind?"

"Bitch, I'll give you two fucking black eyes to go with those bruises on your cheeks. I don't give a shit whether you're pregnant or not. Being knocked up isn't going to save your life—the only thing it might do is prolong it. With what you have in store for you, that's not necessarily a good thing. You'll be wishing for death in the end."

Without buttoning her pants, she turned around hastily, barely making it in time to vomit in the toilet without missing. Donny busted out laughing at her.

"I'm betting there's going to be two pink lines on that stick in about five minutes."

Sophia knew he was right. She also wanted to fight him. Tell him to fuck off. Inform him of his fate once Ramon found him.

But, fear does a funny thing to a person, and she said nothing as she wiped her mouth with toilet paper. She needed to be smart—especially now that she had a little being inside her to keep alive, too.

The man glanced down at the stick on the sink counter.

"Ding! Ding! Ding! We have a winner! Just like I predicted—two lines. Congratulations! You're going to have a future dead Guzman baby! That'll make two dead Guzman kids in less than a year."

Sophia turned around and once again, threw up in the toilet as the other man laughed, "At least we're controlling the population."

Please, Ramon. I need you to find me.

****

Ramon

Jacob's successor, Marcus Hughes showed up with a small team of mercenaries: Eddie Landon, Raul Garcia, and Erik Yu. The men were all retired special ops, who were considered the best in the business, which allowed them to reap a small fortune as private contractors instead of government workers. They seemed to be Marcus' go-to men when shit was gonna get real, which made sense since they'd all been part of the same unit. Eddie, Raul, and Erik had been the only men to come back for Marcus after the government cut him loose when a mission in South America had gone bad. The same mission Dante's wife had gotten him involved in.

Now, Ramon was counting on them to save Sophia.

He sat less than a block away from the house where the Prada purse was, in a van filled with electronic equipment that Jacob and Marcus monitored. Screens with camera feeds from electronic flies—literally. The bugs were micro-sized drones in the size and shape of a common housefly that Erik and Raul had managed to release into the house from attic vents while Eddie stood watch. The men were fucking ninjas, scaling walls, climbing trees, moving along rooflines—all undetected.

"I think I'm going to need a consultation on surveillance sweeps," Ramon murmured when he saw the devices in action.

"Eddie's currently developing a sophisticated detection mechanism that he's looking for an investor for," Marcus said with a grin.

"Would it be able to detect those?" Ramon gestured to the video screens.

"It would, and then it'd zap the power source, so they'd be useless."

"I'm interested. But, let's get my wife home safe and sound first, then we'll talk."

What he was sure Marcus and Jacob were going to charge him, Ramon questioned whether Eddie would need an outside investor. Not that he gave a shit about the money. He'd give his last dime if it meant bringing Sophia home safely.

"She's there," Jacob said into his headset. "Southwest quadrant, small, inner room. Two guards with her, armed, but not exactly on high alert—they're looking at their phones. Looks like Zeta tattoos. Three more armed men in the living room, playing cards. Another one, in a suit, is on the phone. He's probably the one in charge. The rest of the house looks clear."

Ramon asked, "Can you get a closer look at the one in the suit?"

Marcus maneuvered a joystick with ease and brought the man into focus.

"I don't understand. He's CIA, but the men guarding her are Zetas. And so are the ones playing cards—I know those tats."

Jacob leaned back in his chair with furrowed brows as he studied the screen, rubbing his chin like he was lost in thought.

"Either the CIA is double-crossing you—which is entirely possible, or they've got a dirty agent. Also a credible option. Either way, this has the potential to get real ugly."

"I'll worry about that when Sophia is safe."

Marcus, who'd been texting with his men, said, "That should be in about three minutes and thirty seconds. Give or take thirty seconds."

"Any chance the CIA guy can be taken alive?"

Marcus typed on his tablet, then waited a minute. Finally, he looked up. "They said no promises, but they'd do what they could."

"By all means, feel free to fuck him up. I just want him to be able to talk before he's actually dead."

Marcus chuckled. "I'll let you know in a minute."

****

Sophia.

It all happened so fast—and so quietly—that it took her a second to understand what was happening.

A handsome, Asian man stood at her side, while her two guards slumped over on the table they'd been sitting at. She hadn't even heard the gunshot, but the sound of blood as it poured onto the wood from the wound in their heads made her stomach turn.

She looked at the man with the gun and was paralyzed with fear, unsure if she was next. Then he held out his hand and smiled at her softly.

"It's okay. Ramon sent me."

Flashpoint

"How—how did you find me?" she stuttered as she took his offered hand.

His smile morphed into a broad grin when he grabbed her purse off the bookshelf with his other hand. "Just a hunch."

Chapter Forty-Six

Ramon

Jacob hopped in the driver's seat to move the van, backing it into an empty stall in the garage of the house where Sophia was being held. Ramon waited until the garage door had come down before jumping out and rushing inside.

Sophia was being tended to by Erik and Eddie, while Raul was having a 'conversation' with the agent in the suit, using his fists to emphasize his points.

Ramon would get back to that asshole in a minute, he needed to check on Sophia first.

He bit his knuckle at the sight of her bruised face. It was a good thing most of these fuckers were already dead—although Ramon was left extremely unsatisfied at not being the one to have done it.

The asshole in the suit would have to do. And possibly the bastards in the car.

"*Mi amore*," he uttered softly as he kneeled in front of her and gently touched an unbruised part of her face. "Are you hurt anywhere else?"

If they violated her, he would cut their dicks off. He didn't care if they were already corpses. And he'd cut the sniveling agent's dick off while he was alive.

"No. Just smacked around for asking too many questions. Although, Agent Donny promised me my future included wishing I were dead." She bit back a sob, and he wrapped her in his arms. "I can't believe you found me in time."

Her comment piqued Marcus' interest. "In time?"

"He said *they'd* be here soon for me."

The men exchanged glances, then Jacob quietly ordered Ramon's security team, who were on standby nearby, to come help clean up.

"Get her home and take care of her. We'll handle the rest."

Gabriel was waiting for them when they walked outside—and hit the gas the second Ramon closed the rear passenger door.

She trembled uncontrollably, and Ramon felt helpless as he stroked her hair and held her against him.

"You're in shock, baby. It's okay, I'm here. I've got you." He directed his attention to Gabriel. "Have Dr. Topmiller come to the house."

"He's already on his way. Marcus had me call him."

"Thank you for finding us," Sophia whispered against his chest.

"Us?"

"Me and our baby."

"Our baby? *Mi amor*, you're pregnant?"

He was usually a stoic guy, but this day had put him through the wringer, and her revelation had just brought him to his proverbial knees. He needed to keep it together for her sake, but the magnitude of what he could have lost if something had happened to her raced through his mind.

"I was at the drugstore picking up a test when I was abducted. The agent made me take it when the men found it in my bag."

Thank god, that was all they'd found.

"Somehow, today has been the shittiest day of my life, and the best, all in one. You're coming back to the estate. I don't care if you stay in the pool house or a guest room—you're going to be where you're safe and taken care of."

"Why would I stay anywhere other than my bedroom, with my husband?"

****

Sophia

Ramon made sure the doctor examined her from head-to-toe, and peppered the kind Indian man with questions about her and the baby's well-being.

After being assured she would be fine after a few days, and that the risks to her pregnancy from the mild sedative Dr. Swarup gave her far outweighed the harm she'd endure if her body continued to exhibit the symptoms of shock, Ramon put her to bed.

She woke up a few times throughout the night, but quickly fell back to sleep when she realized she was where she belonged—safe in his arms. Where she'd always be safe, she knew Ramon would see to that.

Chapter Forty-Seven

Ramon

When Sophia told him about the agent's comment about two dead Guzman babies, he knew he was the man responsible for Madison's kidnapping, too.

Dante took it from there.

"Turns out, Ol' Donny Boy had been born a Zeta, but was groomed to join the CIA from infancy—even being given an American-sounding name," Jacob said in Ramon's office the next day. "It took a little 'coaxing,' but he spilled everything. How he used his position at the CIA to help further the Zetas with their illegal activities. When the Colombians wanted to align themselves with the Sinaloans, the Zetas tried to make it look like the Colombians were behind Maddie's kidnapping—hoping Ramon's group would go to war with the Colombians and make them vulnerable."

"I kind of wish I hadn't set Martin up with the CIA now."

"Luckily, you've got a patsy with Agent Don. Make a few goodwill deals where Martin profits, and I think you can fix it. You're going to want to keep a tight rein on them, though."

"Bella has to feel relieved," Ramon said. "They found out who took Madison."

"Yeah," John replied. "And he's been taken care of."

"Maddie will be able to live a normal life now."

Jacob laughed. "Well, as normal as a kid could get whose mother is legally dead, but in reality, is alive and kicking ass, and whose father helps run a billion-dollar drug business. Welcome to your future, friend."

"My wife isn't legally dead," Ramon pointed out.

"You're right; that will make all the difference." Jacob rolled his eyes. "I'm sure your kid will get on the school bus every day with all the other San Diego children."

Ramon slumped back in his chair. "*Fuck.* I'm not ready for this. How am I going to keep a kid safe *and* normal?"

John grumbled, "Don't ask Miguel Hernandez for advice about that one."

"Hey, about Layla..."

Epilogue

Ramon

Guzman Enterprises continued acquiring legal businesses and was fast becoming the Mexican version of Berkshire Hathaway. Only they weren't trading Guzman Enterprises stock on the open market. But, Dante estimated they'd be sixty-five percent legitimate by the end of the decade.

Which, fortunately, was good enough for Sophia.

After Ramon divulged Dante's prediction to her, she never again asked about the revenue streams that funded the foundation she continued to run—even as their two children occupied all her free time.

Well, not *all* her free time. There were still the nights after the kids went to bed, and the occasional long lunch she'd take with Ramon in the pool house where he thoroughly worshipped her body. He never missed an opportunity to get naked with his wife, and she never seemed to mind.

As she lay next to him with a sleepy smile after her third orgasm of the night, she cooed softly, "I can't imagine how my life would have turned out if I'd never have met you."

"Me neither, *mi amor*. Me neither."

****

Flashpoint

Bonus scene!

Want to read more about Ramon and Sophia's naughty time on the jet at the start of their honeymoon? Join my newsletter for the bonus scene—for subscribers only! https://www.subscribepage.com/TessSummersNewsletter

****

Does Chachi ever notice Blanca? Their story is coming soon— exclusively for newsletter subscribers!

Fever

"Speaking of longing stares..." Ramon said with a grin. "Is Chachi in today? I need to talk to him."

Gabriel cocked his head. "Yeah, he got here about an hour ago. Everything okay?"

"Absolutely. I just wanted to remind him about our no-fraternization policy."

"We have policies? And about *fraternization*?"

Ramon chuckled. "No, but he doesn't know that."

"You're an evil boss. And that's why you're my hero. But, who is he fraternizing with?"

"You're the head of security—you don't know?"

"Well, I have my suspicions, but there's been no concrete evidence."

"Who do you suspect?"

"Blanca."

"Yeah, that's what I think, too. I actually believe they'd be a good match."

"So, you're saying you approve?"

"Absolutely. I just want to mess with him a little. Like I was telling Sophia—if they think they have to sneak around, it might make it more exciting."

"Or, it could nip it in the bud."

"You've been talking to my wife, too, I see," Ramon said with a laugh. "Like I told her, I won't let the joke go on for long."

"Don't you have an empire to run?"

Ramon narrowed his eyes at the man. "Okay, now I'm *really* starting to get suspicious that you have been talking with my wife... But, it's not often that two people on my staff are interested in each other romantically—at least that I know about—I can't pass up the opportunity when it presents itself."

"I can call Chachi in right now."

Ramon shook his head. "I'm going to Sophia's doctor's appointment. We're going to find out the sex of the baby. But when we get back, I'll just ask him to come to the house with me."

"Don't let it go too long," Gabriel warned. "Chachi is sensitive and will definitely want to follow the rules."

"But will he?"

Coming soon!

Slow Burn

Will John finally get a chance to date Quinn and get his shot at a happily ever after, or will the two remain star-crossed lovers whose timing is always wrong?

Find out in *Slow Burn*. Coming in June.

Ignition
Ensenada Heat, Prequel

Dante Guzman

He knew within hours that Ruby Rhodes, the sexy little auburn haired beauty, who just happened to sit next to him at his favorite bar and flirt with him all night long, was not who she appeared to be. Redheads were his kryptonite—everyone knew it, including his enemies who wanted to see the Guzman cartel destroyed. Just exactly who sent her and why was something he was going to have to figure out. At least playing along with her was enjoyable since part of her ruse seemed to entail sleeping with him and indulging his... let's just say, *darker* desires.

Or maybe that wasn't supposed to be part of the plan, and she broke the rules.

Falling in love with her was definitely not part of his plan, and he was going to have to punish her for making him do just that. Especially after he figures out who she really is and why she was sent to seduce him.

Get it https://tesssummersauthor.com/ignition-1

Flashpoint

Inferno
Ensenada Heat, Book 1

Kennedy Jones

I'm a special agent with the CIA, and I'm good at what I do. In fact, I'm considered one of the best. I can play the role of anyone and eliminating bad guys without them seeing me coming is my forte—which is why I was chosen to take down the head of the Guzman family.

Dante Guzman is a ruthless, sexy, cold-hearted cartel money-man. And now it's my job to study him, learn his likes and dislikes—in and out of the bedroom—so I can gain his trust and access to his uncle, the head of the Ensenada cartel.

I just didn't count on falling into Dante's clutches.

Every second I spend with him he manages to pull me further and further into his world. And the more time I spend there, the deeper I slip into the darkness with him, the more I realize...

I like it.

Dante Guzman

Don't let my good manners fool you—I'm one cold-hearted SOB, and I control the family's monetary affairs with an iron fist. There's no place for weakness in my world. Show weakness, and you die. As simple as that.

So when a petite, feisty, hot-as-hell bombshell storms into my life, I didn't stop to think about the consequences of keeping her. I wanted her, and I always get what I want. Period.

Turns out, the stakes were too high...for the both of us. And there's going to be hell to pay if we're going to be together, to one form of the devil or another.

Get your copy of Inferno!
https://tesssummersauthor.com/inferno

Flashpoint

Combustion

Ensenada Heat, Book 2

> She was meant to be mine—I knew it the moment we met. Too bad I'm about to kidnap her.

Mason Hughes

As a decorated CIA agent, I know better than to kidnap a former colleague's sister and hold her hostage on a ship in the middle of the ocean. The agency tends to frown on that sort of behavior. But desperate times call for desperate measures; I have my reasons, and they're good ones. I'll be forgiven with a slap to the wrist—at least for that part of the mission.

Until I tie Reagan Jones up and can't resist her when she presses her tight little body against mine. That's probably not so forgivable.

Then there's the issue of falling in love with her and refusing to let her go once the mission is over. Definitely not forgivable.

I have no idea what I'm thinking—we can't be together; it's not safe for her. I'm a spy, and she's a feisty art instructor from Fargo. Not exactly the perfect match.

Or is it?

Get your copy of Combustion [here!](https://tesssummersauthor.com/combustion-1)
https://tesssummersauthor.com/combustion-1

Reignited
Ensenada Heat, Book 3

He's known as the CIA's top mercenary fixer. But he can't fix this.

Jacob Smith

Seven years.

Seven long miserable years since he'd ripped his heart from his chest and left it on her doorstep when he walked away from her. But, he'd had no choice.

At least, he'd thought he hadn't. He was too entrenched in the CIA's underground world to safely ever have a wife and family.

But now, after turning his CIA dealings into a *very* lucrative mercenary career, here he was, about to embark on a ten-day cruise with his cabin next to hers, not by coincidence—although she didn't know it yet.

He wasn't known as a 'fixer' for nothing. Maybe it was time to try to fix his broken heart, and hers—if she'd let him. And that was a big *if*, given how he'd shattered hers so long ago.

Get it here!
https://tesssummersauthor.com/reignited-1

Other works by Tess Summers

San Diego Social Scene series:

Operation Sex Kitten—Book One
The General's Desire—Book Two
Playing Dirty—Book Three
Cinderella and the Marine—Book Four
The Playboy and the SWAT Princess—FREE Bonus Book
The Heiress and the Mechanic—Book Five
Burning Her Resolve—Book Six

About the Author

Tess Summers is a former businesswoman and teacher who always loved writing but never seemed to have time to sit down and write a short story, let alone a novel. Now battling MS, her life changed dramatically, and she has finally slowed down enough to start writing all the stories she's been wanting to tell, including the fun and sexy ones!

Married over twenty-five years with three grown children, Tess is a former dog foster mom who ended up failing and adopting them instead. She and her husband (and their six dogs) split their time between the desert of Arizona and the lakes of Michigan, so she's always in a climate that's not too hot and not too cold, but just right!

Contact Me!

Sign up for my newsletter:
https://www.subscribepage.com/TessSummersNewsletter
Email: TessSummersAuthor@yahoo.com
Visit my website: www.TessSummersAuthor.com
Facebook: http://facebook.com/TessSummersAuthor
Twitter: http://twitter.com/@mmmTess
Instagram: https://www.instagram.com/tesssummers/
Amazon: https://amzn.to/2MHHhdK
BookBub https://www.bookbub.com/profile/tess-summers
Book+Main: https://bookandmainbites.com/TessSummers
Goodreads - https://www.goodreads.com/TessSummers

Printed in Great Britain
by Amazon